MALIBU CONNECTION

A BILLIONAIRE MATCHMAKER NOVEL
CHARLOTTE BYRD

BYRD BOOKS

COPYRIGHT

Copyright © 2016 by Charlotte Byrd

All rights reserved.

No part of this book may be reproduced in any form or by any electronic or mechanical means, including information storage and retrieval systems, without written permission from the author, except for the use of brief quotations in a book review.

CONTENTS

Acknowledgments	vi
About Malibu Connection	viii
Prologue	x
Chapter 1 - Logan	1
Chapter 2 - Logan	7
Chapter 3 - Logan	18
Chapter 4 - Avery	26
Chapter 5 - Avery	34
Chapter 6 - Avery	42
Chapter 7 - Logan	51
Chapter 8 - Logan	59
Chapter 9 - Avery	68
Chapter 10 - Logan	77
Chapter 11 - Avery	83
Chapter 12 - Logan	90
Chapter 13 - Avery	100
Chapter 14 - Avery	110
Chapter 15 - Logan	117
Chapter 16 - Avery	123
Chapter 17 - Logan	133
Chapter 18 - Avery	141
Chapter 19 - Logan	149
Chapter 20 - Avery	154
Chapter 21 - Logan	160
Chapter 22 - Avery	166
Chapter 23 - Logan	176

Chapter 24 - Avery   184
Chapter 25 - Avery   191
Chapter 26 - Avery   196
Chapter 27 - Logan   204
Chapter 28 - Avery   211
Chapter 29 - Avery   218
Chapter 30 - Logan   231
Advanced Reader Team   356
Books by Charlotte Byrd   357

WANT TO HEAR ABOUT NEW RELEASES?

Want to know when my next book comes will be released?

Sign up for my mailing list and you'll be the first to know about all new releases!!

You'll also get access to exclusive giveaways, and a chance to be on my Advanced Reader Team: http://eepurl.com/btLdbT

I WILL NEVER SPAM you and you can opt out anytime.

ACKNOWLEDGMENTS

Dear Reader,

Thank you so much for taking the time to read this book. Without you, I would not be able to do what I love. Your support and generosity means the world to me.

I'm particularly grateful to my devoted and dedicated Advanced Reader Team and all of you who have read and reviewed the book prior to its official release.

I'm also sending a special thank you to Mary E. Wolney, Nicole Batalon, Amy Monroe, Lisa Tantsits, and Denise Toups, Amy Shonk, Anne Rse - the wonderful people who found all the typos and errors from one of the last versions of the book. Without you, this work would not be the book that it is! Thank you!

If you would like join my Advanced Reader Team and get FREE copies of my books in return for honest reviews, please email me.

If you just want to let me know what you think about my book, please don't hesitate to write me. I love to hear from my readers!!

Love,
Charlotte
charlotte@charlottebyrdauthor.com

ABOUT MALIBU CONNECTION: A BILLIONAIRE MATCHMAKER NOVEL

I'm Dolly Monroe and I'm a billionaire matchmaker. I like my hair and boobs the way I like my diamonds: big. Why do I do this? I'm really good at it, and I'm a sucker for a happily ever after. Over the last thirty years, I've successfully set up close to 4,000 couples. Over the last five years, the majority were billionaires. Their stories need to be told. These are my favorite ones.

THE LAST THING that Avery Lewis is looking for is a relationship. She has a crazy ex-boyfriend who's refusing to leave her alone and a thriving floral shop near Malibu, California that keeps her very busy. When her friend gives her a gift certificate to Dolly Monroe's billionaire matchmaking service for her 25th birthday, she's more than a little skeptical. The last thing that she expects is to meet the love of her life.

After selling his banking start-up to Google, Logan Davenport is officially a billionaire. He's swimming in money and sex, and that is the way he likes it. But he needs a respectable date to his brother's engagement party. So he finally gives in and lets his eccentric aunt, Dolly Monroe, find him a date. Much to his shock, she sets him up with an opinionated, average-looking, floral shop owner who seems impervious to his charms. Avery doesn't want him, and that makes him want her even more. Before he knows it, he falling in love for the first time ever.

But Logan is keeping a secret. No, he isn't married. No, he doesn't have a child. No, he doesn't have cancer. It's worse than that. Much worse. And when Avery finally finds out, he risks losing the only person he has ever really cared about. Can their love survive his secret?

PROLOGUE

My name is Dolly Monroe and I'm a billionaire matchmaker.

I am 5'10" when I'm awake and 5'5" when I'm asleep. I'm suspicious of women who don't wear heels, just as I'm suspicious of people who call me out of the blue asking for favors.

I have a strict policy when it comes to my hair, one which I've abided to since I was a little girl in West Texas – the bigger the hair, the closer to God. My hair is as platinum as some of my clients' records, and it perfectly offsets the 10-carat diamond ring on my left hand.

I never let my waist get bigger than 22 inches, and I do not have the same restrictions on my breast size. The girls were 36 DD three years ago, and now they're 36 EE. Who the hell knows how big they're going to get in another decade?

I like my men the way I like my purses: in a variety of colors and styles and with a high price tag. My husband, who's also my high school sweetheart, doesn't mind, of course, because my little business makes more than a hefty penny and keeps him in a 20,000 square foot Malibu beachfront house and allows him to spend his days surfing and golfing.

You see, I've been at this for a very long time. I was 13 the first time I did my first set up: my second cousin with my best friend from middle school. They dated through 10th grade, married in 11th, and celebrated their 40-year wedding anniversary last year.

I started my matchmaking business when I was 20 and, at first, I set up average folk like my cousins, then wealthy folk, then millionaires, and now billionaires. This is the only thing I've ever done, and I'm pretty damn good at it. People aren't that different you know. Of course, billionaires come with their attitudes and highfalutin opinions of their own importance, but at their core, they want the same thing everyone else wants: for someone to give a damn about them, not just their money or power. What typically ends up being the problem, however, is that the billionaire (both men and women) think they're going to get this thing from some 20-year-old,

5'11" bimbo, but that's rarely the case. That's where I come in.

Why do I do this?

I'm a sucker for a happily ever after. I believe everyone deserves one, and I can get it for them, if they just get out of their own way and let me.

How can I be so sure?

I have a great track record. I have successfully set up 3,988 couples. That's more than 130 couples per year over 30 years of matchmaking. Not all of them were billionaires, but over the last five years a huge portion of them were. Close to four thousand couples now are living their happy ending because of me. It feels damn good to say that.

And then I made a mistake. I told my publisher friend about this, and she went wild.

"You have to write down some of your favorite stories, you absolutely must. People will go crazy over it!" she said.

So, that's how we got here. This series depicts some of my favorite couples from the last few years. Their names have been changed to protect their privacy, but everything else is as true as it happened from my clients' perspectives. Though each couple eventually found their happily ever after, the road to get there was often difficult and treacherous. But what would life be without a little intrigue and turmoil, right?

CHAPTER 1 - LOGAN

I wake up in the middle of my California king bed with a splitting headache and an aching groin. There are two women lying next to me, both dead asleep. They don't look as gorgeous as they did last night at the club, but I'm used to women's trickery and mystique when it comes to makeup. All those contouring tutorials on Youtube may confuse most men, but I've got three sisters. I know when a nose is made to look a little smaller, lips fuller, eyes larger. And that's okay. Why not look more beautiful if you can? It's pleasing to the eyes, even if it's a little deceitful. But women aren't the only liars. We all are. Men constantly lie about how much is really in their bank accounts by leasing cars that they have no business driving based on their paychecks. And why? To impress women, of course.

I'm lucky this way. I recently sold a small start-up that I founded after college to Google, and the sale officially made me a billionaire. The app allows people to make personal loans to their friends, family, and strangers just like banks and credit cards do and charge interest. It's called BankMe, and whenever I mention the name people generally pretend to have heard of it, even though most of them haven't. I don't mind. It doesn't really matter.

Threesomes are fun. I try to have a couple once or twice a month at least, because they keep me on my toes. Most men want to have two women at once, but I don't want to be just a user. I want the women to have a good time and to enjoy themselves. So, it's important for me to make sure that they do. Last night, however, I made a mistake. I make it a point to always fall asleep on one of the sides of the bed so that I can sneak out without waking anyone up. But last night, for some reason, I fell asleep in the middle. Now, I have to carefully climb out from beneath the blankets without waking either of them up.

I decide to go left, toward the ocean. The girl on the left is turned away from me. I carefully lift the sheet and slide out. Then I climb over her, making sure that I don't pull the sheet too tight so I don't risk waking her up. Just when I'm almost scot-free, she snores and turns around. I hold my breath and freeze. I'm draped over her on all fours, holding myself up by fingertips and tiptoes. Luckily, she doesn't wake up. A moment later, I throw my legs over her and land silently on the floor.

All of this maneuvering is an absolute requirement. I hate morning conversations and make it a point to never talk to the women who sleep over. I'm not so rude as to make them leave in the middle of the night, but I also don't hang around to make them breakfast. Instead, I go outside, grab my board and surf until Marilyn comes by at 8 a.m. to clean, make me breakfast and kick the girls out.

Marilyn is the longest relationship I've ever had with a woman who isn't related to me. Marilyn is from El Salvador, and she has been with me since I lived in a one-bedroom apartment in West Hollywood. Even back then, when I made only $2000 a month and paid about $1300 in rent, I wasn't much of a housekeeper and chose to spend $50 a week on her rather than getting out the vacuum cleaner and doing it myself. My oldest sister likes to say that even back then I was thinking rich. Maybe she's right.

I stumble a little down the stairs on the side of my porch. I live in a 5,000 square foot, four-bedroom house on the beach in Malibu. After the deal with Google, I can afford to upgrade, of course, but this place is enough for me right now. I love it here. The beach is only a few steps away, and it's in the quieter part of Malibu, away from the tourists and the paparazzi. The paparazzi usually don't bother me (who cares about rich techies, right?), but I have been out with more than a few models and celebs and now they're starting to get a little nosy.

I grab the pair of swimming trunks that I keep under my porch along with my board and change into them right there. This has become somewhat of a habit of mine – there's no one out here this early, and I don't think anyone can see me under my porch. Mainly, I change out here because I don't really give a shit. I doubt that anyone will really complain about seeing my 6'1" tan body, my six-pack, which looks like it has been chiseled out of stone, or my large dick.

I grab my board and head toward the water. My head still feels like someone's hitting it with an ax. I definitely had a little bit too much to drink last night. I think it was all because of Allison. Allison was the one sleeping on my right. The thing about threesomes is that usually one of the girls just isn't as hot as the other one, and a part of you has to settle because two are frankly better than one. So that's pretty much what I was expecting when Allison asked if I was interested in partying with her and her friend Samantha last night. But then I saw Samantha. Both of them are equally stunningly beautiful with light green eyes and full, soft lips. They both have infectious laughs, bubbly personalities without being bimbos, and high sex drives. The only thing that's different about them is their hair color – one is light blonde and the other is a dark brunette. As soon as I saw them, I was in heaven, and that was even before they came over and did all those ungodly things to me and each other.

Still, no matter how hot the girls, I have rules for myself for a reason. I follow them religiously for a reason. Let them sleep over, but go surfing before they wake up. Let Marilyn wake them up and put them out. Marilyn is great at delivering early morning excuses and explanations about why I'm not there. He's surfing now, and then he has an early meeting with clients, is her usual one. Today, she'll have to be more creative. Allison knows that I've sold my company and don't officially have a job or any clients to meet with anymore. I'm sure she'll think of something.

I enter the freezing water. There are a few surfers out, and they're wearing wetsuits, but I like the feel of the cold water on my bare skin. It's refreshing and exhilarating. Mornings in Malibu tend to be overcast and a little dark, and the water is colder here than in the rest of Southern California. But I've been living here for close to two years now, and I'm pretty used to it.

When I dip my long yellow board into the first wave, my headache vanishes immediately. I ride the first wave all the way to the edge of the sand and then paddle back out into the blue. I ride another one and another one and another one, and each one makes me feel more alive than the one before.

I stay in the water for close to an hour. Then I shake my hair out before grabbing the board and walking back upstairs. This is one of the perks of having a house on the beach. Back when I lived in West Hollywood, I used to get up at the crack of dawn to beat the traffic, drive forty minutes, park and surf for forty-five minutes before heading back into the traffic and the grind of my life. The irony is that back then I had a job that I needed to get to and had to squeeze my surfing in before it. Now that I don't have a job and actually have time to waste my life in LA traffic, I live right on the beach and don't have to.

CHAPTER 2 - LOGAN

"Hey Marilyn," I say walking into the kitchen, dripping wet.

"Oh, Logan, you're getting all the floors wet!" she exclaims and runs over with a towel. Marilyn is a small, round woman with curly hair who speaks in a thick Spanish accent.

"Sorry about that," I say.

This is a game we play every morning. For some reason, Marilyn doesn't believe me that the bamboo floors will be perfectly fine if they get a little wet, and I pretend that I'm actually sorry about it.

She has already made my smoothie, and it's sitting at the end of the kitchen island. One thing I can tell you is that Marilyn was not happy when I insisted on having smoothies for breakfast. I don't know if it has anything to do with being born and raised in El Salvador, or if it's just a Marilyn thing, but for some reason she doesn't approve of fruit being mashed up into tiny pieces.

"The fruit lose all of their nutrients when they're processed like that," she used to say. "You should eat them cut up, but not processed!"

To which I would smile and laugh and insist on it anyway, even if they no longer had the nutrients. Her response was a shake of the head and something that sounded like a curse to the devil in Spanish.

Luckily, both of us have begrudgingly agreed to disagree, and she no longer tries to convince me to have hot tamales for breakfast. Even though, those suckers are to die for. If you ever the chance to have one of Marilyn Abarca's tamales, do not pass up the chance. You'll think that you died and went to heaven.

"Delicious," I say, taking generous gulps of the berry banana green tea smoothie. Even though she hates the idea of smoothies, Marilyn is the type of person who takes immense pride in her work, and since she must make smoothies, she makes the best fucking smoothies on the planet. Lucky for me!

"Thank you for asking the women to leave," I say.

"Yeah, yeah," she shakes her head. "Logan, you're 30 years old. Rich. Handsome. Why do you need two women for a night? Why don't you try to find one woman for the rest of your life?"

It's funny. My mom asks me the same kind of questions, except that she doesn't exactly know about the threesomes. Something about my mom asking me irritates the hell out of me. When Marilyn does it, I don't really mind. I find it kind of humorous.

"How can I be just with one woman, Marilyn?" I ask, jokingly.

"Then you'll have someone to take care of you. Cook for you. Clean for you," Marilyn says, pushing a rag across the kitchen island, even though it's already spotless.

"But I already have a woman who does that for me," I say.

"Oh yeah? Who?"

"You, of course!" I wrap my arms around her soft, pudgy shoulders and give her a big squeeze.

"Oh, Logan, please!" she pushes me away. "I won't be around forever, you know. I can find other clients, if that means you'll finally get married."

"Are you serious? You want me to get married so much that you'll forgo the crazy salary that I pay you?"

She rolls her eyes and shakes her head.

"I told you it was a crazy salary," she says, pointing her index finger in my face. "No normal housekeeper is paid this much."

"Well, you're not just a normal housekeeper," I shrug. "Not everyone will kick women out of my bed in the morning in such a nice and delicate way that they'll actually come back to me for more."

Marilyn rolls her eyes again and laughs. A big, infectious laugh, the kind that makes the whole world light up.

"You crazy, Logan," she says.

"You know you love me!" I joke. "But seriously, what do you think of Allison?"

"You don't want to know."

"C'mon, please?" I give her kiss on the cheek. She blushes and pushes me away. I know I make her uncomfortable, but in a good way. I think of her as an old, wise aunt, and I really do appreciate her input in my life. Even if I rarely follow it.

"Allison is nice, of course. They're all nice. And they're all in love with you. But you know that already," Marilyn says sprinkling some baking soda on the stove. She insists on using only natural cleaners, even if they require her to do more work.

"Yes, I do," I say, winking at her.

I'm almost entirely air dried by now, and I head toward the master bedroom to take quick shower and wash the salt off me.

"But you don't need a nice girl, Logan," Marilyn yells as I close the door the room. That's one of the things that I love about her – she isn't someone who's threatened by closed doors. She knows that she voice carries, and she isn't afraid to use it.

"Oh yeah? And what kind of girl do I need?" I yell through the door. I've already taken off my swimming trunks and I'm admiring my nicely toned body in the mirror. I love the way the early morning light wraps itself carefully around each muscle in my stomach. I run my fingertips of the each curve of the six pack, which look like little hills protruding out of a 3D topographical map.

"Someone who can put up with all your shit," Marilyn yells and starts the vacuum cleaner. I smile at myself in the mirror. This conversation is over. I turn on my rainfall shower and enter my favorite thing about my house. On occasion, I've shared this shower with a girl or two, but I love this shower so much that I tend to vet women extra carefully before introducing them to it.

Unlike my old apartment shower and bathtub combination, which barely had room for one person, this shower room has space for at least four. The walls are made of beautiful Mexican tile – my favorite – and the floor is made up of little pebbles to mimic the feel of the earth. Water falls directly from the 12 foot ceiling, and there are additional steam nozzles on the side, which I don't use nearly as much as I should. It was this shower that made me finally realize how much money I really had and how far I've come.

Stepping out of the shower, I glance at myself in the mirror. Not bad. Not bad at all. My green eyes catch the light streaming in through the floor-to-ceiling window and sparkle. My face is wet and my eyelashes look a little longer than normal. I never quite got it, but I've had a number of girls note how long my lashes were. A few even admitted how jealous they were of them. I look at them carefully in the mirror. I've always thought that their unusual length made my eyes look a little too feminine, but my one and only serious girlfriend, Sadie, said that they gave me eyes "a kind of ethereal quality." Ethereal. I like that.

I love the tall ceilings in this place, especially in the bathroom. I'm 6'2" and it's nice not to feel like a giant all the time. I flex my six pack and run my fingers over my stomach. Many men would kill for this stomach. I may sound vain – don't get me wrong, I am – but I was a chubby kid and I know what it feels like to hate your body. For some reason, my mom let me eat everything in sight and finally, at the age of ten, I realized that I was a lot fatter than all the other kids at my school. That's when I started working out. I hated how I felt about myself and I really hated how angry and sad I was all the time. My moods were completely controlled by my food and the last meal of sugar and sweets that I had. So, one day, I just decided that enough was enough. I started monitoring my food intake and doing pushups and sit ups. The first six months were utter horror. But over time, I grew to love working out. I loved how strong and powerful my body was becoming. It built my confidence, which eventually turned into pride and cockiness.

I toss my dark straight hair out of my face. Some people joke about $400 haircuts. Say that they're not worth the money, especially for guys, but I'll go to my grave arguing that they are worth every penny. There's no way to even compare the haircut you get at some cheap place like Super Cuts to the one handcrafted by a meticulous Japanese hair artist like my Hiroshi. He takes the time to make sure that every strand is cut just so. So that when my hair does get a little long, they continue to fall in the effortlessly casual way they do now. It's as if each strand knows its exact place on my head and goes there no matter what aggravation I put it through. No matter how many times I run it through the rough surf mixed with sand of the Pacific Ocean. No matter how many times I drive my Aston Martin at 85 miles per hour down the 101 with the top down. None of these things matter. My hair somehow always looks just right afterwards.

Drying myself off, I linger a little bit too long looking at my dick. I've definitely lucked out. It's 7 and a half inches long when erect with barely any curve to it at all. A few years ago, I got into the habit of going in for monthly waxing appointments and getting rid of all hair – and I mean everywhere. The first time I did this, I did it as a joke. I watched porn with this goddess I met in the South of France who held my attention for close to two months, and she asked what I thought about going for the porno look.

"It will make your cock look huge!" she said.

When she came back from the beach the next day, I had a little surprise for her. All of my hair was gone. She went wild for it. Ever since then, I've been getting quite a kick out of seeing the look on girls' faces when they discover that I'm completely hairless. I swear to God, they find it so arousing that the blow jobs now last at least twice as long as before. A few actually said that it makes them feel like they're with a porn star! I guess girls are no different from guys in that way – porn stars fill their fantasies.

I wrap junk in a towel and walk out into the kitchen, where Marilyn is still hard at work cleaning invisible dirt. Honestly, she's such a hard worker. I don't notice half the things she does, but she still insists on cleaning things that basically don't require any cleaning.

"I've been meaning to ask you, how your family? Back in El Salvador?" I ask.

One of the reasons I pay her so damn much is that I know that she sends almost her whole paycheck to her sisters and mother back home. Her father died when she was young and her mother supported her and her sisters on a seamstress salary. She grew up in a one room apartment in the slums of San Salvador and came to America when she was 18.

Marilyn's face turns almost green at my question. Her eyes drop down and her lips curl out of disgust. I know what's going on there. I'm not that uninformed. A month ago, Augusto Sanchez overthrew the democratically-elected President Salvador Cesar. Sanchez was previously in charge of the military, and he took power through a military coup. The attack culminated in the surrounding of the presidential palace and President Cesar's exile. Now, Sanchez has a new military government, which is ruled by the heads of the three armed forces. As the head of the army, Sanchez appointed himself head of the state and started banning all opposition and rounding people up.

"Everything has gone to hell since Sanchez took power," Marilyn says. "Three of my mother's neighbors, our oldest friends, have been taken away in the middle of the night. No one heard of them since. They were probably killed."

"That's terrible," I say.

"I'm so scared for my nieces and nephews. Some of them are very opinionated. They don't know enough to keep their mouths shut. They argue when they need to be quiet. They think all their friends will be their friends. But in that atmosphere of fear, that's not always the case."

Marilyn looks terrified. Her eyes grow large. I can hear her heart starting to beat faster and faster. I wish there was something I could do to calm her down.

"It's going to be okay, Marilyn," I say. It's the only thing I can say. Not because I don't know what else to say, but because I can't say anything. I'm not allowed.

"I don't think so," she says, shaking her head.

"I need to get them out of there somehow. But I don't know how," she says. Her eyes start to tear up.

"Is there anything I can do?" I ask.

"Not unless you know someone in immigration," she says. I don't, but perhaps that can change. Lots of things change with money. I make a mental note to look into this matter in the near future.

"I'm also worried that someone will find out that I work here. For you."

"Why?"

"Because then my whole family will definitely be in trouble. Sanchez is rounding everyone up who is the opposition. And I work here, in America, for a very wealthy man. He might think that it will give my family members resources to oppose him. Even though we won't. Ah, I'm so worried about my stupid nephews. They're so full of pride for their country. They'll do anything. You know how men are. At 20, you think you're invincible. Or worse yet, you believe that there's sense in dying for your country."

She shakes her head and walks away. I know she wants to be alone now. I let her.

Again, I wish that I could ease her fears and anxieties. I can. All I have to tell her is who I really am. What I really do in my spare time. But I can't. It might jeopardize the whole mission. So, instead, I just stand there quietly, trying to offer my sympathies from afar.

CHAPTER 3 - LOGAN

I'm dreading this lunch. We've had it planned for some time. Apparently, Sadie has something very important to tell me. Why we couldn't do this on the phone is beyond me. Or better yet, text message. I don't see why text messages get such a bad rep nowadays. They are efficient and to the point. And if you want emotions, just add an emoji.

Sadie and I make plans to meet at Salvatori's. A ridiculously overpriced Italian restaurant on Rodeo Drive with excellent wine and so-so pasta. Though I have my suspicions that I might be the only one who has ever noticed, because I might be the only one who still eats carbs out in the open in this city. Salvatori's isn't my favorite place, it's not even in my top ten, but Sadie likes the atmosphere, and it is her choice. Even though I'm the one who's going to pay for it.

I walk into the restaurant and tell the hostess my name. She takes me to my table where I order a scotch. Sadie is late, as always. I don't think I have been out with her for one meal when she wasn't at least fifteen minutes late. Sadie adores Coco Chanel and believes in the importance of making a grand entrance. I agree, of course. Except that this is a dinner. Something of a business engagement.

I drink my scotch, scroll mindlessly through the Google News feed and occasionally look up at the door. Finally, I see her. I glance down at my watch. Burberry with a nice cloth strap. I can afford much more, but I have a weakness for this British company. Something about its quiet understated style turns me on. Sadie is only five minutes late. Wow, she wasn't kidding. This must be important.

We give each other a brief hug and an air kiss. There's no kissing on the cheek in this town – only pretend air kisses. Real kisses, even those on the cheek, might mess up the makeup and definitely don't mesh well with the contouring.

Sadie's legs are so long that they hit the top of the table as she sits down. She's a Victoria's Secret model, which means she's 5'10" tall. Add to that her obligatory 5 inch Louboutin heels.

"Traffic was horrid," Sadie says. She grew up in South Africa and went to boarding school in England. Her accent is all over the place, but it's beautiful and soothing. I smile and nod. I don't mention the fact that she only lives 15 minutes away.

"I ordered you a watermelon martini," I say.

"Awe, thank you," she smiles. "I wish I could."

I furrow my brow. I don't know what this means. Sadie is not the woman to miss a drink. Ever. When we dated – however, briefly – she didn't go one night without a glass of wine or three.

"Okay," I say slowly. "So what did you want to talk to me about?"

The waiter arrives and asks us our order. I order the lobster bisque and she orders the spicy tuna. Not really Italian, but they carry it and it's delicious. Sadie doesn't even bother to open the menu. It's what she always gets here.

After the waiter leaves, I don't ask her my question again. Instead, I just wait for her response. Her eyes have a hard time meeting mine. They are all over the place. As if she has something to apologize for. I try to think of what this can all be about.

Sadie is my longest relationship ever. We dated, exclusively mind you, for three whole months. That's three months during which I didn't sleep with anyone else. It may not sound like a lot, but I don't make that kind of commitment lightly. Our breakup was a mutual decision. I know that everyone says that, but it's true. I was thinking of calling it off for about a week, before she brought it up at dinner one night. Why did we break up? I don't know. Just wasn't feeling us anymore. I wouldn't say that it got boring. Just a little bit predicable. We ran out of things to talk about after a few dates, and the sex was only really good for the first two months. After that, it required a lot of work. Work that neither of us were willing to put up.

"Okay, I have to tell you something," Sadie says.

"I know, I'm waiting."

"You don't have to be a dick."

"I'm sorry," I say, and I am. I'm just getting a little impatient. And I still don't know why all of this couldn't be done on the phone.

Sadie takes a deep breath. She leans forward and looks straight at me. Her long, straight hair falls over her shoulders, cradling her gorgeous breasts. She's wearing a strapless dress, which perfectly accentuates her small waist and curvy body. She's not curvy by normal standards, but she is by Victoria's Secret standards. Sadie's has beautiful olive skin and the coral necklace around her long, delicate neck perfectly complements her skin tone.

"I'm pregnant," she says.

"What?"

"I'm pregnant."

I shake my head. "What? How?"

"You know how," she shrugs.

"Is it…" I'm about to ask if it's mine, but I wisely stop myself before finishing that sentence. Of course, it's mine if she's telling me about this. Why else would she be informing me, and not the real father?

"Yes, it's yours!" she hisses, just as our plates arrive. We don't speak again until the bus boys carefully place our food in front of us, grind the pepper and sprinkle the plates with the right amount of parmesan cheese.

"How did this happen?" I ask. "We were careful."

I'm always careful. I know lots of rich guys who don't care, but I'm too smart for that. If I have kids, and that's a big if, I want to be there for them. I'm not going out there and getting a bunch of women pregnant and paying for thousands of dollars in child support for nothing.

"I guess not careful enough," she shrugs.

"But I thought you were on the pill. And I wore a condom."

"I am on the pill. But you didn't wear a condom every time. Don't bullshit me," she says.

Shit. She's right. There were a couple of times at the end of our relationship when we were just caught up in the moment.

"So what happens now?" I ask. I'm trying to be as tactful as possible. I have my doubts that this baby is mine, but getting Sadie pissed off right now isn't the solution. I'm not even sure that I can do a paternity test right now, so there's no need to even get into that.

"I'm going to keep it," she says. Definitely. This isn't up for debate. She isn't giving the baby up or getting rid of it. She's only telling me now because the decision has been made.

"Okay," I say as definitely as possible. I match her decisiveness, even though that's the last thing I'm feeling at this moment.

Suddenly, Sadie breaks down. The façade of determination and strength crumbles before me. Her face gets flushed and her eyes tear up.

"What am I going to do, Logan?" she whispers, stuffing large amounts of her spicy tuna salad into her mouth. She's gulping them down so quickly, for a second, I worry that she's going to choke.

"What do you mean?"

"I can't have this baby. I'm only 25. I wasn't one of those models who got on the catwalk at 14. This has been a struggle for me. So if I have this baby now…my whole life is over."

I take a deep breath. She needs a rock right now. She needs someone to tell her that it's all going to be okay. I can be that person.

"It's going to be fine," I force myself to say. "But are you sure you're pregnant?"

"Yes, I'm sure. I took like a million tests!" she explodes. Wrong move. Mascara is running down her face along with the tears. She rubs her eyes and makes the mess even worse.

"Oh shit, it's getting into my eyes." Sadie takes out her compact and wipes it away. Then she takes a deep breath and returns to me.

"What are you going to do about this?" she asks.

"What do you want me to do?"

"Are you planning on being a father?" Sadie's no longer sad. Somehow, her disappointment and fear morphed into anger at me.

"Well, frankly, I don't know," I say as honestly as possible. "I hadn't really considered a baby until this very moment. Not sure how it's going to fit into my schedule."

Bad move. Awful. The worst part is that I knew that it was the wrong thing to say as I was saying it, but I couldn't stop myself.

"Not fit into your schedule! Are you insane? You don't do anything. You just live off your billions. And you're unemployed," Sadie yells. Couples at tables near us turn to look at us.

"Keep your voice down," I say quietly. "I'm not unemployed. I just sold my business."

"And what do you do now?" she asks.

"I'm in between things," I say. That's the best way I can explain it. She doesn't know the truth, no one does. So to her, I don't do anything. That's the way it's going to have to be.

The rest of the dinner proceeds as expected. Sadie vacillates between being upset with herself, me, and at being pregnant, and yelling at me for not wanting to be a father. She's not wrong about that. I don't want to be a father. I definitely don't want to be a father to my ex-girlfriend's baby, an ex who I wasn't very keen on seeing again at all, but there's something else to all this. What Sadie doesn't want to admit is that she doesn't really want to be a mother either. Finally, after close to an hour, dinner finally ends. I get the check and we say our brief goodbyes while waiting for the valet.

CHAPTER 4 - AVERY

Oh my God! Oh my God! Oh my God! I'm not going to get these done in time! I look at my phone. I have an hour left before Roberto, the driver, has to pack the centerpieces up and drive them to the wedding venue in Malibu. I'm working as fast as I can, but the flowers are still not cooperating. The design is simple enough: opaque ivory white vases with a band of thick yellow ribbon around the bottom. The splash of yellow is the perfect complement to the yellow and white flowers inside the vase and acts to extend the crisp color scheme of the wedding decor.

When I went over this design with the bride and groom three weeks ago, I thought that it would be a walk in the park, since the vases aren't see-through.

That means there's no need to worry about the arrangement of stems. Those can be such a hassle! The bride wanted something simple and yellow and this was supposed to be a breeze.

I like to have my centerpieces done completely the night before, but unfortunately there was some sort of tulip emergency, and they didn't get here until this morning! We're lucky they came at all.

"Don't worry, it's going to be okay," Cynthia mutters under her breath. Cynthia is my assistant and oldest friend. She's usually the one that's freaking out all the time, but this time she's the one staying calm. Not a good sign.

I cut the stems in the sink and carefully arrange the jonquils, sweet peas, ranunculus and finally the tulips in the second to last centerpiece. Cynthia has already laid them out for me and made the first ten centerpieces. I look at my phone again. We only have five more minutes before Roberto shows up. We need at least ten minutes to look over each centerpiece and make sure that it's perfect.

My mind and hands have never worked so well together. I'm cutting, arranging, coiffing, and adjusting at record speed. Even though Cynthia is the type to talk endlessly when she's nervous or anxious, she knows better than to disturb me now. A few minutes later, Roberto arrives and everything is almost ready. There's only one more centerpiece left to check.

"Wow, I can't believe you got it all done," Cynthia says.

I take a step back from the table. My light turquoise long sleeve shirt is drenched in sweat. The apron I'm wearing is barely covering it and, even though I've known Cynthia for many years, I hope she doesn't notice.

Cynthia and I help Roberto load up the van.

"Why don't I just go to the venue myself?" she asks. "You can stay here and relax."

I've never not gone and set up the centerpieces myself, but this has been a very stressful job and I'm leaning toward letting go of some control.

"Are you sure?" I ask.

"Yes, of course!" She has a surprised look on her face, like she can't believe that I'm actually going to let her do this.

"I'm going to make it perfect," she adds.

I know she will. She's even more of a perfectionist than I am.

Cynthia and I have known each other since we were 13. Her parents are like my second parents, and I practically lived with them after the accident. My parents died in a car accident, the summer after we graduated from University of Southern California. I had a job lined up at a boutique investment bank in downtown LA, but after the accident, I couldn't take it. I didn't do anything for a whole year, and Cynthia and her family took me in and cared for me. I was 22, way beyond the legal age, but after their death, I became a lost teenager again. It took me close to two years to finally feel normal again. Or as normal as I could.

After Cynthia and Roberto leave, I decide to make myself sangria. I don't drink often, but I'm in the mood right now. I cut up apples and oranges into squares and toss them into a pitcher and add three tablespoons of organic brown sugar. After muddling everything with a wood spoon, I add a cup of orange juice and a third of a cup of brandy for taste and muddle it again. Then I dump a bottle of Albero Spanish Red, a dry Spanish red wine, and taste it. It needs something else. I add a splash more of brandy and a little more brown sugar to sweeten the mixture. After adding ice and garnishing the rim of the pitcher with orange segments, I pour myself a glass and go out onto the porch.

This account is the biggest one I've had to date. The bride's parents are spending more than $500,000 on the wedding. When I showed them around my shop and showed them my proposal for the centerpiece designs, I was certain that there was no way that they were going to go with me. I have excellent designs, don't get me wrong, but I also have a little shop in Topanga Canyon, not some fancy storefront in Malibu or Beverly Hills.

Topanga Canyon is a rural canyon nestled between the northern suburbs of Calabasas and Woodland Hills and the lavish ocean front homes of Malibu. It's not a cheap area by any stretch of the imagination – you can hardly buy a house here for less than $800,000. The reason people live here and love it is because of its unique culture. Rural chic, Cynthia likes to call it. There are no developments, and there are a lot of old ranch homes. The new houses that pop up are architecturally interesting and unique. Lots of people have horses and chickens and shop for all of their food in organic farmer's markets.

After my parents' untimely death, I got $200,000 from their life insurance and decided to do what I always dreamed of doing: open my own floral shop. I found a small space on South Topanga Canyon Boulevard, in a little shopping center with its own unique flair. My floral shop, The Flower Patch, is sandwiched between Hidden Treasures, a vintage clothing store, and Quilts!, a quilt supply store. I got a great deal (for this area) when I signed a five-year lease for both the commercial space downstairs for The Flower Patch and the small studio apartment above. The studio apartment is technically not zoned for residential living, but the 88-year-old owner of the shopping center was kind enough to rent it to me for only $1000 a month, which is a steal. And this way, I don't have to commute or pay much more in rent somewhere in Calabasas or Malibu.

When I first opened The Flower Patch, I thought that I would have to run it in the red for at least 6 months, but much to my surprise, lots of locals started to come in for their weekly flowers and the two nice women who ran Hidden Treasures and Quilts! also spread the word to their customers. Before I knew it, I was making a nice little profit and had time and money to think about expanding into weddings. For the floral industry, weddings are where it's at. Flowers for weddings are typically marked up 35 to 55 percent, and that may or may not include a 20 percent mark-up for the design.

When I first ventured into weddings, a few months ago, all I did was charge a little bit less than my competitors in Malibu and Calabasas, and I started to have a lot of referrals and walk-ins. Twelve months later, the problem was keeping up with all the demand rather than drumming up business. That's when I finally started paying Cynthia (she was a thankless volunteer and a cheerleader before then) and hired Roberto, and my two part-time assistants, Peyton and Brie. I could probably use a few more assistants, but the space won't allow it. It's crammed as it is when just Cynthia and I are in the room.

Cynthia thinks it's time to expand – maybe look for another location – but I have a three-year lease, and the rent here is unbeatable. If I move, then I probably won't be able to charge the same prices. Or worse, I might end up being just another run-of-the-mill flower shop. Here, I'm embedded in the local culture. I know my weekly customers, and they're the ones sending me my wedding business. No matter how good expansion sounds, I've decided not to consider it until closer to the end of my lease.

A few hours later, Cynthia comes back. I pour her a glass of sangria, and she joins me on the porch. She hands me her phone and shows me the pictures of the centerpieces from the reception hall.

"The bride was ecstatic," Cynthia says. Unlike most people in Southern California, she doesn't use superlatives very often, so I know she's not exaggerating. "And the mother-in-law. You should've seen her face."

"I'm glad," I nod.

She hands me the check. They already paid the down payment, and this is the rest of what they owe me. The sum brings a smile to my face. I take out my phone, scan it and deposit it immediately. A few months ago, one of my customer's checks bounced, because I waited until Monday to deposit it instead of taking care of it that Friday. It took two months to finally get the money from her, but in that time, I have learned a very important lesson. Now, I deposit all checks as soon as I get them.

CHAPTER 5 - AVERY

"This is the best sangria I've ever had," Cynthia says, finishing her glass and pouring herself another. We are sitting on the little porch in front of my apartment. It's not so much a porch as a walkway leading to the stairs downstairs, but I'm the only one up here so I've decorated it like it's my porch. I bought a pair of natural wood Adirondack chairs and painted them myself. I'm sitting in the bright yellow one, and Cynthia's occupying the bright blue one. The pitcher of sangria stands between us on a small side table. I had purchased from the thrift store downstairs. I like it, because it's from another world altogether. The legs are sleek, like midcentury modern, and the top is made up of tiny little pieces of Mexican tile. It is as if someone had broken a colorful piece of pottery and then glued all the pieces on top of the table.

"It is quite good," I nod. Sangria is one of my specialties. I'm not actually a big fan of wine, but wine with fruit, brandy and brown sugar is hard to pass up.

"So…" Cynthia says, turning to me. Her eyes sparkle mischievously.

"So?" I ask. "So what?"

"Happy birthday!!" she yells.

"Oh that," I mumble.

"Oh, c'mon. It's your 25th birthday! We have to celebrate."

I sigh. 25 years already. I should be more excited, but for some reason I'm not. Frankly, I was hoping that she would forget all about it.

"I'm too tired to celebrate," I say. It's not a lie. I am exhausted. Working on those centerpieces and taking care of all the customers who have been coming in for the last couple of days have really taken it all out of me.

"No, absolutely not," Cynthia shakes her head. "You're not getting out of this that easily. I have reservations, tonight. Well, actually in an hour," she says looking at the time on phone. "At that place in Malibu that you like."

"The one with the ocean view?" I ask. That doesn't really narrow it down. Almost all restaurants in Malibu have an ocean view, but Cynthia and I know each other very well.

She nods. "The one with the blue shutters."

"Well, if it's the one with the blue shutters," I say with a shrug. "How can I say no?"

"And before we do that, I have something else for you."

"We said no presents," I remind her.

"That was before your business was doing so well that you actually gave me a job! You're getting this present. And I'm certainly expecting a present from you in a couple of months."

I smile. Cynthia reaches into her large Louis Vuitton purse and rustles through it, looking for something. I do not pay Cynthia enough for her to be able to afford a Louis Vuitton – their bags start at as much as I pay for a month of rent for my apartment – and this one is about double in size, so it must cost at least double if not triple that. Cynthia has always enjoyed the finer things in life and even before she started working for me, she spent all of her money from bar-tending on purses and shoes. It also helps that her parents don't mind helping her out a bit, or a lot, to cover the necessities like her car and her apartment.

Cynthia finally emerges from her bag with an envelope. She holds it up above her head.

"Okay. But before I give this to you, I want to tell you that this was nearly impossible to get. I know that this isn't your style or anything, but I want you to give this a chance. This woman is very good at what she does."

I have no idea what she's talking about, but I nod anyway. She hands me the envelope. Inside, I find a beautiful white card with elegant script that reads 'Happy Birthday.' I open the card. A small postcard falls out onto my lap. The front of it says, *Dolly Monroe, billionaire matchmaker*. The back reads *Good for one free consultation*.

"What is this?" I ask.

The inside of the card also has a few kind words from Cynthia in her elegant handwriting, but I can't focus on that right now.

"Well, I was thinking about what to get you for this very important birthday. I was sort of reflecting on your life, and I was thinking that despite what happened a few years ago with your parents, you have a lot to be thankful for. Your business is very busy, much busier than you ever thought it would be, you have amazing friends, mainly me, and there's really only one thing missing."

I wait for her to finish her thought.

"A man! And not just some guy, a real man."

"So you got me a consultation with a matchmaker?" I ask. "Can't I just go online to get a date?"

"Yes, you can. But I don't want you to just find some guy. I want to help you find the one. And a little birdie told me that this woman, Dolly Monroe, well, she's the best!"

I look at the card again. It is very thick stock and a rich color of ivory. As someone who recently spent a little money on designing and ordering business cards, I know that this one cost a pretty penny.

"Does she have a website?" I ask. I want to look her up right away.

"No," Cynthia says with a coy smile. "That's the thing about her. She's very exclusive. She doesn't advertise to the public. It's all word of mouth."

"I don't get it," I say.

"I don't know either. But there's a phone number on the card. You have to call it and make an appointment. Then she'll tell you her address. A friend of mine used it."

"Did she find someone?"

"She found her husband," Cynthia says.

"Oh, you mean Isabel?" I ask. Cynthia nods. I don't know Isabel personally. She's a friend of Cynthia's from this place in Belize where her parents have a vacation condo. Isabel is from Texas, and her claim to fame is that she married a very rich rancher in West Texas. And they are apparently insanely happy.

"I didn't know this then, but Dolly apparently set them up. It's part of the contract that the couple isn't supposed to talk about her until after some time passes. Not sure why."

"So this Dolly, she's a matchmaker? And that's all she does?" I ask.

"Yes. But not just some matchmaker. A billionaire matchmaker."

"But I don't want to meet a billionaire," I say.

"You don't want to meet a billionaire? Are you crazy?"

"No, I don't really want to meet anyone right now. Let alone, some rich prick with a Hollywood attitude who thinks he is God's gift to women."

Cynthia shakes her head.

"This is your gift from me. I want you to at least give it a chance. Just meet with her. Will you do that?"

I sigh. I don't want to. Cynthia should know better. The thing is that my resistance doesn't even have anything to do with Dolly or the men she would match me with. It's all me.

"I don't think I'm ready," I say.

"You're ready. I know you are."

I don't have to tell Cynthia what I'm thinking. She knows it all too well. Cal, my ex, and I broke up almost five months ago, but he still won't leave me alone. I met him through Cynthia – they work at the same restaurant. We dated for three months, and then things got too intense for me. He always wanted to know what I was doing and where I was going. He went as far as putting a tracker on my phone to check up on my whereabouts. Real stalker. When I finally decided that enough was enough, he choked me until I passed out and just left me there. I could've died. I would've if my neighbor didn't invite herself over without knocking and ask to borrow some eggs. It was she who found me and called an ambulance.

It was over for us after that. Or so I had thought. I took out a restraining order. The judge ordered him to stay away from me. So far he has, but I still get the sneaking suspicion that, though I haven't actually seen him, he's around and watching me.

"This is going to be good for you," Cynthia says, taking my hand into hers. "Something positive in your life. Who knows, maybe you'll even have fun."

"You know, not everyone can be as happy as you and Todd," I say. Cynthia has been with her boyfriend, Todd, since we were all freshmen at USC. They are two peas in a pod – best friends. I haven't even seen them fight, once! My parents were like that too.

"Maybe not everyone. But I know you can. You deserve it. And I want to help you to find him."

"And you think that this billionaire matchmaker can help me?" I ask.

"I know it's silly. But what if she can? She has a great track record. She used to set up regular people way before she set up billionaires."

I look at the card once again.

"Okay," I finally say. "I guess I'll give it a shot. About time that I moved on, right?"

CHAPTER 6 - AVERY

My appointment with Dolly Monroe is three days later. Her assistant gives me an address to a pop up office in Malibu. I don't really know what a pop up office is, but her assistant fills me in. Apparently, they are offices that are used occasionally, on as needed basis.

"Why doesn't she have a permanent place?" I ask.

"Because she mainly conducts business from her home, but she does not give out her address to just anyone."

I guess that makes sense. Though, a Starbucks would do just as well.

I pull into a small shopping center just off Pacific Coast Highway. There are many little boutique shops with overpriced clothes and jewelry on the bottom. I go upstairs and knock on the corner door.

A tall, slender woman with bored eyes and sky-high heels opens the door.

"Hi, Avery Lewis?" she asks without taking off her sunglasses.

I nod. She shows me inside. I'm wearing flats and this girl is about eight inches taller than I am. I think almost every guy I've ever dated is shorter than she is, and they were not short.

"Dolly will be with you in a minute."

The assistant sits back down at the desk and disappears behind her Mac laptop. Just as I'm about to sit down in one of the chairs against the wall, a petite blonde woman with too much makeup comes out and invites me in.

"Hi there! I'm Dolly, pleased to meet you," she says in a thick Texas accent.

"Hello, I'm Avery," I shake her hand.

She leads me into a large space with floor to ceiling windows. There's a large white desk facing the entrance near the window with nothing on it except an iPad, a small pink notebook and a pen. Dolly sits down across from me and motions for me to take the seat in front of the desk. Behind her, all I see is the vastness of the Pacific Ocean and a blue sky without a single cloud.

"So, tell me about yourself Avery," Dolly says. She's wearing a professional linen blouse, but because her breasts are so big, she looks more like someone playing a businesswoman in a porn film. Her waist is also small enough to look like it belongs to the impossibly tiny Audrey Hepburn.

I tell her that I grew up in Calabasas and attended USC, majoring in communication. I briefly mention my parents' untimely death and my blooming business, The Flower Patch (no pun intended).

"Oh my God, I know your place. There's this little restaurant in Topanga Canyon that I absolutely adore – The Inn of the Seventh Ray! They have the best brunches on weekends."

"Yeah that place is one of my favorites."

"I always see your place on my drive up, and I've been meaning to pop in for some time now. I love your signage," Dolly says.

"Thank you, I really appreciate it. It took a while to get just the right design."

"It's surprisingly difficult to capture 'rural chic,' as my assistant Cynthia calls it," I say. "It took us almost a month to come up with just the right typography and color scheme to portray the feeling of farm-fresh flowers and high-end, elegant and contemporary designs."

"Well, you've captured it perfectly! That's exactly what your sign says."

I really appreciate her saying this. I may not know anything about Dolly, but I do know that she did not get where she is right now knowing nothing about business. Any business, especially ones as personal as hers and mine, require a lot of attention to detail and sending out just the right message to your clients.

"Can I ask you something?" I ask. "How did you get into the matchmaking business?"

"I actually discovered that I've a knack for this when I was in my teens. A long, long time ago. I set up a few kids in my high school, and they really hit it off. I grew up on a ranch in West Texas. There were a lot of wealthy people around, but our ranch was barely making ends meet. So after I married my high school sweetheart at 19, he got a job in the oil industry, and we moved east to Dallas. That's when I decided to start doing matchmaking professionally. And it grew from there."

"Oh wow, that's impressive. Is your husband still in the oil industry?"

"Oh no," she laughs, getting up from behind the desk. "Would you like a cup of coffee?"

I nod. Dolly walks over to one side of the room where there's a large Starbucks-style coffee machine.

"I'm having a cappuccino. You?" she asks.

"That sounds perfect," I say.

"I know my assistant can do this, but making my own coffee is one of those pleasures in life that I don't delegate to others. When I was really young, growing up on a dusty mesa where canned beans made up the majority of any meal, I read in Time magazine that people in Paris and Rome sit around coffee shops all day drinking their cappuccinos and espressos. I didn't know what those things were, but to me that was the height of sophistication. I dreamed of one day going there and getting a job at one of those coffee shops. Now, I own a coffee shop in the Latin Quarter of Paris and in Trastevere in Rome, but I still don't do too much sitting around in coffee shops. Ah, childhood dreams die hard, huh?"

The more I talk to Dolly, the more I like her. I love how straightforward she is. She doesn't seem to have any pretenses. Yet, she's something of an enigma. For one, she looks like a total bimbo, even a trophy wife for some really old and wealthy man. Her tight black pencil skirt accentuates every curve, showing off quite an impressive butt for a woman of her age. Speaking as a girl who hardly ever wears heels, I'm in awe at how easily she maneuvers around the office in her five-inch Louboutin pumps with the signature red lacquered sole. It's as if she's wearing sneakers.

"Oh yes, you asked me about my husband," Dolly says sitting down. "No, he quit the oil industry in his early thirties. The matchmaking business was making so much by then it didn't make any sense for him to be out on the rig for a month at a time anymore. He got into real estate."

"And you two are still together?" I ask. And then I catch myself. "I'm sorry, I don't mean to be rude."

Dolly throws her head back and laughs with her whole body. "Oh no, that's quite alright. Yes, we're together. We've been together since we were in high school. Many, many happy years."

"Wow, that's...amazing. Especially, in this town."

"Eh, people say that marriage requires work, but if you ask me, if you find the right person, it doesn't. It's easy if you marry your best friend," she says.

"I've never heard anyone say that before."

"I know. It's not the right thing to say. But in my experience, marriage should be fun. It's an optional experience. If it's not fun, why do it?" she shrugs. "Trust me, if it required work, my husband and I wouldn't be together anymore. I'm a hard worker, but I limit my work exclusively to my business. I say, you wouldn't work hard at being friends with someone, so why would you at love?"

I nod.

"Of course, there is one rule that both people should abide by," she adds.

"What is it?"

"Keep the fights clean and the sex dirty."

I take a sip of my cappuccino, letting all that set in. I don't know if she's right or wrong, but whatever she's doing it's working for her.

"So, tell me a little bit about your dating history," she says.

I shrug. It's hard to know where to start.

"I've had a few boyfriends in college. One lasted a year, the other a couple of months. Then I dated this guy, Cal, for a bit last year. He asked me to marry him. I said yes at first, but called off the wedding soon after."

These are definitely the highlights over what happened.

"Any reason in particular?" she asks.

"It wasn't a very healthy relationship. He was…too controlling. Always wanted to know where I was," I say. I pause for a moment. I don't want to go into more details. "I'm sorry. It's a little bit hard to talk about that. Let's just say that I'm glad that I'm out of that relationship for good."

"Okay, I understand," she nods, sympathetically. From her demeanor, I get the sense that she actually does get it.

"So, how does this work?" I ask, changing the subject.

"Well, I have a roster of possible men. I talk to you, get to know you a little bit. Ask you what kind of guy you're looking for. And then I use my judgment. Sometimes I match you with someone exactly to your specifications, but that's not always the case."

"Really?" I ask.

"I listen to what both parties want, but I also rely on my own judgment. For instance, I find that men often rely too much on physical attributes. They think that they want one type of woman, but when they meet someone completely different, that's a great match for them based on their personality, they fall for her."

"That makes sense."

"Since we're on the subject. I have one important question to ask you," Dolly says. I nod and wait.

"What kind of net worth are you looking for?"

"Excuse me?" I ask.

"In your date? In other words, how low of a net worth are you willing to consider? This is important because I have a lot of clients and it gives me a ballpark of where to start."

"Are you serious?" I ask. My blood starts to boil. My face gets flushed and my fingers grow ice-cold.

"Is this really the operation that you're running here? Setting up sleazy old men who are only after looks with gold diggers who are only after money?"

"Avery—" she tries to interrupt me, but I'm on a roll. I grab my purse and head toward the door.

"You know, you really had me going. I actually liked you. I thought it was so sweet that you and your husband have been together since you were both in high school. I really fell for your whole rags to riches story. But now I see that this, this whole thing, is nothing but a front for some sugar daddy business. You don't care about love. You want to know what net worth I'm looking for? I don't give a fuck. How about that for a net worth?"

I walk out steaming. Luckily, there's no elevator to wait for. I'm parked right next to a personalized parking spot that belongs to Dolly Monroe. The car in the spot is a Maserati. It confirms everything I just said up there.

"Avery, please," Dolly catches up to me when I'm already in my Prius, about to pull out. She knocks on my window. Against my better judgment, I roll the window down.

"That was a test. You passed the test," she says, trying to catch her breath.

"What?"

"I ask all the women that to make sure that they're not just looking for a sugar daddy. That's exactly what I don't want. You passed the test. And given that little display in my office, I think I know just the right guy for you."

CHAPTER 7 - LOGAN

Stephanie doesn't know how to sail, but none of them do. What she does know is how to be impressed with my sailboat and my sailing abilities. We don't go out too far, just around the harbor, not far from Marina del Rey, but it's enough to get Stephanie's panties wet. She has had herself draped around my neck for close to an hour now, acting very impressed with everything as I let her steer. Stephanie is my perfect date. She's blonde, tan, vapid and polished. She knows almost every beauty product at Sephora and how to expertly use it, and she knows barely anything else about anything else.

Stephanie is from Orange County. And though I usually don't like to date girls that far away – the commute is awful – Stephanie loves driving the new

Beamer, she got as her college graduation present from her daddy, and she is always game to party. As much as I wish it were, today is not a Netflix and chill kind of night. It's not a hookup. Stephanie is my date. I'm having dinner with my younger brother and his girlfriend. They have something very important to tell me, and apparently, it can't be done over the phone.

Don't get me wrong. I love my brother. Liam is a great guy, but we're completely different. Liam loves the nine to five lifestyle, which in his profession is more like the nine to seven grind. After college, whilst I bummed around, backpacked through Central America and Europe and started my company, he went to law school and focused on getting the right internships. Liam has always been very career-oriented, rather than entrepreneurial, and that's what makes my dad get him more. My father isn't someone who really understands my lifestyle. He knows that I no longer need to work, but he doesn't really get why I don't. Liam and my dad are two peas in a pod. Honestly, I think Liam would probably say no to all my money if that meant that he still had a job.

As you can probably guess, when I hang out with Liam, I need a buffer. That's where Stephanie comes in. His girlfriend, Kora, is an okay buffer, but I've known her for so long that she's practically family now. Liam met Kora in Oberlin, the small liberal arts college in Ohio where he studied Economics. After graduation, he took an internship at Citibank in New York City, until he realized that he didn't want to go into finance after all. He switched to law, which my father had been harping on him to pursue for years. He's been singing the same song to me, but I was wise to ignore him even after I grew up. But Liam's a natural. He graduated from University of Michigan and then came back to the LA area to practice law. Kora followed him all around the country. She completed her Master's degree in Education and supported them working as a middle school teacher while he was in law school. Now, he supports her. They're a nice couple, really. I don't have anything against them. Except that we have hardly anything in common.

I look down at my Omega watch. We have half an hour before we have to be at the restaurant. I guide Stephanie's hands as we pull into the slip.

"We're back," I whisper into her ear. She giggles and flashes me a smile of her pearly whites.

"What should we do now?" she asks. Suddenly, she's acting shy. All this time on the water, she was flirting like hell. Okay, I'll bite, I decide.

"I can think of a few things," I say, wrapping my arms around her. She's standing in front of me, with her back to me. I push away her windblown hair and kiss her neck. Little goosebumps run up her spine. I feel them with my tongue. She tilts her head back and moans a little. I run my tongue from her earlobes to her collarbone. Then I flip her around and press my lips onto hers. She responds right away, forcing her tongue into my mouth. I pull her toward the cabin, taking extra precautions to make sure that she doesn't bump her head. I have learned that injuries are not romantic, no matter what all those romantic comedies try to tell you. I push Stephanie onto the bed. When I don't climb on top of her immediately, she pulls on my shirt. This is going to be a good night. Even if everything else tonight goes wrong, this is going to be so right.

After we are both more than satisfied, we get dressed and get off the boat. We took a little longer than I thought, so I hurry Stephanie along. She ends up re-applying her lipstick and blush as we walk to the restaurant in the harbor. Women's ability to multi-task never ceases to amaze me.

Stephanie is wearing a designer black dress with spaghetti straps. It's so short, if she bends over I'll see the lower part of her perfectly toned butt cheeks. Stephanie is a yoga enthusiast with a body to match. For a moment, I hesitate. I want to go back to the boat and tear that dress off her again. Then I spot Liam and Kora somewhere in the back of the restaurant. It's too late. I wave hello.

Unlike Stephanie, who isn't afraid of the self-tanner, Kora is so pale that she looks ill. Her jet-black hair is cut short, and she's wearing hardly any makeup. She has nice bone structure and a pretty enough face, but a little bit of makeup would go a long way to making her look beautiful. My brother is no different really. He has the same cheap haircut and is wearing a crumpled old suit. He doesn't care about fashion one bit and only wears suits because they're required for his line of work. He doesn't seem to know that there are new lines of suits coming out each season and has worn the same two suits since law school.

"Hey there!" Liam gets up and gives me a warm hug. After giving Kora a kiss on the cheek, I introduce Stephanie and we all sit down.

"It's very nice to meet you, Stephanie," Liam says, glaring at me. "I wish my brother had told us that you were coming."

I smile. What he really means is that he wishes that I had told him so that he could tell me to not bring her. Well, she's here for me. Not you.

"Nice to meet you too," Stephanie says in a high, peppy voice, completely oblivious to Liam's half-assed compliment.

Liam and I each order a scotch and Stephanie and Kora order lemon drops. We make small talk about the weather and the traffic – usual LA stuff – before I finally broach the subject of why I'm here. I've waited long enough for them to bring it up.

"Not that I don't love catching up with you two," I say finishing my scotch. I motion to the waitress to bring me another. Alcohol is pretty much essential if I have to spend time with my family.

"But what's the big news already? I'm dying to know."

"Well, the big news is that…" Liam looks at Kora. Her eyes light up and she sticks out her left hand.

"We're engaged!" They say simultaneously.

"Oh my God! Congratulations!" Stephanie gets so excited that she spills her drink putting it back onto the table, before grabbing Kora's hand.

"Oh my, this is beautiful. Two carats?" she asks.

"Two and a half," Kora smiles.

"Holy shit!" Stephanie yells. She isn't a girl with much of a filter, but the expression on Kora's face says that she couldn't be happier with Stephanie's exuberance.

"He did really good. You did really good, Liam!" Stephanie says approvingly. "And the diamonds on the sides, nice touch!"

"Logan?" Liam turns to me. Stephanie has ushered in the kind of level of excitement that I can never match. At least, not about this.

"Wow, congratulations!" I say as peppy as I can. Apparently, it works because Liam smiles.

"How long have you two been together?" Stephanie asks.

"A long time. Seven years," Kora says. Kora's been trying to get Liam to marry her since they have graduated from college. Honestly, I'm shocked that it took Liam that long to keep her at bay.

"Wow, that's a long time," Stephanie says. "I say you really deserve something more than two carats for waiting so long. Why did it take you so long to ask this gorgeous girl to marry you?"

Wow, Stephanie really doesn't have a filter. I'm actually starting to enjoy this. I turn to Liam and watch him squirm.

"Yeah, Liam, why did it take you so long?" Kora joins in on the fun.

"You know why. Because I was in law school. And then I just started working. There were a lot of things to figure out."

"Well, I'm glad you finally figured them out," Stephanie announces as if she has known Kora her whole life.

"Hey, why is everyone interrogating me? I'm only 27. Logan there is 30 and has never had a relationship that lasted longer than two months."

"Ah! Is that true?" Stephanie gasps dramatically.

"My therapist says I have commitment issues," I say. I don't have a therapist, but I've noticed that people like the sound of that. Like I'm admitting that

I have a problem, and I'm trying to resolve it. It makes me sound like a good guy.

"Well, at least, you're working on it," Stephanie says with a sigh.

"Man, I can't win, can I?" Liam jokes and we all chuckle.

"I think you've already won," I say raising my glass. "I'd like to make a toast to you, Liam and Kora. Despite all the jokes, I know that you two have loved each other for a very long time. You have been through it all together, and now you're finally coming together and making it official. I couldn't be prouder of you as my little brother. And I couldn't be happier to welcome you, Kora, into our family as my future sister. Here's to you!"

Liam's eyes get a little misty and Kora cries outright. Even Stephanie tears up. I don't really mean a word of what I said, but those were nice words, huh? I like Kora okay, but I think she can do better than my brother. He works too hard and doesn't do anything for fun. Everything is such serious business with that guy. He's got way too many hang-ups and anxieties, and now poor Kora will have to put up with them for as long as they live. Or as long as they stay married. But I couldn't very well say any of that. I'm not that much of an asshole.

CHAPTER 8 - LOGAN

As I predicted, that speech I made last night at dinner really endeared me to Stephanie. We had a wild night on the boat afterwards, and she said that she was even open to the possibility of inviting a friend or two into our bed. And she knows the perfect girl – her college roommate! That was music to my ears. I've been looking for some variety in my threesomes, and I've noticed that it's more effective if the girl finds the other girl to join us. That way I don't look like a slime ball.

Stephanie had an appointment with a plastic surgeon about a possible breast augmentation down in Newport Beach the following morning, so she took off at three a.m. to beat the traffic and get an hour or two of sleep. Apparently, canceling it was out of the question – she has been waiting for it for a month. Watching her drive away in her white BMW convertible, I suddenly wondered if I was in love. Everything about that girl is perfect physically. She doesn't want to stay the night and she's into threesomes. What more does a man want? What more do I want?

Instead of sleeping on the boat, I decide to take the opportunity and drive back to my place in Malibu, also to beat all the traffic. I cruise down Pacific Coast Highway at 80 miles an hour and arrive at my house in record time. After stripping off all my clothes, I fall into a dead sleep.

"Well, well, well," I hear a woman's voice somewhere in the distance. "It's almost eleven and Mr. Logan Davenport, an unemployed billionaire, is still asleep."

The woman speaks in a thick West Texas accent while tapping her heel on my marble floor.

"I had a late night," I mumble into my pillow.

Click. Click. Click. She walks across the floor, grabs the remote to the blinds and pulls them up. The sun hits me like a brick. I grab another pillow and cover my face with it.

"I had a late night, Aunt Dolly," I moan.

"Yes, I can see that. But half the day is nearly gone already."

"I can because I'm retired," I say, rubbing my eyes and finally sitting up. "I can do anything I want to do."

Aunt Dolly smiles a wide toothy smile. Her veneers are bright white and her matte red lipstick is perfectly applied. There isn't one line on her face, and her hair is as big and platinum as ever. "The bigger the hair, the closer to God," is a popular saying in Texas, but Aunt Dolly takes it to a whole new level.

"You may be retired, but you are also only 30 years old. You can't just do nothing all day."

"I don't do nothing. I surf. I go out to lunch. I go on dates."

I do plenty of other things too, which I can't really mention to her. Or anyone else for that matter.

"Oh I know all about your dates," she waves her hand dismissively. I chuckle and sit up in my bed. I can't really get out from under the sheet, because I'm completely nude. Noticing my conundrum, she walks out of my room.

"I'll wait for you in the kitchen," she says. "I have to talk to you about something important."

I pull on a t-shirt and shorts and follow her out. Marilyn is in the kitchen cooking something delicious on the stove.

"Why did you let her in?" I ask jokingly.

Marilyn turns around.

"Because it's Dolly," she says with a smirk. "I always let in Dolly."

Aunt Dolly smiles and tosses her hair with attitude.

"But I'm the one who pays you."

"Not enough to not let in Dolly!" Marilyn announces.

I roll my eyes. Marilyn adores Dolly. They've been friends ever since she came to work for me. If she wasn't so happily married, Dolly would undoubtedly set her up with one of her millionaire clients, and I'd be out of a great housekeeper.

I follow Aunt Dolly out to the porch. Marilyn brings us a tray of fruit, juice and coffee. The Pacific Ocean is unusually calm today. The sun is blistering hot and there are three pretty girls frolicking in the waves. I yearn to grab my board and join them.

"I found the perfect date for you," Aunt Dolly announces. I shake my head. Not again. Aunt Dolly has been trying to set me up with someone for years. And for years, I've politely declined her offer.

"I'm not really interested in meeting one of your gold diggers. I can find plenty of them myself."

"I do not deal with gold diggers, you know that," she says sternly. This is a sore subject for her. I know I'm being unfair. She is careful to weed those girls out. She refuses to meet my gaze. I know that I've offended her. This conversation won't go any further until I apologize.

"Okay, I'm sorry. But I can find my own dates," I say.

"She's completely different from anyone else I've ever met. And definitely not like all those stupid, hot girls who are just after your money, who you find so charming."

"So she's not hot?" I ask. "Thanks."

"She's not a model, no. But she's plenty gorgeous."

"She sounds boring."

"Oh trust me, she's anything but boring."

I want to ask her more about what she looks like, but I know that will make me seem shallow.

"So what's so special about her?"

"It's hard to explain. She's got this zest for life. This attitude."

"So she's a bitch?"

"No."

"Zest for life? What's that a euphemism for? Opinionated? Overbearing?"

"Exciting."

I shake my head. I'm not convinced.

"How old is she?"

"25."

"What does she do?"

"What do you care? None of the girls you date have jobs."

"Good point," I laugh.

"It just so happens that she runs her own business. She has a floral shop in Topanga Canyon."

Hmm, that's interesting. I've never been with anyone from Topanga Canyon before, but I've heard the rumors about the hippie girls who live there. They are very open-minded, sexually adventurous. I want to ask Aunt Dolly about it, but I don't know how to phrase the question delicately, so I don't look so much like an asshole.

"Is she one of those love the earth, flowers in her hair girls?"

"Are you asking if she's a hippie?"

"I guess."

"I don't know. She definitely bathes and shaves if that's what you mean."

"That's not exactly what I was getting at," I mumble.

"I don't really know anything about her politics," Aunt Dolly says, trying another angle. Now we're way off course. I don't care about politics. I mean, I have my own opinions, but I've noticed that there are open minded and sexually adventurous girls on both sides of the political spectrum, so I don't discriminate.

"What makes you think that we're going to be a good match?"

"Because she'll keep you on your toes."

I'm intrigued. Not so much by the fact that Aunt Dolly thinks that this girl will keep me on my toes, but by the fact that she lives in Topanga Canyon. Plus, she runs an actual business. That will be quite a change – to go out with someone with a job!

I take another sip of my orange juice and look over at Dolly. She stands out like a sore thumb, but it's not just in Malibu. With that hair and jewelry and boobs, she would stand out anywhere. Aunt Dolly is my mom's half-sister. My grandfather left my mom's mom and moved to seek his fortune in West Texas and married Dolly's mom. I met Aunt Dolly for the first time when I was 14 when she just showed up at our door in Chatsworth, California. My mom, who likes to wear sweats around the house, was horrified because Aunt Dolly was dressed in Chanel from head to toe. We have been close ever since. She's outgoing, exuberant and knows how to have a good time. She loves to spend money, but she also loves to give it away. Despite the clothes, the jewelry and the shoes, she has absolutely no attitude. She doesn't act like she's better than anyone else and has a heart of gold.

When she arrived in Los Angeles, Aunt Dolly's matchmaking business was already making close to half a million dollars – and that was in the late 90's – but it really took off once she got established here. That's when the millionaire and billionaire clients started to come around.

"Don't take this the wrong way, but I've always found what you do a bit odd," I say chucking a grape into my mouth.

"I know."

"I just don't really get why people would pay you so much money to find them a date. Can't they do it on their own?"

"What I do is not find people dates. It's so much more than that. I set them up with people who are their best fit."

"And they don't find these people themselves?" I ask. "Don't people know what they like?"

"Okay, how about this for an analogy," she says tapping her long nails on the table. "People can pick out their own clothes, right? They know what they like."

"Yes."

"But there are people out there who are professional stylists. That way when you go out to a premier or some fancy party, you can look your best. You may know what you like, but you're not someone who deals with clothes exclusively. You don't know all the latest styles and fashions. So you hire this stylist to curate a collection of options for you so you're not overwhelmed by all the choices. You're paying the stylist for their opinion."

"I guess that makes sense," I concede. "But what about all those online dating sites? Aren't you afraid that you will be replaced by a computer? An algorithm?"

"No," she shakes her head confidently. "I can't be replaced by technology, because computers aren't sentient beings. Yet. When that happens, we'll talk."

CHAPTER 9 - AVERY

Two weeks later, I receive a call from Dolly Monroe. She calls me directly and says that she has a date for me. She doesn't tell me much about him except that we're going to his brother's engagement party and that I should wear heels.

"Of course, I'll wear heels," I say. "It's an engagement party."

"Okay, then. I just wanted to remind you, because you wore flats to our meeting and I wasn't sure if you make that a habit or not."

I chuckle to myself a little. With comments like that, she reminds me of my mother. She was also suspicious of women who didn't wear heels. She never understood my desire to be comfortable, especially when it came to going out.

"A woman should look like a woman, right?" I say into the phone.

"What?" Dolly asks. "Well, yes, of course."

"I've heard that before."

"From a wise woman, I'm sure," she says and hangs up.

Two days later, I'm in a total panic. My date with Logan is tonight, and I have absolutely nothing to wear. Why did I put this off to the very last minute? Why did I think that my closet would magically manufacture the perfect outfit for a stranger's engagement party at the precise moment when I need it? I leave work really early – at 4 pm – and leave Cynthia in charge of the place. She wants to come upstairs and help me dress up, but I tell her that I need some time to shower and think first. I have exactly two hours until he arrives. If I'm lucky, he'll be late.

I jump into the shower and wash my hair. Ever since those dry shampoos came out, I've become somewhat of an addict. In high school and college, I used to wake up early, take a shower and do my hair and makeup. I actually used to devote at least an hour and a half to this regimen every day! But now that I have my business, I don't really have time for any of that anymore. No, that's not true. I still have time. I just don't have the patience.

Massaging conditioner into my scalp, I take a deep breath. I really should do this more often. I try to remember the last time I washed my hair. It must've been at least 3 days ago. Oh my God! Has it been that long? It's not really as disgusting as it sounds. Even though my hair gets pretty greasy the day after I wash it, dry shampoo takes care of all that grease. I hate to admit it, but this isn't even the longest I've ever gone without a wash. The record was last month during a particularly stressful wedding when I went for seven days without a wash.

After getting out of the shower, I tie my hair up in a towel and sit down to apply my makeup. I give myself some time to do this, because I actually find the experience quite soothing and relaxing. It's as if I'm meditating. When my face is all done, with fake lashes and contouring, I dry my hair and then curl it to give it some more body. I seal it with some hair spray and look at myself in the mirror. Not bad, actually, except now is the difficult part. Figuring out what to wear.

I briefly consider the possibility of pants. I can almost hear my mom turning in her grave and Dolly gasping in shock. But no, I'm not thinking about slacks or something like that. Skinny jeans or leggings. Something to show off my butt in, but still be comfortable. But I have no idea how dressy this engagement party will be, so I need to play it safe. Skinny jeans might not be appropriate, no matter how cute the pumps.

I move on to dresses. I have three to choose from. One red, one black, one blue. All above the knee and tailored around the waist. The red one is strapless, the blue one has spaghetti straps and the black one has thicker, more traditional straps. I try them all. I only have one decent pair of black heels to wear, but luckily they will go with any of the dresses. The black one makes me feel like I'm either too formal or going to a funeral, and the blue one is a little tight around the bust, so I go with the red one. It has built in cups, which frame my breasts quite nicely, and I've heard somewhere – probably Dr. Oz – that both men and women respond well to red worn on dates. Okay, fine by me. I put in a pair of matte, silver hoops and a large cocktail ring on my right hand. It's from H & M, and Cynthia says that it makes me look flirty. That works for me.

After I'm pretty much ready, I take a selfie in front of the full-length mirror and send it to Cynthia.

She sends back a plethora of smiley faces, champagne drinks and firework emojis. I know that the outfit is a hit.

At 6 o'clock on the dot, there's a knock on my door. Right on time. It's an unusual thing for an LA guy to show up on time, there are just way too many excuses about traffic to take advantage of. I'm impressed.

When I open the door, I see a gorgeous, tall man before me. He's dressed in an expensive suit, but he doesn't look a bit uncomfortable in it. The charcoal-gray pants bring out his sparkling green eyes and compliment his dark thick hair. He has a tan of a surfer and brilliant white teeth, which decorate his luscious kissable lips. When he gives me a hug, I feel the hardness of his body, his chiseled abs and pecks.

He introduces himself as Logan Davenport. I think I say that my name's Avery, but who the hell knows. Wow. I had no idea that Dolly Monroe knew hotties like these.

"So this is your place?" he asks as we walk downstairs. I nod. "Dolly said that you own a flower shop."

"She told you that? She didn't tell me much about you."

There's a BMW parked in the far corner of the parking lot. And I confidently walk toward it. But he stops and points to his Prius.

"You drive a Prius?" I ask.

"Yes, do you have a problem with that?" he smiles.

I try to conceal how shocked I am. I thought he was a billionaire or at least a millionaire. I was certain that he would be driving at least a Maserati.

"No. It's just that I drive a Prius too," I say and point to the blue 2015 model in the parking lot.

We get into his white Prius and rush down Topanga Canyon Blvd toward Malibu.

"So do you actually live there?" he asks.

"What?"

"Above your flower shop?"

Seriously? This is what he's asking me?

"Yes. I actually live in a studio apartment," I say sarcastically. "I have a good deal on it, and I don't have to commute far to work."

"That's not what I meant," he says.

We're not getting off to a good start. How can someone this hot and attractive be such a dick? We drive the rest of the way until we hit the ocean in silence. Finally, I get sick of it.

"So, what do you do?" I ask as he turns onto Pacific Coast Highway.

"I'm sort of in between things right now."

I shake my head.

"What?" he asks.

"So, you're unemployed?" I ask. Now, it's my turn to insult him.

"No, not really," he shrugs.

"People with a little bit of money always say that."

He smiles his beautiful smile. I don't know if I want to kiss him or punch him right now.

No matter how much I love what I do, I can't help but feel envious that some people can just have money and do nothing all day. I mean regular people wish we had the luxury to do that? To just bum around and surf and go out and do basically nothing while we try to find ourselves again?

"I started a company a few years back," Logan says. "It got very successful, and I ended up selling it to Google. So now I'm just trying to figure out what to do with my life."

Logan talks on and on about the details of his start up and how it allowed people to borrow money directly from their friends and family, not just a bank or a credit card. I listen, but end up getting lost a little in his long eyelashes and deep, soothing voice. It doesn't hurt that he also smells intoxicating, like some sort of heavenly mixture of ocean waves and eucalyptus.

We arrive at the restaurant a few minutes later. I've driven past this place numerous times, but I've never been inside. It's right on the water, with outdoor seating facing the ocean. Almost every single thing in the restaurant is white except for the blue trim around the windows. It has an ultra-modern design, which I don't usually love, but it somehow fits this place. The tablecloths are white and very expensive to the touch, the menus are an off-white color, and all the waiters and the waitresses are dressed in white. The party is already in full swing by the time we arrive. The hostess shows us to the deck, which is decorated with hundreds of yellow lanterns and flowers. It's a little cold – about 60 degrees – but there are outdoor heaters all over the place to warm up the guests. I'm no longer regretting not bringing a shawl with me.

Everyone who greets us give me a warm smile and a hug. I still don't know about Logan, but his family is definitely very nice.

"Hey, you made it!" Dolly comes over to us. She's dressed in a hot pink suit that is probably tailored to accentuate her figure and is wearing a humongous diamond on her left hand.

"Hey, what are you doing here?" I ask.

"I'm his aunt," she says. "You didn't tell her?"

Logan shrugs; he looks a bit lost.

"Dolly's your aunt?"

"Yep," he nods.

Before we get the chance to get further into this, the couple of the hour comes over. Logan introduces me to his brother Liam and his fiancé, Kora. For some reason, I was expecting some six-foot-tall model with a bubbly personality, but instead I met Kora. Kora is exuberant and effervescent and smart. She made me laugh within a minute of talking to her. Honestly, I had forgotten that girls like her still exist. Her husband-to-be also seemed nice – very different from Logan. Straightforward, not so showy. Normal, somehow. He's of course not as good looking as Logan is, but he seems to have a good head on his shoulders.

For a moment, I excuse myself and turn around to get a plate of food. The three of them continue to talk, and I hear Kora say,

"I like this one Logan. She's really different from your usual lot."

That puts a smile on my face.

CHAPTER 10 - LOGAN

I arrive at the address that Avery gave me on the phone. At first, I don't think that I have the right place, but then I see the sign for The Flower Patch and remember that Aunt Dolly said that she lives above it. I make my way up the dirty stairs, wondering how anyone could live up here. I don't mean to be such a snob. It has been only a few years since I lived in my one-bedroom walk up in West Hollywood, but this place is a real dump. The door is all scratched up, and the railing is half falling down. I'm not even sure if this place is legal to rent out. Just as I get all down on myself for finally caving into Aunt Dolly and letting her set me up with one of the insane women who use her service, I knock on the door and see Avery for the first time.

My heart jumps out of my chest. She has almond-shaped hazel eyes and long light brown hair which curls nicely around her voluptuous breasts. I have seen enough fake and real breasts to know the difference right away and hers are definitely not fake. She's about five-foot-five and 110 pounds. Not a flamingo, but a nice womanly shape nevertheless.

Usually, I have no problem making small talk, putting on my charm to woo a girl, but something about this one leaves me tongue-tied. I mumble something about how nice she looks, but it doesn't seem to register. Instead, she comments on my Prius, which I frankly took because I didn't want to move my other cars to get to the Maserati. She asks about what I do. I can't very well tell her the truth, so instead I go on and on about my old company. This usually impresses the girls, but she doesn't seem impressed. She looks bored and annoyed. Like I'm some rich guy who no longer has to work for a living while the rest of the world has to.

After we arrive at the engagement party, things go from bad to worse. Aunt Dolly is there, and Avery looks mad that I didn't tell her that she was my aunt. I probably should have, but for some reason, for the first time in my life, I'm tongue-tied. At a loss for what to say. I'm like one of those losers who stumble and mumble and say things that don't make any sense. Over explain. Under explain. Let long moments of silence pass me by without a word. What. The. Fuck?

"So, Dolly didn't tell you that she was my aunt?" I ask when Kora and Liam finally leave us alone. Focus, Logan. Turn on the charm. You know how to do this. You're a natural.

"No," she shakes her head. Her hair falls off her shoulder, exposing her cleavage a little more. She's no model, but she definitely has the goods. And in that short, tight little red dress, they look like chocolates that I'm dying to unwrap.

"Sorry about that. I thought you knew."

She shrugs. She's about to look away somewhere in the distance, but I tilt my head toward her and look straight into her hazel eyes. Now, I have her.

"You know, I'm not sure if I told you this earlier, but you look beautiful tonight. Stunning, actually."

A small smiles begins at the corner of her lips. I lick my lips. Her eyes light up. I feel an energy between us. Finally, I'm on the right track.

"Thank," she begins, but then clears her throat. "Thank you."

I stare into her eyes, trying to peer into her soul. I do this with all the girls, but with Avery, I'm actually doing it earnestly.

"You know, you don't look so bad yourself," she says looking me up and down.

I like the feel of her approving gaze all over my body. I know I look good, but it's always nice to hear it from the person you want to pin against the wall and do bad things to.

The tone of the evening becomes more serious for a moment, and I know that it's that time.

"Excuse me for a minute," I bring her hand to my lips and give her a little peck. "But I have to make a toast."

As I walk away, I feel the burn of her gaze on me. She's watching me. Falling for me. I'm back!

With newfound confidence, I grab a glass of champagne and clink the glass. When the roar of the crowd quiets down, I start.

"As many of you know, I'm Logan, Liam's charming older brother. Liam has been my brother since my mom brought him home from the hospital, put him on my lap and said here he is. Your brother. To which I said, 'That's not a brother. That's a baby!'"

Everyone laughs. I look at Avery, who also seems pleased. Her smile gives me butterflies. I take a deep breath and continue.

"Liam and I went through the usual rough patches – fighting over girls, fighting over cars, fighting in general. We didn't have very much in common. Still don't actually. And then came Kora. Liam met Kora in college freshman year at Oberlin. I first met her when she came out to visit him for spring break. Speaking as someone who knows how to do Spring Break right, I knew that they were meant for each other when they spent the whole week in each other's arms on the couch at our parents' house. They were like two peas in a pod.

"I was a cynic back then – Who are we kidding, I'm kind of a cynic now – but back then, I was even more of a cynic. As much as I loved Kora, and as much as I thought Liam loved Kora, I thought that it would never last. Not all the way through college. Not through law school. And definitely not through all those early years of practicing law.

"But as it turned out, I was wrong. And Liam was right. Not the first time! Kora was just the perfect girl for Liam. Kind, attentive, persistent and persuasive. Honestly, man, I have no idea how you got away with not marrying her for so many years!

"What I'm trying to say, rather inarticulately, is that I may not know much, but I do know one thing. Liam loves Kora and Kora loves Liam. I guess that's two things. They're a perfect couple and I know that they will make each other very happy for many years to come.

"To Liam and Kora, and the wonderful life they have ahead of them together!"

Everyone claps and drinks. With tears in her eyes, Kora gives me a warm hug and a kiss on the cheek. I look across the deck at Avery. She looks impressed.

CHAPTER 11 - AVERY

After listening to his speech, my opinion of Logan completely changes. I see him in an entirely new light. Instead of some rich, cocky guy with nothing to do during the day, he suddenly becomes a part of a family. Both Liam and Kora were touched by his speech. Kora even cried! Maybe he doesn't show this part of himself often, but at least it exists.

"You have quite a way with words," I say to Logan when we're alone. The rest of the party moved away from this side of the patio, toward the dessert table. It suddenly feels like the whole world has fallen away, and it's just us, the cloudless sky, the bright yellow moon and the sound of calm waves falling onto the sand.

"Thank you," he says moving closer to me. The moonlight illuminates his luscious lips and plays with the sparkle in his eyes. There's a mysterious quality to them that draws me in.

Logan moves closer to me. He licks his lips and reaches toward my neck. The touch of his fingers along my jaw speeds up my heart rate. It feels like any second now it's going to jump out of my chest. Slowly, his fingers make their way to my mouth and run along my bottom lip. His fingertips feel soft and rough at the same time. I look into his eyes. He leans even closer. I feel his breath on my lips and close my eyes. Our lips touch.

His lips are effervescent. At first, the kiss feels like the kiss of a butterfly. Delicate. His tongue is foreign, yet familiar. He tilts my head back and drops his. He kisses my neck. Slowly. Deliberately. The hair on the back of my neck stands up.

Our bodies get closer and our legs touch. I love the feel of his silk pant leg on my bare skin. Logan's hands caress my shoulders. He pushes me back against the railing and our kiss gains momentum. It's no longer fragile. We're no longer breakable. Passion sweeps through me, and I push back against him. His hard, toned body welcomes me in, but doesn't give much. He pushes me back. Harder this time. This time, the railing digs into my back. It's a bit painful. It might even leave a bruise, but it feels so good.

"Logan?" I hear someone say his name. "Logan?"

Reluctantly, he pulls away from me.

"Are you serious?" the girl says. I can't see her very well, she's standing in the shadows, but I know one thing. She's gorgeous. In her heels, she's just as tall as Logan and all legs.

"What?" Logan asks unapologetically. I don't know who this is, so I try to create some separation between us. But he puts his arm around my waist and pulls me back.

"What are you doing here?"

"It's my brother's engagement party. A better question is what are you doing here?"

She ignores him. Instead, she walks closer to me and extends her hand.

"Hi, I'm sorry for being so rude. I'm Sadie," she says in a high, peppy voice. I nod, introduce myself and shake her hand.

"I'm the mother of Logan's future child."

If I had a glass of champagne in my hand right now, I'm certain that I would have dropped it.

"What?" I mumble.

"Shut up, Sadie," Logan shakes his head.

"Oh, he didn't tell you?"

I turn to Logan. He looks lost. His eyes search my face for some sort of response. My ears start to buzz, and I get a nagging pain in the back of my head.

"Sadie is my ex-girlfriend," he says. "She just told me about this pregnancy. I don't even know if it's mine."

"You're such an asshole," Sadie says tapping her foot on the floor.

"This is our first date, Avery. I wasn't keeping this from you. It just wasn't the right time to tell you. We hardly know anything about each other."

"I have to go," I mumble. Logan tries to come with me, but I push him away. "Leave me alone."

I don't know how to process this. I've heard about this happening, of course, but I never thought that it would happen to me. Millions of thoughts rush through my mind. Why didn't he tell me? He's such a dick! Sadie is right. It is our first date. I don't know anything about him. Did I really expect him to open with this?

Somewhere in the background, I hear Sadie and Logan arguing. They definitely sound like exes. And if this baby is Logan's, do I really want to do deal with this? Is this how we're supposed to start our relationship? What relationship? This is our first date. Suddenly, we're in a relationship?

Agh!

I want to scream and pound my fists on something, but I'm at a party. An engagement party, of all things. And Kora and Liam are so nice. I can't make a scene. Keep it together, Avery.

I decide to drown my sorrows in cake and alcohol.

"Is everything okay?" Kora walks over to me, putting her arm around my shoulder. Oh my God. Is it that obvious?

"Yes," I mumble and stuff some cake into my mouth. "Wow, this is delicious." And it is. It's some sort of magical chocolate, red velvet, cheesecake concoction. I'm certain that if I could eat the whole thing that all of my problems would go away.

"What is it with food that makes me think that it can make all of my problems disappear?" Kora asks. I look at her. It's as if she can read my mind.

"Oh please, don't stop, I'm just talking about myself."

We both crack up laughing.

"Unfortunately, through a lot of trial and error, I have found that after I stuff myself silly, none of my problems are really gone. I'm just ten pounds heavier and everything is even worse," I say.

Kora nods.

"Are you okay?" she asks.

I might as well tell her. I doubt that I'll ever see her again after tonight. What's the harm, right?

"I really like Logan," I say.

"Did he do something bad already?"

"No, not really. I mean yes, but it was before me."

"What?"

"I just saw Sadie."

"His ex?"

From the look on her face, I'm pretty certain that she doesn't know what's going on.

"We were kissing and it was this perfect kiss. And then Sadie came over."

"She's his ex. They broke up a while ago," Kora says.

"I know. That's what he said. But then she said that she's pregnant."

Kora takes a step back. "Oh, wow. I did *not* know that."

"Apparently, he just found out."

Kora takes a deep breath. "That's intense. I don't really know what to say. But I like you, Avery. A lot. You're very different from the usual girls that he goes out with. So, I just want to take this opportunity to warn you about Logan. He's a great guy, don't get me wrong, but he doesn't always treat the women he dates well. He isn't a cheater, he's too honest for that, but he's not one for long-term relationships either."

I nod. That's pretty much what I thought.

"I'm not sure what you're looking for with him, or why Dolly even set you two up, but he has a history. And now, apparently, a future baby mama to boot."

CHAPTER 12 - LOGAN

I've kissed a lot of girls, had a lot of first kisses, but the magic that I felt with Avery from the first moment that our lips touched, I've never felt before. It wasn't just sexual attraction – though there was a ton of that as well. It was something more than that. A chemical connection. I've wanted to kiss her ever since I saw the way she looked at me while I was giving my speech.

And then Sadie had to come over and ruin it all. She's such a bitch. I don't know what I ever saw in her. I'm not even sure that this baby is mine. Sadie wasn't exactly a loyal girlfriend. How can she be so sure?

And now, Avery is talking to Kora. Kora may have teared up at what I said, but Kora and I don't have the best history. She wasn't always my biggest fan. She doesn't approve of my romantic life, even though she knows that I never cheat on anyone. I'm very honest about who I am and what I do. I don't do long term relationships. I'm not interested in that. At least, I haven't been for years. Kora is the type of woman who is very suspicious of perpetually single men. It's as if she doesn't believe that a man can be a bachelor and happy about it. It's as if all single men are there to break women's hearts and break up marriages. Well, I never date anyone married. I haven't even dated anyone who was dating anyone else. I don't like the drama, and I don't need it.

Suddenly, my phone rings. I pull it out and see that it's my other phone. Shit. I never get calls on it unless it's something important. I'm not in the best headspace for it, but I can't not answer.

"Yes?"

"We need you in Playa del Carmen, Mexico on the 17th of next month."

I look down at my calendar.

"I'm actually going to be nearby in Tulum for my brother's wedding that weekend."

Kora and Liam have waited for seven years to make it official, and now that they're engaged, they have decided that they couldn't wait the customary year to plan everything. They are going to do the whole thing in less than two months. My gift to them is that I'm picking up the tab for everything, including the wedding planner, and it's no skin off my nose if they want to get it done so quickly. The wedding planner, however, is more than a little miffed. If it all goes smoothly, there's a big tip in it for her for the rush job.

"The target will be on his yacht for his niece's birthday party that day."

"I actually put in for some time off that weekend."

There's a pause. I know I said the wrong thing.

"You don't get time off. You're an agent, and we need you there."

Well, technically, I'm a spy. If you want to get even more technical, I'm an assassin, but the CIA frowns on that kind of literal interpretation of my job description.

"Right," I say.

"I'll be in touch with more details later," he says and hangs up.

I take a deep breath.

I'm really getting sick of this job. I'm counting down the days until my contract runs out in two years, and I can actually enjoy my life as a civilian. A very rich civilian, at that. The funny thing is that I actually got involved with the CIA completely by accident. I was at one of those career fairs that the University of Southern California puts on for its students every fall and spring. I had no idea what I wanted to do with my life after graduation, so I was walking around and talking to all the recruiters. And the CIA was there. I gave them my resume, and a few days later, they called me in for an interview. After a few rounds of interviews, I took a bunch of tests. I should've known right then and there that this wouldn't be a good fit. I do great on tests, always have, but I hate them. I have no business working at any organization that's based on tests.

Apparently, I did quite well on the tests, and they moved me further along. More tests followed. Then ten weeks of training and fieldwork. Then a special agent from a special branch of the CIA came to talk to me. He knew I was trying to do my own thing – building my start up, travel around the world – so he had a proposal for me. Join his unit and I wouldn't have to work full-time. Just on on-call basis. Fulfill a mission or two a month, get a full-time salary, and be free the rest of the time to do my own thing. The only thing was that I couldn't tell anyone about what I actually did, being a spy and all. You have to remember, I didn't have any money then. I wanted to travel and see the world. I had a kernel of an idea for my start up. It sounded like the perfect job.

Well, eight years later, it's not so much. Despite my best efforts, I'm apparently quite good at this, and I've moved up within the unit. Though I only do a few missions a year now, they still call on me for pretty much every complicated mission they have. And this one, in Mexico, is not going to be any walk in the park, that's for sure.

I spot Avery by the dessert table. She's all alone and looks much calmer now. Perhaps, it's a good time to approach and explain.

"I want to go home," she says before I get the chance to open my mouth.

"What?"

"I want to go home. Will you take me home?" She taps her foot on the floor, impatient. It reminds me of Sadie. I cringe.

"It's still early. You don't want to stay a little longer?"

"No. After finding out that my date is going to have a baby with his ex-girlfriend, I've had just about all I can handle."

She walks toward Liam and Kora, gives them each a brief hug, and says that she has to go. They thank her for coming, and she and Kora exchange numbers. I want to stop her, but we're already on our way out.

"I'm sorry. Avery, I'm sorry," I run after her. She shrugs, but continues steadfastly toward my car.

"What do you want me to say? I just found out. I honestly don't know for sure if it's mine."

"And what are you doing in the meantime?" she asks, turning to face me at the passenger door to my car.

"What do you mean?"

"Are you going to her ultrasound appointments? Are you going to go to her Lamaze classes with her?"

"I have no idea," I shrug. I haven't given that any thought whatsoever.

"Well, if it is your baby, you probably should. Otherwise, you'll miss out."

"Okay, fine," I nod. "Maybe I will."

"I'm not really sure if I want to date someone with a baby on the way." She gets into my car and slams the door.

Now, I'm completely lost. I have no idea what is the right thing to say or do. I follow her into the car.

"What do you want from me?"

"I want you to drive," she says looking straight ahead. "I want to go home."

I start the car and pull out of the parking lot.

"This is what's going on from my perspective," I say, taking a deep breath. I've never worked this hard with a girl. A real change for me.

"Sadie and I dated briefly. I thought she was cheating on me. We broke up, largely because of that and partly because we weren't a good match. I don't have any proof of this, but she didn't deny it either. Then a couple of weeks ago, she insisted on meeting for dinner. And that's when she told me that she is pregnant. I have no idea if that baby is mine, but it's all her decision. I'm fine with whatever she decides. I don't have a say in it, I know that. I also can't find out if the baby is mine until it's born. So I won't know for nine months."

She nods, but keeps looking straight ahead. From her demeanor, I know that she's listening. So, I continue.

"I know that this is a complication. For us. But I also know that I want to see you again. I'm not someone who's keen on relationships, which I'm sure my future sister-in-law filled you in about, but I feel something for you. Something completely different."

"What do you mean?"

Finally, I have her attention!

"I like you, Avery. A lot."

Luckily, there's a red light. I turn to face her.

"I like you a lot. You don't know me very well, but I never say that. Never."

"I don't want to date someone who has a baby momma," she whispers, turning to face me.

"I know," I shrug. "I wouldn't either, but there's nothing I can do about that right now."

We turn onto Topanga Canyon Boulevard and disappear into the hills.

"What do you want me to say?" she asks.

"Nothing. I just want you to know that I felt something in that kiss we shared. I felt a lot. And I'd like to see you again. And I'm sorry about what happened with my ex. But I have no interest in being with her, regardless of what happens with the baby."

"What are you going to do if it's yours?" she asks.

"I'm going to step up and be part of its life. I'm going to see the baby and build a relationship. I don't love the idea – don't get me wrong – but I don't want my child to grow up without a father. Especially, when I can easily participate in his or her life."

Honestly, I didn't know that's how I felt until this very moment. Goosebumps run down my arms at even the thought of being a father. But that's the right thing to do. I know it.

I don't say anything else the rest of the way. Neither does she. I do look over at her occasionally, though, and I feel her stealing the occasional glance at me as well.

I pull into the parking lot by her apartment and park next to the only other car in the lot, her Prius. She gets out of the car, and I follow.

"You don't need to walk to me to the door," Avery says.

"I know," I say, following her. I'm not sure if my presence is welcomed, but I'm trying my best to make up for the wrecked night.

When we reach her door, she turns to face me. I take a step forward. We're so close to each other, I can feel and smell her peppermint breath on my lips. If she didn't want me this close, she could take a step back. But she doesn't.

"I'm sorry about tonight," I whisper. I lean closer to her. At first, her eyes look past me, somewhere in the distance, but a moment later, they meet mine.

"I'm sorry too," she whispers.

I don't know what that means. Does she want to see me again but won't because of what happened? Or does that mean that she's just generally sorry about what occurred?

"Can I call you?" I ask.

She doesn't reply. It's now or never. Just go for it, I say to myself. I press my lips to her lips and bring her closer to me. At first, she doesn't respond. But then, the moment takes over, and she kisses me back. I push her against her apartment door, cradle her head in my hands. I let my hands run up and down her body. I'm pleased when she doesn't stop me. A few moments later, I pull away.

"Can I call you?" I ask again.

She's breathless. After a few moments, her eyes manage to focus on mine.

"Yes," she whispers and gives me another little kiss on the lips. "Against my better judgment, yes," she adds.

I smile as she opens the door to her apartment. I want her to invite me in. I pray and hope for it, but I'm not surprised when it doesn't happen.

"You better call," Avery says and waves goodbye, before closing the door in my face. I nod and smile. I'm definitely going to call. This isn't some empty promise that I typically make other girls. Avery is different. So different, in fact, it's frightening me. I walk back to my car with shivers running down my spine. What is this? Anxiety? Fear? I've never felt this way about another person before. I don't know whether I want to curse Aunt Dolly for matching us or give her a huge tip. What the fuck is going on? I turn up Guns 'n Roses and race back down to Malibu in a state of awe.

CHAPTER 13 - AVERY

The following morning, I tell Cynthia everything that happened over our Starbucks coffee. I don't hold anything back. I tell her the good and the bad, and about these crazy feelings that I have developed for Logan during just one date.

"He's kind of a dick. You should've seen how he looked at my apartment – like he felt sorry for me – but then he's sweet. You should've heard what he said to his brother in his engagement speech."

"But he's having a baby? With his ex?"

"Yes, that is a problem.'

"But it may not be his," Cynthia says.

"It may not. But it may be, and I don't know if I need that kind of drama in my life."

"On the other hand, it's his ex, and he doesn't seem to like her very much. How much drama could it be? So he'll pay child support and see the kid every other weekend. That's not too bad. Plus, it'll show you what kind of dad he can be."

I choke on my coffee, burning the roof of my mouth.

"We had one date! Are you really talking about his future potential as a father?"

"Hey, one date is all it takes."

"What do you mean?"

"One of these days, you're going to go on a date with someone who you'll end up spending the rest of your life with. It may be Logan, it may not. But you don't know," Cynthia says.

"You're freaking me out," I say. "Why didn't you get any muffins? I want a muffin."

"Oh, I forgot. No worries, the bakery across the street has way yummier ones." She grabs her wallet and heads toward the door.

"No, I was just kidding," I say. "You don't have to get me a muffin. I'll get one later."

"It's fine," Cynthia says. "I really want one too. I'll be right back."

I'm left alone surrounded by a sea of flowers. One of the things I love most about flowers is that, no matter how alone I am, their presence always brings me comfort. Especially daffodils and daisies. They aren't the fanciest flowers by a long shot, hardly anyone requests them for bouquets, let alone centerpieces, but they are the friendliest. Whenever I look at them, I can't help but smile. They're a constant reminder that everything will be okay. The world isn't such a bad place, as long as daffodils and daisies continue to flourish.

There's a knock on the door. Cynthia's hands must be too full with muffins and coffee to open it herself. I head toward the door, but it opens before I get there.

"Hello Avery," he says in his sultry voice. Cold shivers run down my spine. I'm still clutching a loose bouquet of daffodils and daises, which I was just enjoying. Only now, I'm grasping it, squeezing the life out of it.

"Cal," I whisper. "What are you doing here?"

My voice breaks a little at his name. My mouth runs dry. I take a deep breath and finish the question with strength. He can't see me wither.

"I wanted to see you. I miss you," he says. He's shorter than Logan, but still much taller than I am. He recently got a buzz cut, which makes him look even more menacing.

"You can't be here," I say.

"I know, but this girl I was with broke up with me, and it made me realize how much I've missed you." Cal comes closer to me. Much too close. I back away.

"You were seeing someone?" I ask. Perhaps there's hope that he can be someone else's problem now. Not that I want some other unsuspecting girl to have a stalker, I just don't want him stalking me anymore.

"I know, I'm sorry. I shouldn't have. But after you took out that restraining order on me, what could I do? Will you forgive me?"

What. The. Fuck?

"You can't be here," I say in the most confident and self-assured voice that I can manage to muster. "The restraining order is still in effect."

Suddenly, I'm backed against the wall. Freshly cut tulips press into the back of my head. Cal leans close to me, putting his hand on the wall behind the tulips. The only thing that's separating us is the bouquet of daffodils and daisies, I hold in my extended hand as if it were a weapon. We're so close that his significant beer belly presses against them, pushing their heads toward the floor. Not a great weapon.

"I miss you," he whispers. Out of the corner of my eye, I can see that his arms are stronger now than they were before. More defined. He has started to work out. His bicep flexes a couple of times and my knees grow weak. I'm not sure I can hold myself up for much longer.

"What are you doing here?" Cynthia marches into the store. Her authoritative voice makes both Cal and I flinch. "You can't be here. She has a restraining order out against you. I'm calling the police."

"I was just checking in with my girl," Cal says, backing away from me.

"Well, she doesn't want you checkin' in. You're lucky that you're not in jail right now doing time for assault," Cynthia says, taking out her phone. "I'm calling the police."

"Fine, fine, I'm leaving," Cal says. "I miss you, Avery. Call me."

I let out a big sigh of relief when the door shuts closed behind him. I find the nearest chair and collapse into it.

"Yes, hello? I need someone to come out to make a report about a violation of a restraining order…No, he's not here anymore. He just left," Cynthia says and gives the police our address.

"What are you doing?" I ask when she hangs up.

"The police will be here within the hour. They said that you have to report each violation of the restraining order. And that's what we're doing."

I'm so happy that she's here. Not just for making Cal leave, but also for calling the cops. I'm not sure I'd have the strength to follow up as quickly as she had. All the adrenaline pumping through my body has vanished, and I feel too weak to utter a single word.

'Thank you,' I mouth.

A COUPLE OF DAYS LATER, Dolly and I meet for lunch to discuss the date – to conduct a post-mortem, of a sort. She had called the day after the engagement, right after Cal left, but I was in no mood to talk. I even asked Cynthia to text her back for me and schedule something for later in the week.

I meet her in her office. She's dressed in a loose-fitting light pink pant suit, which she pulls off marvelously. It hugs her in all the right places and does not make her short legs look stubby, which is almost always the case with me. It's probably all the heels, I decide. In addition to her gigantic diamond wedding set, she's also wearing a diamond ring on the right ring finger. It's in the shape of a bow tie, and she's wearing it right at the tip of her nail, near the first knuckle.

"I love your ring," I say. "I've never seen a knuckle ring like that."

"Oh, thank you for noticing," she extends her hand so I can get a closer look. "It's a new creation by this talented young designer out of Santa Barbara. It's part of her very first collection, coming out this summer. It's not available anywhere yet."

I nod. For a second, it feels like she's actually telling me all of this because I might go out and get one. As if it's something that she got at Target, and it's actually something I can afford. When I glance back up at her, I know that she's not showing off one bit. She's simply sharing, because I had showed an interest.

"I'm going to make myself a cup of hot chocolate. Real dark chocolate, nothing instant. You interested?" Dolly walks up to her coffee machine.

"Yes, sure," I nod.

"I've had the best hot chocolate one time when I was in Tulum, Mexico. This tiny Mayan woman ran this little stand on a street corner, and it was the most delicious thing I've ever tasted. I was looking through some of my old travel pictures this morning and was reminded of it, so I thought I'd give it a shot."

She hands me a photo album titled "Tulum."

"This was only a few years ago, so all of my pictures came from my phone, but I'm an old fashioned one. There's nothing like looking at photos in a photo album," Dolly says as I flip through her pictures. The photos are gorgeous – Instagram quality. Beautiful cliffs and ruins running into the bluest water I've ever seen.

A few minutes later, when I'm 100% certain that my next vacation – if I can ever manage a week away from the shop – will be to Tulum, she hands me my cup of hot chocolate. It's dark and rich and flows as if it were lava. I take a sip. Wow. Dolly has upped her drink game. If her cappuccinos were simply delicious, her hot chocolate is heavenly.

"This is amazing," I say, taking two more quick sips. It's so good, I'd be done with the cup already, if it weren't so hot.

"Yes, it is quite good, isn't it?" she says, taking a sip. "Not quite like in Tulum, but very good."

"You must've had a blast on this trip," I say.

"Tulum was one of the last cities built and inhabited by Maya between the 13th and 15th centuries. They called it Zama, the City of Dawn, because it's on a bluff facing east. If you only ever see one sunrise in your life, it should be in Tulum."

"You're making me jealous," I say. "I'd love to go there someday."

"It just so happens that I heard that you made quite an impression at the engagement party."

Oh that. I sit back down in my seat.

"And not just on Logan. Also on the bride and groom to be."

I nod.

"I liked Kora and Liam a lot too."

"Well, they liked you so much that Kora called me a few days ago and asked for your address. She's sending you an invitation to her wedding. In Tulum."

I stare at her. I can't go to the wedding! But it is in Tulum. A great excuse. No, focus. Don't get distracted. You can't go to this wedding.

"Why didn't you tell me that you were his aunt?" I ask Dolly. I catch her off-guard. I want to see her squirm, but she barely blinks.

"I don't tell the women very much about the men before the date. It's one of my policies. But between you and me, it's because I've never set Logan up on any dates before. He's not really my client. Just my nephew. He has never asked me to set him up before. In fact, I had to fight him on it."

"Why did you?"

"Because I had the sneaking suspicion that you two were perfect for each other. The minute that you stormed out of my office when I asked you about net-worth."

"So you know what happened?" I ask. "On our date?"

"Yes, Logan has filled me on the details. But now I need to hear it from you."

"Did he tell you about his ex, Sadie? That she's pregnant?"

"Yes, he did mention that part."

"So? What am I supposed to do with that? I can't go out with someone who has a baby."

"That's very judgmental of you," Dolly says.

"I don't know anything about babies."

"You don't have to. Besides, he doesn't have a baby now. It might not be his, and even if it were, that's not an issue for at least eight more months. Enough time for you and Logan to go on another date and figure out how you feel about one another."

I shake my head. When she puts it that way, it doesn't sound like a big deal. So, why does it feel like it is?

"What did Logan say?" I ask.

"I can't tell you that," she shakes her head. "You need to tell me how you feel about him first."

I take a deep breath. Finish the last bit of my hot chocolate. "I thought he was a dick, at first. But then, I liked him. He's a very good kisser."

Dolly smiles with her whole body. Her brilliant white teeth nearly blind me.

"Ah! I knew it," Dolly says.

"But I can't go to this wedding," I say.

"Just think about it."

CHAPTER 14 - AVERY

The following day, a kid who looks like he is barely old enough to drive shows up in the floral shop. It's too early for prom and too late for a winter formal.

"May I help you?" I ask, waiting for him to ask me to pick out a bouquet for him for his girlfriend.

"I have this box for you but you need to sign for it."

"Oh okay," I nod. He's a messenger. I look outside. There's no FedEx or UPS truck out there, and he's definitely not from the US Postal service. For a second, my heart drops to my stomach. What if this is something from Cal?

"Can you wait here for a second while I open it?" I ask. And then realize that if this is a bomb, then it would be all my fault that he would die along with me.

Luckily, it's not. Inside the package, I find an invitation that has been carved into a thin piece of birch tree. It's about cardboard-thickness and, at the top, there are L + K with a heart around them.

"Can I go now?" the kid asks me. I had forgotten that he was still here! I give him a small tip and he leaves.

I pick up Liam and Kora's wedding invitation. I guess Dolly was right. I did make an impression. The wedding is in a month, and I have to let them know my decision as soon as possible. What is my decision?

If I go to the wedding, then I'll definitely see Logan there, and that's not necessarily a bad thing. We have texted a lot over the last few days, but it never really went further than that. He didn't ask me out again, and I didn't initiate anything either. Texting is the safe thing to do. I don't have to see his beautiful eyes. I don't have to say no in person, and if he asks me out again, it's easier to say no in a text.

I hear a little ring. Someone opens the door to the shop. I put the invitation away and gather my thoughts. I can't just obsess over Logan all the time. I have a job to do here.

"Logan?" I ask.

He stands before me, looking straight into my soul.

"Hi," he says, coming closer. He looks down at his feet and then back at me. I find this display of vulnerability utterly charming.

"I thought I'd give texting a rest for a bit," he announces. I nod. I look him up and down. He's dressed in a pair of tight light blue shorts that accentuate the tightness of his perfect butt. The lightweight, loose, button-down shirt is buttoned only half way down his chest, exposing his hard, tan pectoral muscles. I'm not sure how he looks hotter – in a suit or in flip-flops. Both are very easy on the eyes.

"So this is where you work?" he asks, looking around. "It's beautiful."

I smile and clear my throat.

"Well, you know. They're flowers. It's their job to be beautiful," I say.

"Hmm…I don't know. I'm not sure it's a job if they can do it so naturally."

Our eyes meet. After a moment of silence, we both crack a smile. I walk around the counter.

"Want the grand tour?"

"Of course."

"Roses are over there. Baby's breath here. Tulips in the back. This is where I make centerpieces. And this," I turn to the counter. "This is where the customers pay me."

He continues to smile. The grin on his face is warm and inviting, and it's all I can do to not run into his arms and press my lips onto his.

"It's nice to see you again," he whispers. "I've missed you."

He takes a step forward until we're close enough to kiss. For a moment, we don't touch. It feels like the longest moment of anticipation. And then he takes my hand in his.

"It's nice to see you again," I manage.

"I wanted to come see you...well, I wanted to see you. But I also wanted to tell you that I'm going to be out of communication for a bit. It's a work thing."

"Okay," I nod.

"And I also wanted to ask you to be my date to my brother's wedding."

He touches the tips of my hair, plays with it haphazardly. I wonder how long we're going to stand here before he kisses me. I'm having trouble focusing on anything he's saying.

"What?" I ask, when I finally register that he's talking about taking me to the wedding.

"I want you to be my plus one," he says, looking into my eyes. They look like they're made of crystal – I can see my reflection in them.

"I got my own invitation," I say.

"What?'

"I just got it today. Liam and Kora invited me."

"Oh great. So you don't want to go with me?"

"That's not what I said."

He takes another step forward. I didn't think that it would be possible, but somehow he manages to get even closer to me – without kissing me.

"I'm just saying that I don't have go as your plus one."

"I never said you did. I just wanted you to know that I wanted you to."

Why does he have to be so charming? And hot? A few strands of hair fall into his eyes. And suddenly, I can't help myself. I reach out and brush it away. The next thing I know, we're kissing. It's me who makes the first move. I pull his neck closer to me. I stand up on my tiptoes and bring my lips to his. He reciprocates right away.

He pushes me against the counter, wrapping his strong hands around my waist. After pulling me up a little closer to him, and moving my hair off my shoulders, he runs his tongue down my neck.

"Go to the wedding with me," he whispers into my ear in between the kisses.

"I don't know," I whisper.

"Why?"

"It'll just be our second date. I can't go away with you for the weekend, to your brother's wedding for our second date."

"Why?" he kisses my collarbones and buries his head in my cleavage.

"Because...because," I tilt my head and moan. I can't focus. Words don't make any sense to me anymore. I just want to rip off his clothes and for him to rip off mine.

"Because it doesn't seem right," I manage to finish a thought.

He lifts his head from my cleavage and bats his eyelashes at me. I roll my eyes. He lifts me up and sits me down on the counter. He spreads my legs with his hard body, resting his hands around my waist.

"Our first date was at their engagement party. What's more appropriate than having our second date at their wedding?"

I think about that for a moment. Of course, I want to go with him. I want to see him again, more than anything. Still, the Sadie factor is still weighing heavily on my mind. I don't want to bring her up. There's no other news. There's no way to know anything until the baby is born, and that's not going to be for a long time.

"Okay," I finally cave. His eyes light up, "but only because Kora and Liam invited me directly."

He kisses me again. He tastes like salty peanuts. When he pulls away, I pull him closer. We continue to kiss until his lips spread into a wide grin and don't close again.

"What?" I ask, sort of kissing his teeth. "What's so funny?"

"So, let me get this straight, you don't want to go as my date to the wedding?"

"That's not what I said."

"You should let me know, because I'm taking my plane to Tulum. And if you're going as my date, you're more than welcome to come with."

A private plane! I've never been on a private plane before. My heart skips a beat.

"But if you don't, I'd be more than happy to recommend a cab company that can pick you up from the airport *after* you fly coach."

I roll my eyes. "You think you're so charming," I say.

"Yes, yes, I do," he shrugs. I playfully push him away, but he doesn't budge an inch. Instead, he presses himself closer to me, and we lose ourselves in another passionate kiss.

CHAPTER 15 - LOGAN

I was toying with her. Of course, I wanted to kiss her. More than anything. But I wanted to see that she wanted it as badly as I did. She was such a flirt over text, but my experience tells me that some girls can say the dirtiest things in texts and not have anything to show for it in real life. Our texts didn't get dirty, but they were fun. Still, I wasn't sure how surprising her at her shop would go. It could've been a total disaster. Luckily, it wasn't. She said yes.

I try to make the kiss last as long as possible. I hold her by her waist and bury my head in her bosom. They are just the right size. And natural. Perfect. She tastes of wine and fruit and chocolate. I lick my lips after we pull away.

"You taste delicious," I say. She blushes.

"I had some sangria earlier. And chocolate," she puts her hand over her mouth. I pull it away, and kiss her beautiful lips again. I want to rip off her shirt and hike up her skirt. I want to fuck her. Hard. From the look in her eyes, I'm pretty sure that she'd let me. Maybe even close down the shop so that we aren't disturbed. But I'm running late. I already stayed much longer than I should have.

Reluctantly, I pull away from Avery.

"What's wrong?" she asks, tilting her head and flashing me a smile. My knees feel wobbly. I know I'm in trouble.

"I have to go."

"Noooooo." She pulls me closer.

"I know, I'm sorry," I push away. Shit. Why did this have to happen today of all days?

"Where do you have to go? You don't have a job!"

"I do have a job. An obligation. It's a pretty serious one too," I look down at my watch. I'm late. Really late. He hates lateness. Doesn't tolerate it.

"What is it?" she asks, jumping off the counter. She crosses her arms across her chest. She pouts her lips. If only I didn't have to leave right away. I have a few ideas of how I could make that pout disappear.

"It's difficult to explain," I say. I don't want to lie to her – wow, that's a first – but I can't tell the truth either.

"I'm going on a very important business trip tomorrow. I won't be able to stay in contact. Not constant contact."

"Why are you telling me this?" Avery turns away from me and pretends to work on a centerpiece.

I turn her around.

"Because I don't want you to think that I'm ignoring you. I like you Avery. A lot. But I can't stay. I have to go. I have a meeting with my director, and I'm running late. Tomorrow I have to leave. I'm not sure when I'll be in touch again, but I will pick you up for the wedding. I promise."

She shakes her head, as if she understands. In today's age of constant contact and almost infinite technology, it's a little hard to explain why I'm going to go pretty much underground for a month, but this is the best explanation that I can offer.

I bend down to her ear. I move hair off her shoulders and kiss the back of her neck. She moans a little. I want her to remember these words.

"I like you, Avery. A lot."

I RACE THROUGH TOPANGA CANYON, breaking all speeding records. Here, the problem is not so much the police hiding behind curves, but the curves themselves. The road is windy and steep.

It's not advisable to go faster than 50 miles per hour. I'm meeting Franklin Truman on a park bench on the Santa Monica Pier. I'm late, of course. It's only by fifteen minutes, but fifteen minutes is like two hours in Truman time.

"I was about to leave," he says, looking straight at me. I don't apologize. That would be admitting a mistake, and that's a big no-no with Truman. To him, an apology is a sign of regret, and regrets are unprofessional.

Santa Monica Pier is swirling with happy families and pets. Everyone around us is having fun and smiling.

"This isn't the best place to meet if you wanted to fit in," I say. "Given your propensity to stare ahead with a serious expression on your face."

He turns to me. I know better than to expect a sarcastic smile from him. Franklin Truman has no sense of humor. I've never seen him smile or even make a joke. Perhaps that's one of the requirements of being the director of Daffodil, but I have the feeling that I'd run it completely differently. Daffodil is the name of the secret organization within the CIA I made the terrible mistake of joining all those years ago. Part-time work, my ass.

"Augusto Sanchez has already started to consolidate power," Truman says. "He's had at least five ministers who helped him conduct the military coup arrested. Many have disappeared. None of our operatives on the ground know how many civilians have vanished. He has completely taken over the newspapers and the media. Analysts are saying that he's well on his way to becoming the next Kim Jong-Il."

I nod.

"We have intelligence that suggests that he's going to be on his yacht on the night of the 18th. Are you still going to your brother's wedding?"

"I'm the best man."

"Fine, that will do. It might actually be a good cover as to why you're there."

"A convenient cover is not really what I'm looking for that weekend," I say. Truman ignores me. My wisecracks used to get under his skin. He used to take them very personally. Over the years, he has learned to pay them no attention.

Truman is in his late 50's, but his body looks like it belongs to a 70 year old. He doesn't take care of himself - he eats too much and drinks too much. He has no sense of style or fashion. He's wearing a relatively new suit, but the collar is open and the shirt is crumpled. The pants look like he has slept in them for three days straight. If I didn't know any better, I'd say that he's some put upon traveling salesman, a Willy Loman type.

"They are expecting you in D.C. tomorrow."

"I'll be there. Of course, I have nothing better to do than to go through more useless tests."

Testing and training is very important in the CIA, and it's especially important in Daffodil. What they conveniently forgot to mention to me when I signed my contract with them is that, though I'm only obliged to complete a certain number of missions a year, each mission also comes with extensive training, planning and testing components. There are tests on stress and concentration, fatigue and general physical discomfort. There are tests on conventional firearms and tactical training and, of course, analytical training. The training and testing vary depending on the depth and the scope of the mission, but they do have one thing in common: they are all a major pain in the ass.

"Don't forget the bag," Truman says, getting up.

"Now, when have I ever forgotten the bag?" I hiss back. That one was just to irritate him. I've never met any other agents from Daffodil – it's not like we have conventions every year to discuss our career paths – but I really hope that I'm the most annoying one that Truman has to work with. Anything short of that, and I'd be disappointed in myself.

CHAPTER 16 - AVERY

Logan's appearance is a breath of fresh air this afternoon. After he leaves, all the air seems to have been sucked out of the room. I'm just about to close up shop. Cynthia is off today, and I am left all alone for what seems like the two longest hours of my life. I can't concentrate on anything. It requires all of my effort just to arrange the one bouquet that I've already designed. And I actually consider closing early. Wow. He must've really made an impression because I never close early. Ever.

I want him back. I want him to come right back here, put his arms around me and press his lips onto mine. I want him to take me upstairs and to do all sorts of bad things to me. If I had known that he was leaving on a business trip for a month – a whole month! – I would've demanded that we go on our second date sooner. I would've closed the shop earlier so that we didn't just make out like teenagers, but actually took off our clothes and got serious. Shit. Why did he have to be such a gentleman? Does he not think that I can hold my own? Does he not see me that way? Does he not want me?

No. He wants me. If there's one thing I know, I know that. I could feel how much he wanted me while we were making out on the counter. I brush my hand over the counter wistfully. I felt it pressing against me through his shorts. And I liked what I felt. It felt big and strong.

"I need to take a shower," I say out loud.

"Mind if I join you?"

Shivers run up my spine. Could it be? No, it couldn't. He had left.

"Hi," Logan walks out of the shadows.

"Hi," I whisper. "I thought you had to go."

"I did. But I thought I'd stop by before my flight. Just to say hi."

He comes behind the counter. He stands so close to me, I can see strands of his hair move as he breathes.

"Just to say hi?" I ask.

"I wanted to see if you'd want to go on a second date with me now."

"Instead of waiting a month?" I ask.

He nods, playing with the ends of my hair.

"What do you have in mind?" I ask, not moving an inch. Slowly, he puts one arm around me, pulling me closer to him. The fingers of his other hand softly trace the outline of my face. His thumb brushes along my lower lip. At that moment, something takes ahold of me, and I lick him. I don't even really know what I'm doing, and half expect him to push me away and walk out. His breathing pauses for a moment. I look up at him, my eyes searching his. Perhaps that was a step too far, but instead of shock and awe, a wide grin spreads from the corner of his lips to his whole face. His eyes light up with excitement.

Logan stares into my eyes. It feels like he can see right through me. The moment lasts both for a second and forever. I shift my eyes to his mouth. I want to feel it on me.

He's breathing harder than usual. I stop breathing altogether.

Kiss me, kiss me, kiss me, I say silently over and over. Why is he taking so long? Is he asking my permission? He didn't need it before.

As if it were possible, he takes another step closer to me. I close my eyes. He leans down and kisses my lips. Gently. He brushes his tongue along my lower lip. Our tongues intertwine, and become one. He pushes me against the counter, and I push back. I love running my hands along his fit, strong body. I love feeling his arms all around my body. He grabs my butt, squeezes, sending shivers through me. I bury my hands in his soft hair. I'm making it a total mess, and I wouldn't have it any other way.

"Wait," I mumble. I'm getting tossed by passion as if it's an ocean wave. I'm only vaguely aware of the fact that we're still in my shop. And the front door is still unlocked.

"What?" he moans, nibbling on my earlobe.

I moan along with him. I want to tear off his clothes. But not here.

"Logan," I whisper. Finally, he pulls away. Looks directly into my eyes.

"I'm sorry. You're right. We should stop."

A pang of anger flashes through me.

"I don't want to stop, silly," I say kissing his neck. Who is this person? It's as if confidence is oozing out of me.

"You don't?" He smiles with his eyes.

"I just want to go upstairs. We can't do it here, a customer might come in."

Logan holds me by my waist as I lock up and head upstairs. He drapes his hot, tan body on mine, grabbing at all of my bits.

"Okay," I turn around to face him, "but before we go in, you have to promise not to make fun of my place."

"What are you talking about?" he asks, kissing my neck.

"It's a studio. A very small studio. I don't know the last time you were in a place like this, but it's not one of those large, spacious studios that poor people always have in the movies or in television shows. I don't pay much rent and it looks it."

"I don't care," he whispers. "I don't care if we do it outside by the trashcans, I just want you."

I stare at him. Kind of insulted. He catches himself.

"Okay, that's not what I meant," he says. "I just meant that I totally understand. I used to live in a one-bedroom apartment in West Hollywood. I know that money doesn't go very far in this town."

I sigh. He wraps his arms around me again.

"I'm not going to laugh, Avery. You don't have to be embarrassed. About anything. Not with me."

Reluctantly, I open the door to my place. I don't know why I'm so self-conscious about this place. Luckily, I was feeling a little bored last night and cleaned the whole place top to bottom. The apartment is basically a large rectangle of about 300 square feet. My bed is against the left, directly across from the kitchenette. I have a mini-fridge, which is about a few cubic feet bigger than the one I had in college, and a hot plate. The hot plate is technically illegal, but there is no stove, making the whole apartment basically illegal, so my landlord and I have an understanding. He doesn't report me, and I don't report him.

"Will you excuse me for a second?" I ask and head toward the bathroom. "Make yourself comfortable. There's some water and orange juice in the fridge."

In the bathroom, I flip on the lights and take a deep breath. The only thing I really hate about this place, and I mean really hate about it, is that there's no bathtub. I love taking baths. As a child, I spent hours and hours in the bathtub – reading and playing and listening to music. Here, I only have a crammed stand up shower, with low ceiling, which barely fits one person. On more than one occasion, it made me feel so claustrophobic that I had to hurry up and wash the conditioner out of my hair before I was really ready, because my heart started to beat so fast that I felt like I was going to have a heart attack. After brushing my teeth, I walk back outside.

Logan is sitting on my bed, with his back to the headboard.

"You know, I like what you've done with the place," he says looking around. "It's cozy."

I smile, roll my eyes.

"I'm serious," he says. "I particularly like these lights."

He's referring to my paper lantern string lights, which I have strung along the top of my curtains. The sole window in my apartment makes the place more than a little dark and I needed a way to bring more color and life into the place.

"Thanks," I nod. "So, do you want to go to your place instead?"

Logan shakes his head and takes my hand in his. He pulls me down onto the bed next to him.

"Thanks for inviting me here."

"Against my better judgment."

"I know, and that's why I appreciate it," he says, looking around. "And I really do love what you've done with the place. It has so much color and light, despite...everything."

Despite how small it is. Despite the fact that it has only one window, and the front door opens directly into my bedroom. But I really do appreciate him saying that. From the tone in his voice, I know that he means it.

"Now, let's take off this sweater, shall we?" he says quietly. It's lightweight and sheer, and it falls off my shoulders with just one tug. He tosses it on the chair next to the bed.

He leans over and kisses the top of my shoulders. I tilt my head back.

"I want you," he whispers. My heart skips a beat. He runs his fingers down my neck and over the top of my breasts.

The muscles within me clench and don't let go. Then he leans over and pulls me toward him. I expect him to kiss my lips, but he doesn't. Instead, he kisses the top of my head, gently. I close my eyes, and he kisses my eyelids. They flutter underneath his lips, and I shiver. And then slowly, he grazes his lips with mine. I kiss him back, but he pulls away and kisses my neck. Slowly. Lingering over each kiss. Then he took a deep breath, inhaling me.

"I love the way you smell," Logan whispers.

"What do I smell like?" I ask.

"The perfect combination of sweetness and sex," he says looking straight at me.

My heart drops. I don't know how to respond.

Holding my gaze and refusing to let me go, Logan unclasps the front of my bra. My breasts rejoice in their newfound freedom, and he catches one with his hand. He kisses the top of it and then the nipple. He stays there for a while, getting to know each curve. He is gentle at first. My body throbs for his, and he quickly realizes that I'm not very interested in him being gentle.

"I want to spend a weekend with your body," he whispers. "So I can know every detail of it. Love each inch of it. Find out how every part of you works."

I take a big gulp.

A moment later, our clothes disappear and we're both naked.

He plays with me before he enters me. He pulls me against his hips and he pushes himself inside of me. I moan into his mouth. I brace myself against his biceps, which pump with each thrust. I bury my hand in his hair – it's soft and messy, and I make it even messier. He pulls my hair gently as he rocks inside of me. We fuck until we are both so intensely fevered that the world outside of us becomes a blur.

I DON'T HEAR BACK from Logan for a few days after that one afternoon together. He warned me that he would be out of touch. I assume it'll be okay, but I didn't realize just how much I would crave more contact. I want to see him. I want him to put his arms around me. I want to kiss him. I want him inside of me.

Get it together, I say to myself, checking my phone for the millionth time today. He said he can't text or call for a while. Why are you freaking out?

I just need a distraction. I arrange a few bouquets, go out for some coffee, eat a muffin.

"Carbs and sugar are not a solution, Avery," I say out loud as I toss the last of the crumbs into my mouth. And then, suddenly, my phone beeps.

I miss you, Logan texts. *I hate it here and I want your mouth.*

I want you too, I text back. *I miss you, too.*

Tulum can't come soon enough, he texts.

How's it going? How's work?

Fine. Boring. How's your cunt?

I drop my phone and feel my cheeks get flushed. Shivers run down my spine. I smile. He's being coy. Cocky. More cocky than usual. Space and distance would do that.

Avery? I'm just joking, he writes after I don't respond for a minute. *Are you offended?*

No, I'm not offended. I just don't know what to say. I've never sexted before.

Wet. How's your dick? I text.

Hard, he writes. *I want to smell you. Inhale you. Eat you up.*

I want to ride you, I text.

Shit. So so sorry for cutting this short. But I have to go. Rain check? he texts.

Sure.

I put down my phone. The door opens and Cynthia comes in, startling me. I take a deep breath. I'm covered in sweat. I have large stains under my arms and along the bottom of my breasts.

"Oh my God, Avery," Cynthia says. "Why don't you just turn up the air conditioner if you're that hot?"

CHAPTER 17 - LOGAN

I wait for Avery on my plane. I sent a car for her so that she doesn't have to drive. We haven't seen each other since that one earth-shattering afternoon in her tiny apartment. I've never felt this drawn to anyone before. My mind keeps swirling back to her. What she tastes like. How she laughs. The way her lips curl upward, as if in a smile when she gets upset. I crave her. I need her. I'm not someone who's used to needing anymore.

When her car pulls up, my heart starts to beat a little faster. I nervously play with my cufflinks. I'm wearing a button-down shirt, a gray tie and matching charcoal-gray pants. I brush my fingers through the back of my hair – I just got a new haircut, and I feel a little naked now. It's a bit too short for comfort.

After a month away in cold and perpetually overcast Washington D.C, my tan has faded a bit. This must be remedied ASAP. My body is starved for sunlight, warmth and Avery. I glance down at my phone absent-mindedly, listening for her footsteps going up the plane.

"Ms. Lewis? My name is Kim, and I will be your flight attendant this evening," Kim introduces herself.

"Oh please call me Avery," I hear her say. "Is Logan here?"

"Avery," I say, walking up to her. I put my arms around her and give her a warm hug. I can feel how fast her heart is beating through her dress. After pulling away, I kiss her. Her lips are soft and responsive, but after a month apart, the kiss is rather chaste. Both of us are keenly aware of Kim's presence.

I show her to the seat across from me. She's wearing a short grey dress with long sleeves. Her legs are toned and bronzed and adorned with red heels, which match her nail polish and lips perfectly.

"I've missed you," I say quietly.

"I've missed you too," she says. I've completely forgotten that when Avery smiles, she smiles with her whole body. I want to grab her, pull her close to me and kiss her properly, but I restrain myself.

"Wow, this plane is beautiful," Avery says, looking around. "Are we the only ones going on this flight?"

"That's the best thing about private planes. You don't have to travel with anyone you don't want to."

Her hazel eyes sparkle in the light.

"Is this real leather?"

I nod.

"What can I make you to drink?" Kim's comes over. She's leggy, with large breasts and very easy on the eyes. She's my perfect type, but I've never made a move. I don't sleep with the help. This wasn't always my policy. Last year, I made the mistake of sleeping with my old flight attendant, Cherry – that was actually her name! – and when I got bored, I had to pay her a pretty extensive severance package to get rid of her. I couldn't very well bring dates on my private plane with my ex-hook up serving us drinks.

"I'll have a dry martini, well, you know how I like it. And you?" I turn to Avery.

She's staring at Kim's cleavage. I don't blame her. Her breasts are more than a little mesmerizing.

"I'll have a sangria. If you have the ingredients."

"Oh yes, of course," Kim smiles. Kim's the ultimate professional even if she doesn't really dress like one.

"She's very pretty," Avery says disapprovingly.

"Yes, she is," I say, "but not as pretty as you."

Avery rolls her eyes, as if she doesn't believe me. Her self-esteem is something that I'm really going to have to work on. The only unattractive thing about her is her lack of confidence.

"So how was work?" she asks.

I sigh, looking away into the distance.

"Tiring," I say. "Boring. Not very interesting."

I don't know how else to describe what happened over the last month. I've participated in more tests and training than I ever care to again. I've never been through anything that exhausting before, not even when I just started. I guess they know that my contract is expiring and there's no way in hell I'm going to re-up. So they decided to drain me completely – emotionally, physically, and mentally. I don't really understand the rationale though. Wouldn't you want your agents to go out into the field, on very dangerous missions, well-rested and in full control of their faculties? All those analysts and scientists and they don't know the first thing about being a human being.

Kim brings us our drinks and disappears.

"Wow, this is so good," Avery says, taking a sip of her sangria, following it up with a big gulp.

My martini also goes down nicely. In addition to all the annoying tests, I also haven't had a drink in a month. This one both exhilarates and relaxes me.

"Are you looking forward to the wedding?" she asks.

"Not as much as I'm looking forward to doing some of those things we talked about over text."

Avery blushes, looking away. Was that a bit too far? I scrutinize her face for signs. No. She likes it. She's trying to pretend that she doesn't, but I can see that she does.

A COUPLE HOURS LATER, we land in Tulum, Mexico. The nearest commercial airport is in Cancun, about two hours away by car. Here's yet another perk of flying private. We step off the plane. The air is thick with moisture. My eyes, which often get dry in California, feel satiated.

"Oh wow," Avery says, inhaling the world around her. "The air smells like the ocean, doesn't it?"

I take a deep breath. A thick aroma of salt and flowers overpower my senses. The starchiness of my collar lets go a little, relaxing under the humidity.

"I feel like a movie star in the 60's," Avery whispers as we walk down the stair ramp. "Not many of them get off planes like this anymore, do they?"

I smile and wink at her.

"In that dress, you could pass for a movie star anywhere."

She blushes and stumbles a little.

The airport faces the Caribbean, and far in the distance, I see its unforgettable blueness calling to me. I've always loved the Caribbean. The Pacific has its charms, but the water there is cold and unwelcoming in comparison to the Caribbean. Right now, I wonder why I still live in Malibu at all. I could live anywhere I want. We're not anywhere near the beach, but the Caribbean is definitely making quite an argument. I wonder what Avery would think of that?

Shit. Did I just really think this? We've had two dates. This weekend is technically only our third. And yet, the closeness that I feel toward her is unlike anything I felt for anyone else. I crave her. Want her. I feel myself becoming needy around her. You know what? Fuck Dolly. Why the hell did she have to introduce me to this marvelous creature? I was fine going through life a bachelor. I was fine with my life the way it was before. Basically one endless fuck fest interrupted by a few nice dinners and a couple of three-martini lunches.

"Are you okay?" Avery asks. I must've blanked out. I don't remember the last thing I said.

"Yep, fine. Just taking it all in."

"If this is the airport, I can't imagine what the rest looks like," she says looking around. We landed on a small runway surrounded by thick jungle on both sides. To make the airport, they literally cut a strip away in the green.

"What is that sound?" Avery asks.

"Which one?"

Everything around buzzes with life. There are ibises walking around and crickets and other insects singing on top of their voices. Southern California is by all accounts a desert and, though there's a lot of life in the desert, it doesn't buzz, thrive or thump all around. There are insects and bugs, but they don't make their presence known loudly. Not like here.

A car is already waiting for us. The driver carries our bags and places them carefully in the trunk.

"You have quite a lifestyle here," Avery says.

"Oh, you like what you see?"

"Of course, who wouldn't? First class is definitely the way to go."

"I have a secret to share with you," I say, putting my around her shoulders and giving her a small peck on the cheek. "This is better than first class."

She shakes her head and bursts out in a sexy little laugh.

"The cockiness that comes with it does leave much to be desired," she says.

"I'm not so sure you believe that," I say, laughing. I grab her waist and tickle her until she admits defeat.

CHAPTER 18 - AVERY

After checking into a deluxe waterfront suite at the Jashita Hotel in Tulum, I freshen up, change and hurry downstairs to Liam and Kora's rehearsal dinner. Logan, the best man, went downstairs earlier to participate in the rehearsal. Our suite is large and spacious and has everything you could ever want – even a private terrace with an outside shower! I peel off my travel clothes and wrap myself in the hotel-provided robe made of the finest Italian linen. The view of the Caribbean from the terrace is breathtaking. We are steps from the whitest beach I've ever walked on. Before I start getting ready, I spend a good half an hour lounging in the Mayan hammock on the terrace, listening to the waves calmly crashing into the sand.

Makeup and hair are a little bit of a challenge here. The humidity in the air makes my face a little too shiny and makes my makeup run a little. My hair, which is typically razor straight and fine, has suddenly found some body and decided to curl up in all directions, looking unruly and completely out of control. After I take care of these problems, I pull out the dress that I got exactly for this trip. It cost $250, on sale – way too much – but I wanted to look perfect both nights.

The dress is a Draper James original, Reece Witherspoon's new clothing company. It's the color of a Louisiana lilac, powder blue, and it's a gorgeous striped and printed organza with silk lining. It's sleeveless with a delicate slit down the front and comes with a thin white belt, which perfectly cinches the waistline. The way it flares out a little bit at the hips perfectly complements my figure and hides all the flaws. After putting together my whole look, I glance at myself in the mirror one last time. I look good. Put together. Classy. Sophisticated. With a touch of fun.

The rehearsal dinner is held downstairs on the patio. A soft Caribbean breeze from the ocean caresses the guests with kisses, and I thank God that I decided to use hairspray in my hair before I left.

I see Logan across the patio, chatting with his brother. He waves me over. He is dressed in a sharp linen suit with light brown loafers and no socks. The drink he's holding in his hand is almost empty, and his demeanor is relaxed.

"What a beautiful party," I say coming over to them, and giving Liam a brief hug. "Thank you very much for inviting me."

"Thank you for coming. Did you get a drink?" he asks.

"No, not yet."

Just as I say that, a waiter appears as if out nowhere and offers me the dinner's signature cocktail – watermelon vodka martini. It's smooth and refreshing and puts me in an even more vacation mood.

"How do you like you room?" Kora asks, giving me a brief hug.

"Oh my God, it's amazing!" I gush. She laughs.

"I know, right?"

The rehearsal dinner apparently went really well, and Kora hardly seems nervous at all about tomorrow.

"Honestly, I don't know how you're holding up," I say as the guys move away from us, chatting about golf. "I'd be such a wreck."

"I don't know," Kora shrugs. She's wearing a bright blue wrap dress, which brings out her eyes. "I think that I've been waiting for this so long that I'm just super happy that it's finally happening."

"Have you been getting any sleep?"

"A lot, actually. I don't know if you know, but Logan's paying for this whole thing, and he insisted on hiring us a wedding planner. She has been a lifesaver. She knows exactly what to do and how to do it. She presents me with just a few choices and I pick one. She's really a relief. If we didn't have her...this whole thing would take over my life for a year."

I smile. I had no idea that Logan was paying for this – very generous indeed. Especially for someone who doesn't seem to be particularly keen on the whole idea of marriage.

"I'm so glad that everything's working out," I say, and can't help but give her a hug. For some reason, I feel a strange connection to Kora. We don't really have anything in common, and yet I feel like she's a kindred spirit. Someone who I just get innately, regardless of how long we have known each other for.

FOR DINNER, all the guests are served with their own freshly-caught lobster on a bed of rice and spices, and we're treated to a slideshow of the bride and groom and their families and friends through the years. Logan appears in a number of these pictures – there's the freckled six-year-old, the smart-mouthed eleven-year-old, the cocky seventeen-year-old. There are pictures of Logan's mom and dad, Liam and their three sisters, who I've only met briefly during cocktails, because they were too busy running after their husbands and kids. I don't mind. This is only our third date.

After the slideshow, while I'm still digging into my lightly buttered and utterly delicious lobster, Logan gets up and gives another touching and eloquent speech. This time, he talks about how much Liam means to him and how he would not be the person that he is today were it not for his brother. Most of the women in the audience tear up, including me.

"Are you okay?" he asks afterwards, as he sits down next to me.

"Yes," I nod, wiping a tear. I hate when I get this sentimental, but words make a big impact on me. "That was just so sweet, what you said."

Logan smiles and puts his arm around me, giving me a brief squeeze.

"No, you're the one who's sweet," he says.

Waiters come around with the dessert: cheesecake served with an assortment of local fruit – mangos, pineapple, star fruit, and bananas. The combination of tart and sweetness sends shivers down my spine, and I finish two whole slices before I'm able to stop myself.

Logan's phone beeps. When he looks at it, he gets a concerned look on his face. He excuses himself and goes out onto the patio.

As I contemplate whether or not I should go get yet another slice of that wonderful cheesecake, I catch Sadie talking and laughing somewhere in the background. She looks just as stunning as the last time I saw her. She's dressed in an incredibly short satin dress, with delicate straps. It looks like lingerie, and it doesn't look like she's even wearing a bra. Despite that, her breasts are perfectly framed and erect. Why does she have to be Logan's ex? I think to myself. Of all people, why does the mother of his future child have to be so perfect?

If whether or not I had another slice of the cheesecake was a question before, it's not anymore. I feel crappy about myself, and I only know of one way to drown that sorrow.

Kora catches my arm right before I get to the dessert table.

"Hey, come here. I have to tell you something," she whispers under her breath. I follow her to a dark corner of the room, away from everyone.

"I just heard from Dolly that Sadie's had a miscarriage," she says with excitement. "I'm sorry, I know it's terrible that I'm so excited, but I just really didn't like that woman and couldn't imagine her being the mother of my niece or nephew."

"She had a miscarriage?" I ask slowly, trying to grasp what that really means.

"Yes."

"Are you sure?"

"She told Dolly herself. I think she's going to tell Logan tonight."

"Oh wow," I mumble.

"C'mon, aren't you excited? Please smile or something, so I don't feel like such a horrible person."

I smile. It's genuine. I am actually happy.

"Okay, good," Kora gives me a brief hug.

"How is she feeling?"

"Who? Sadie?"

I nod.

"Fine, I guess. I mean she looks like she's having fun."

We both glance in her general direction. She's draped around an older gentleman and laughing at every single thing he says as if he's the funniest comedian on earth.

"Yeah, she does seem fine," I say. Kora takes a step back, staring at me.

"Where the hell did Dolly find you?" she asks.

"What do you mean?"

"I mean you are way, way, too good for Logan. I love him to death. But you're way too good for him."

"I am not," I say, shyly.

"Let me tell you this, unless he has changed tremendously in the month that you've known each other, you need to be careful. Logan likes the ladies. He has never had a serious relationship in his whole life, for crying out loud."

"I don't think you're being very nice," I say, suddenly feeling very protective of Logan.

"I'm sure that he'll agree with me," Kora says, crossing her arms across her chest. "Wouldn't you Logan?"

I turn and see him standing directly behind me.

"Agree with you on what?" Logan wraps his hands around my waist.

"I was just telling your girl, Avery, here that she's too good for you."

"And I was trying to convince her that I'm not," I say looking up at him.

"Oh no," he shakes his head definitively. "You're definitely too good for me."

He kisses me on the cheek.

"See?" Kora says and walks away.

CHAPTER 19 - LOGAN

My other phone beeps during dessert. As I reach for it, I'm grateful that Avery doesn't know me well enough to know that this isn't my usual phone. It's a text from Truman.
Call me.
I excuse myself and go out onto the patio. There are a few couples here, smoking and drinking and kissing, but it's a little bit more private than the dining room. When Truman picks up, he starts talking right away. I don't even get the chance to say hello.
"Sanchez's yacht will be off the coast of Playa del Carmen tomorrow night. I'll send you the exact coordinates later."

I do the math in my head. I need to leave the wedding by 2 a.m, at the latest. The plan is to take a speedboat most of the way and then paddle a dinghy the rest – so that his bodyguards don't hear me.

"He's hosting a birthday party for his niece and, from what we know, he's not coming ashore. The job is to do this quietly. Make it look like an accident, if possible. Do not take care of anyone else."

I clench my fists. Why does Truman feel the necessity to tell me this? I'm not one of his rogue agents who takes innocent civilians out left and right. In fact, I've gotten reprimanded for not taking shots when I should have just because innocent people were present.

"Any questions?" Truman asks.

"No."

He hangs up without a good-bye.

My mind is still on what I have to do tomorrow as Avery walks up to me.

"Hey stranger," she says.

I turn to face her. She looks radiant. I love the way her eyes sparkle in the moonlight.

"Everything okay?" she asks.

No. But it will be, I say to myself and lean down and kiss her. She tastes sweet and lemony. I lick my lips after I pull away.

"The cheesecake was delicious," she announces.

"Do you want to get out of here?" I ask. She nods.

Back in our suite, I sit down on the edge of the bed and pull her onto my lap. I move her hair off her neck and kiss it. Gently. Softly. She moans a little from pleasure. Little goosebumps form under my lips, and I kiss them away. Her arms are delicate, but powerful. She's no waif. Her hands dig into the sleeves of my suit. She tosses off her heels. I wrap my arms tighter around her small waist and pull her closer. The feel of her butt on my dick makes my erection grow bigger and bigger.

I grab at one of her breasts. She responds with a louder moan. I unzip her dress and pull it over her head. I undo her bra and free her breasts. They fall naturally into my hands. She turns to face me and removes my jacket. When Avery pulls my tie over my head, she catches it on my mouth and we both crack up laughing.

I bury my fingers in her long, soft hair and pull her close to me. I kiss her from her neck down to her nipples. I bite down softly on her left nipple, and she cries out in pleasure. I can tell that she likes it a little rougher. I'm going to give her what she wants.

I flip her back around on my lap and pull her back against the headboard along with me.

"You're as light as a feather," I whisper into her ear. She turns her head and kisses me hard, pushing her tongue into my mouth.

She tries to turn around, but I stop her.

"This is about you," I say. She smiles, closes her eyes and lets go. I position her in front of my dick, facing away from me and spread her legs open with my hands. She leans into me as my fingers run down her thighs and find her special spot. She moans harder this time. She pushes on my legs with hers as she moves up and down in pleasure. A few times, she clenches her thighs, but I push them open again. She moves up her feet, opening wider. I bury my fingers within her and start to move faster and faster. Her body responds and rubs harder against my dick. The faster my fingers move, the more energy builds within her.

And then she lets out a big powerful moan. I feel her orgasm pulsate through my fingers and her body starts to shake. A few seconds later, her body goes limp on top of me.

"How was that?" I ask.

"Amazing," she whispers. "I can't feel my legs."

After she climbs off me and lies there motionlessly, I pull off my pants and socks. Now, we're both naked. I lean down over her and kiss her from her lips down to her thighs. Inside her thigh, I linger for a moment, inhaling her sex.

"What are you doing?" she asks, closing her legs, self-consciously.

"I love the way you smell," I say and pull them open. I press my lips onto her and tongue her wetness. She's so deliciously wet.

I pull away for a moment to get a condom.

"Oh my God, did we use one last time?" she gasps.

"Of course," I smile. Relief sweeps over her face.

After the condom is on, I thrust myself inside of her. Avery lets out a moan and her eyes roll to the back of her head.

I thrust into her again and again, and we start to move in rhythm. She cries out a little with each thrust, making me swell up more and more, as if that were possible. When I start to feel like I'm getting close, I cradle her head and kiss her hard. I feel her body quiver below mine. Her moans get quicker and quicker, and she yells out my name. Suddenly, my whole body convulses and gets tight. I come and empty myself into her.

CHAPTER 20 - AVERY

The following morning, I wake up when the sun kisses my eyelids slightly. I feel the bed next to me. Logan is gone. He said that he was leaving to go golfing with Liam this morning. I look at the time. It's after ten. I really slept late. I can't remember the last time I slept in this long! I wrap myself in a bathrobe and make my way to the patio. The smell of the ocean calls to me. After doing a few sun salutations and one very stiff downward facing dog, I go back inside and change into a bathing suit.

I practically run into the water. Unlike the Pacific Ocean, which can be bone chilling even in August, the water temperature here is much more to my liking. It's lukewarm, and I don't shiver once getting in.

"Oh my God, this is amazing," I exhale jumping into the waves. I dive under the water. When I open my eyes, I see a school of colorful yellow and black striped fish swarm around me. They nip at my hair and give me little kisses on my hands. I dive down over and over and let the movement of the ocean rock me into a state of utter relaxation. About an hour later, I finally get out of the water, reluctantly, and head back to our room.

"Hey!"

"Oh my God!" I jump back a few feet, clenching my chest. "You scared me!"

"I'm sorry," Kora says, sitting down on the bed. The room is perfectly put together again. The bed is made. The fruit bowl is refilled. Pillows are plumped. How the maid managed to get it all done so quickly, I have no idea.

I don't have a towel, and I'm dripping water all over the place. I head to the bathroom and wrap myself in a towel.

"What's up?" I ask, coming back out, It's only now that I notice that Kora's already wearing her wedding dress.

"Oh wow, is this your dress?" I ask the stupidest question on earth. No, she just walks around in beaded white dresses for the hell of it.

"Yes," she nods. Kora's dress is formfitting, strapless and with a long, delicate train. I'm sure it looks gorgeous spread out, but pooled at the bottom of the bed, it looks like she's drowning in a cupcake.

"I love the lace," I kneel down before her and examine the intricate work.

"It's all hand sewn," she says. I expect her to stand up for me and model a little, but she doesn't move.

"I don't want to get it all wet," I say, standing up and moving away.

"It's okay. I'm not even sure if this wedding is happening."

"What?" I drop my towel. Kora doesn't even notice. I pick up my towel, secure it around myself again and sit down on the bed next to her.

"What are you talking about?" I ask, putting my hand around her shoulder.

"I'm just not sure about this whole wedding. Liam and I have been together for so long. What if it's the wrong thing to do?"

"How could it be?"

She looks at me. Her makeup is a total mess. One of her fake eyelashes is falling off. Both eyes are blackened all around from the smeared tears. In movies, the brides always cry in a delicate, non-eye makeup smearing sort of way, but this is real life, and it's not a pretty sight.

"I was just thinking about this all night," she says in between sobs. "I'm pretty much pushing him into this. And after seven years, maybe it's the wrong thing to do. Maybe he'll regret it in a few years and then what? I'll be even more heartbroken."

"So, this isn't about you having second thoughts?" I ask.

"No, not entirely. Well, yes, perhaps," Kora says, wiping her eyes. The back of her hand is dirty and she looks for a place to wipe it off. I guide her away from the lace on her dress and onto my towel.

"How do I know that I actually love him? I don't feel butterflies anymore. What if I'm not in love with him anymore? What if I'm marrying someone who's a stranger?"

"Well, the one thing you know for sure," I say squeezing her hand. "Is that you're not marrying a stranger. You and Liam have been together for a long time. You know him. And you know that he loves you."

"How do you know?"

"Because I've never seen anyone look at a woman like he looks at you. He oozes love for you."

"Really?" Kora's eyes light up.

"Yes," I nod. "And those butterflies. You'll feel those again when you walk down the aisle."

"And what if I don't?"

"If you don't, then you can just write them off to something you feel when you don't really know someone. Relationships are different in the beginning than they are later on. But what you two have is so much more solid and strong. Butterflies come and go."

"But what if I never feel them again?" she asks.

What the fuck is with these butterflies? I say to myself. But I can't just leave her hanging. I have to convince her, not remind her, of who they are as a couple and how much love they have.

"You will feel them again when you two do something that you've never done before," I finally say.

"Like what?"

"Like when you buy your first house together. Like when you find out that you're pregnant. Like when you decorate your nursery. Would you like to do those things with Liam?"

"More than anything," she says through the sobs.

"See. That's my point exactly! Butterflies are just things that happen when something is new. In the beginning, it's the relationship itself. Everything about it is new. Everything you do with that person is magical, because you haven't done it with anyone else. And later on, you'll get those same butterflies when you do new things together. Experience something exciting."

"Maybe you're right," Kora mumbles, wiping her tears.

"Maybe? Maybe? No, I am right," I say confidently. She cracks a smile.

"I think I should head back. The makeup people have their work cut out for them."

I nod. She doesn't even know the half of it. I give Kora a warm hug and watch her walk away.

CHAPTER 21 - LOGAN

I am sucks at golf. I don't know why the hell he has dragged me out here at the crack of dawn to play a round. My favor to him is that I'll play with him, not that I'll let him win. I'd prefer sailing. The resort has a beautiful restored, fifty-footer sitting out front. I love the spray of the ocean in my hair and the warmth of the sun on my face. Here, on the golf course, the sun feels more like it is scorching my face as a punishment.

I'm driving the golf cart. Liam looks ahead absentmindedly.

"How are you and Avery doing?"

"Fine," I nod. Are we really here to talk about that?

"You seem really happy with her? Is she a keeper?"

I look at him. Scrutinize his face. What is the meaning of this? But Liam looks genuinely interested.

"I like her. A lot."

"I know that's not something you often admit."

"No, it's not. But honestly, it's not something I ever really felt before."

"What do you mean?"

"We just have this connection, you know. I feel like she gets me. And I get her."

Liam smiles, nods. I turn the conversation back to him.

"I'm sure that's exactly how you felt with Kora," I say. And then I catch myself. "I mean, I'm sure that's how you *feel* about Kora."

"It was and it is, I guess."

"That doesn't sound too convincing."

Liam doesn't respond.

"Did you two have a fight or something?"

He shakes his head.

"No. Nothing major, anyway. I just don't know if this is the right thing to do."

"What? The wedding?" I stop the golf cart.

"Why are you stopping?"

"There's no one here anyway. What's going on?" I ask. I've never heard him talk like this. I'm not the biggest fan of Kora, but I know that he loves her. Something big is up. Unfortunately, I'm not the guy to handle it.

"It's just that she has wanted to get married forever."

"I know. She has been quite a nag."

"I wouldn't call it that," Liam says, "but yes, she has been a little annoying."

"Why didn't you?" I ask. This is something I've been meaning to ask him forever. He and Kora have been together for many years. And by together, I mean tied at the hip. They were practically married as is, they just never bothered to have a party or do the paperwork.

"Why didn't I what?"

"Why didn't you want to get married? I thought you two were solid. You never dated anyone else. And neither has she. Not that I know of, of course," I say.

"No, we have been faithful. Very faithful, actually."

I didn't know there was such a thing – too faithful – but okay.

"I never knew that you wanted to be with anyone else," I say it in the most polite way that I can.

"I never did. And I don't now."

"So what's going on?"

"I don't know," Liam shakes his head. "I guess I'm just scared. I mean, it's just going to be Kora for the rest of my life. One woman. Wouldn't that scare you?"

"Well, yes, of course," I shrug, "but I'm completely different from you. You were with Kora and no one else for years. And you didn't have any second thoughts. You don't want to be with anyone else. Getting married isn't going to change that."

"It won't?"

"No," I shake my head. "Besides, if anything changes between you two and you no longer want to be with her, there's always divorce."

He looks at me, and we both crack up laughing.

"You're such an asshole," he says through the laughter.

"I'm not the one thinking of standing up my bride on our wedding day," I joke. "C'mon let's play some golf."

AFTER A FEW LONG and blisteringly hot hours on the golf course, I get back to the room for some peace and quiet. I look at my phone. I'd like to go for a swim and then make love to Avery again, but there's not much time. Besides, she's nowhere to be found. Instead, I sit back against the headboard and do something that I've never done before: research the target that I'm supposed to eliminate tonight.

Don't you just love that kind of language? Instead of a person, a human being, we say 'target.' Instead of kill or murder or assassinate, we say 'eliminate.' It's supposed to make things impersonal, but the people in the government who have created that language are not the ones actually tasked with the elimination. They aren't the ones who pulled the trigger. They aren't the ones who have to watch the target's family gather around and try to bring him back to life. No, to them they are just numbers. Successes or failures. But no amount of detached, corporate bullshit speak is going to make them that to me.

I scan some articles about Sanchez from the New York Times, The Telegraph and some other uncensored South American newspapers. From the English-speaking newspapers, he comes off a dictator. A strong man who consolidated power based on his control of the military and his charisma. Basically, a fascist. But the Spanish-speaking newspapers are probably more spot on. Ever since he took power, thousands of young people have disappeared never to be heard from again. There are rumors of secret torture camps in jungles. Not one person who has been arrested has been found. The families have given up all hope. The major newspaper from Buenos Aires repeatedly refers to him as 'The Butcher of El Salvador." And I know that they do not exaggerate and do not flirt with the truth the same way many American and English newspapers do.

Fine, I decide, turning off my phone. As much as I don't agree with political assassinations and as much as I hate my job, I have to do this. I can't screw this up. Sanchez has to go. And, if I retire after this mission, perhaps taking out this guy isn't so bad.

CHAPTER 22 - AVERY

"Wow, you look..." Logan says, trying to find the right words, "amazing."

I smile. He's actually speechless. I wasn't expecting that, but it's a nice surprise. I never thought that a man who seems to have everything – he does have a private plane – would be left speechless by an average girl like me. I glance at myself in the mirror. Though, I have to admit, I do clean up nice.

I'm wearing a light pink dress, which is crafted in organza with panels of lace and tulle. Cynthia helped me pick it out and said that it was perfect because it managed to balance a simple silhouette with feminine drama – whatever that hell that means. Personally, I like it because it's sleeveless and tight-fitting, accentuating my waist and bringing extra attention to my cleavage. You can never go wrong with that. It's cut right above the knee, bringing attention to my sun-kissed legs.

"You look really good too," I say, giving him a brief hug and peck on the cheek. He wraps his hand around my waist, pulling me close to him, but I press my index finger onto his lips before they reach mine.

"Uh, uh, uh," I say flirtatiously.

"Oh c'mon," he shrugs his shoulders from exasperation. "You can't look this good and not let me kiss you."

"Do you know how long it took me to do this makeup? I'm not a natural at it, you know. And I just got the lipstick just right."

He smiles and extends his arm to me. I take take it and we proceed out of the suite.

"Look at us," Logan whispers. "We already sound like an old married couple."

He's right! Oh my God! The idea sends shivers down my spine. He can't be serious. I look up at him. I expect to see an expression of panic at what he had just said, but instead he seems to be at peace with it. It's a joke, of course, but then it's not a joke. We walk the rest of the way to the wedding in silence.

I love how dashing and handsome Logan looks in his classic fit, light beige suit. The light blue tie brings out his eyes and, after a day in the sun, a bit of his old tan is coming back. As he leads me down the long, marble staircase, I feel like a princess.

The lobby of the hotel blends in with the outside world. Its twelve-foot floor-to-ceiling windows are always open, blending seamlessly with the sand and the ocean outside. The light breeze, which sways the kneeling palm trees, enters the lobby, consuming the senses with an aroma of salt and freedom.

The ceremony is held outside in a tropical garden. Logan shows me to my seat and goes up to the front to stand with Liam. I look around in awe. This lush, sun-drenched setting is arranged in such a way that it allows nature to take the lead. There are rows of white chairs facing the ocean, and the simple bamboo arch is decorated in dahlias. The palms in this area of the garden seem to kneel inward, as if by design, to create more intimacy for the space. The ceremony itself is romantic and touching. Liam and Kora wrote their own vows and neither can get through theirs without crying. This makes everyone at the ceremony tear up, including me.

After cocktails at the beach, we are lead back to the dining hall for the reception. Tall candles with matched and mismatched brass candleholders dot the dining hall, making the place feel magical. Calligraphed escort cards topped with delicate crowns complement the nature-centered theme, and eclectic vintage chairs make the place feel historically romantic. The tables are topped with many different tapered candles and lush, low centerpieces of dahlias. Single-blossom accents wind their way down the length of the table. The color palette of a spectrum of soft greens and creamy tones with notes of blush and coral matches the surroundings.

"Isn't this place just magnificent?" Dolly comes over to me.

"Oh my God, it's gorgeous," I say, giving her a warm hug. She's dressed in a tight, lavender dress and adorned with large diamonds around her neck, ears and hands.

"I'm glad that you decided to come," she says. "You look beautiful."

"Thank you," I nod.

"I hate to admit this, but I think you were right about Logan. We do seem to make a good match."

Dolly's eyes light up.

"It's definitely a risk," she says, "but I'm glad to hear that it's working out."

"What do you mean?"

"Well, you know, Logan doesn't have the best reputation when it comes to women. I mean, women love him and he loves them. But for a long time, I had my doubts that he would be happy with just any one woman."

I take a deep sigh. Perhaps, he won't be.

"But after talking to him about you. Let's just say that you have made quite an impression."

"What did he say?"

"He said that you make him feel like no other woman ever has."

"Oh wow," I smile. "That's...nice to hear."

"Hey there," Logan comes over and gives me a kiss on the cheek. "Aunt Dolly."

"Logan," Dolly says raising her eyebrows with a mischievous look on her face.

"I hope you two aren't gossiping about me," he says.

"Oh you know me better than that," she waves her hand. I'm not sure how big the diamond ring is that she's wearing on her left hand, but it looks heavy.

"Of course, we were gossiping," Dolly smiles at him. Logan shakes his head.

"Then I hope you were saying something nice."

"Of course," she says.

"Avery?" he turns to me.

"Actually, Dolly here was telling me that you apparently have the hots for me," I say. I've had two glasses of champagne already, and it has gone straight to my head.

"I have the hots for you? Is that what she said?" he asks, jokingly. "I'm sure that's exactly the words that she used."

"Okay, so she didn't say that," I say, smiling at Dolly. "What she said is that I apparently make you feel like no other girl ever has."

"Oh my, Dolly. You've been bad," he wags his finger at her. "That was a private conversation."

"I know I'm sorry," she shrugs.

"Well, is it true?" I ask. I would never have had the courage to talk like this if I weren't a little tipsy. They don't call it liquid courage for nothing.

Logan looks straight at me. His eyes narrow, as if he's evaluating if I really want to know the answer. For a moment, I feel like he's going to say no, but then he flashes his pearly whites at me.

"Of course," he says with total confidence. "I haven't met anyone like you before."

I smile. We are locked in a moment. When I finally catch myself and look around, I see that Dolly has disappeared.

"She left," Logan whispers not breaking eye contact with me. His gaze is intense, and it sends shivers down my whole body.

"She really knows the right time to exit," I say.

"Well, she is a professional."

It's one of those exchanges where we are talking about one thing, but thinking another. The words don't matter, and I don't even know why we're saying them, except that there's the social expectation that something needs to be said.

His eyes finally let go of mine and travel down to my lips and then my neck and toward the top of my breasts. I can feel his gaze on me. It is so exhilarating and erotic that my feet grow numb.

"Do you want to go somewhere?" he whispers. I nod.

A few minutes later, we're alone in our suite. All the windows and the doors to the patio are open, and there's a nice salty breeze circulating around the place. Moonlight streams in turning everything in the place a mysterious silver-grey tone. Neither of us dares to turn on the lights.

I head toward the bed, but Logan stops me in the middle of the room. He leans into me. His fingers run along my jawline and bury themselves in my hair. Slowly, he removes some of the hairpins and lets them drop. They make little dinging sounds when they hit the floor. He takes a step closer to me. I feel the unevenness of his breath on my lips. I wait for our lips to touch, but he surprises me. He demands that I wait. Instead, he leans down and runs his lips over my neck. Gently. Quietly.

I bury my hands in his hair and pull his head toward mine. I have to taste him. I have to touch his tongue with mine. When our lips finally meet, shivers run down my body. His tongue feels rough and strong. He grabs my face and kisses me more passionately with each breath. He's kissing me as if he's trying to prove something. I like it. A lot. He devours me, and I devour him.

Suddenly, he pulls away from me, and takes a step back. His eyes run over my body, from top to bottom. I try to approach him, but he puts me back into place.

"What..." I'm about to ask him what he's doing. But he puts his index finger on his lips.

"Shhhh," he whispers. He walks around me and unzips my dress. It falls effortlessly to the floor. He undoes my strapless bra and then grabs at my breasts. Slowly, with kisses, he makes his way to the front of my body and places one of my nipples into his mouth. He's gentle at first, carefully playing with it, as if it were a bing cherry. Warmth courses through my body, and I feel like I'm running a fever. My knees grow weak, and I lean on him for support. His body is hard and sturdy, and it holds me up seemingly without much effort.

In the meantime, Logan's kisses intensify. He moves on to my other breast, squeezing my nipple in between his teeth, and toeing the line between pleasure and pain. I remove his jacket and tie and unbuckle his belt. His underpants fall to the floor. My hands feel rushed, and they shake in anticipation. At first, he doesn't cooperate, but eventually gives in. I run my fingers over his hard abs, each pectoral muscle is illuminated by the light of the moon. He looks photoshopped. For a brief second, I worry about my own less than perfect body, but when he kneels down before me, placing all of my breast into his mouth, all of my insecurities vanish.

He pushes aside my panties, and spreads me open. He runs his fingers over me, teasing me before thrusting them inside. I tilt my head back. He runs his lips along my thigh, then up to my navel and then down again.

"You taste so good," he says licking me. Another wave of warmth runs through me and this time, I'm certain that I'm going to fall down. He isn't holding me up anymore, and my legs are too weak to do it for me. With what seems to be my last ounce of strength, I pull away from him and grab his large cock. It pulsates and throbs in my hand. I run my fingers over its every line and curve. His eyes roll to the back of his head. I pull him toward the bed. Another moment later, he's inside of me. Neither of us can toy with each other anymore. My fingers dig into his shoulders.

"Avery," he whispers over and over.

"Logan," I moan into his ear.

Our hips move as one.

"I'm getting close," I whisper.

"I love you," he says. A moment later, my legs grow completely numb and my toes bury themselves into the bedspread. A warm, soothing sensation spreads through my body. A few thrusts later, Logan says my name a few more times and then collapses on top of me.

CHAPTER 23 - LOGAN

While I'm trying to catch my breath after one of the most intense orgasms of my life, my mind runs a mile a minute. Did I really just tell her that I loved her? I've never said those words in my life to anyone. Well, not anyone except my mom, dad and siblings. Definitely not to a girl. But Avery isn't just a girl. She's a girlfriend. Wow, even that word, girlfriend makes the hair on the back of my neck stand up. It sounds so official.

I get up and go to the bathroom to brush my teeth.

"You okay?" Avery asks from the bedroom.

"Yeah, fine."

I stare at myself in the mirror. Not really fine at all. She does not know this, definitely doesn't even suspect it, but I've just crossed a threshold. Took a big step. Not one that I ever thought I would.

I wash my face, rubbing it hard with a towel. I look at myself in the mirror again. Everything about me looks the same. Even my tan is coming back. There's the beginning of those nasty little crow's feet around my eyes. There are the strong, broad shoulders that are perfectly balanced with the narrowness of my waist. I seem the same, but I don't feel it. What is this feeling? And why does it make me feel like I'm suspended in weightlessness? As if I'm scuba diving in that middle section, far enough from the bottom of the ocean floor and too far away from the surface that I don't see either the ground or the waves.

And then it hits me, perhaps this is what it's like to actually care about someone? Maybe this is what it means to be in love?

I walk out of the bathroom. Avery is sitting on the bed, wrapped in a bed sheet. Her hair is all messed up, her makeup is a little smeared and I've never seen anyone so beautiful before. Her knees are pulled up to her chest and she's holding something in her hand.

"Someone called you," she says. I glance at her hand. That's my other phone. Shit.

"I was going to get it for you, but when I searched through your jacket, I found two." Avery takes out her other hand and shows me both of my phones.

"Why do you have two phones?" she asks.

I don't know what to say. I freeze.

"Logan! Why do you have two phones?" she asks again, this time less patiently.

"I have to have another phone for work."

"For work? What work? You don't work."

"Yes, I do," I take the phone from her.

"What do you do?"

I stare at her, waiting for my mind to kick in. I'm trained in this. I know how to lie. Expertly. Just say something already, I say to myself. Anything.

"There are certain business opportunities that I'm investigating," I say looking straight into her eyes. Most people are afraid of direct eye contact. Look right into her eyes and don't blink, I remember what my training has taught me. That's how most people determine if you're telling the truth. "These companies have privacy concerns. So they gave me another phone to use in all of my communications."

She nods.

"Okay," she finally says.

"You don't believe me?" I ask, changing my tone. I sit down next to her and put my arm around her. "It's nothing, really."

"No, I believe you," she lets out a deep sigh. "I'm sorry. I was just really surprised. And then when I saw the phone, I freaked out a little."

"I know," I smile. "But it's really nothing very interesting. They just tend to call me at various times of day and night. Not courteous like that."

"And you're thinking of doing business with them."

"They have some very interesting ideas," I say.

I brush her hair from her face and lean in to kiss her. At first, she doesn't kiss me back, but then she reciprocates and I know that she believes me.

"Can I have my phones please?" I ask, pulling away.

She hands them to me.

It requires a password to open, so I know that she couldn't see who called or read any of the text messages that Truman might have left. But if he called me so close to the mission, I know that it can't be good.

I enter the passcode.

Where the fuck are you? Call me back ASAP.

Truman does not use language like that often, and I've never seen him text with this kind of urgency. Whatever it is, it's not good.

"I have to make a call," I say.

Truman starts talking almost as soon as I press send.

"Where the hell are you? Doesn't matter. There has been a change of plans. Sanchez isn't going to be on the boat. We just got word that he's staying at the same resort as you. Room 117. First floor. He's there alone. There's a guard by the door, but we don't think there's anyone on the side facing the ocean. We'll never get as good of a chance to get to him as we have now."

"Got it."

"I don't think this needs saying, but you don't need to wait until 2 a.m. Go now."

"Okay."

I hang up the phone, take a moment to collect my thoughts. Going now is a little bit of a problem. Avery is here, and she's already suspicious, but there's no other way around. Getting Sanchez here is much easier than on that boat, and there's no one else around except his guards, which makes civilian causalities not much of a problem. I hate missions in which women and children are around the target. I don't want to hurt or injure any innocent bystanders and make poor decisions as a result.

"I'm really, really sorry," I walk into the room shaking my head, "but I have to go."

"Go? Go where?" Avery asks.

"It's work. There's this emergency that I have to take care of." I buckle my belt and put on my dress shirt.

I had another outfit lined up for the mission, but with Avery being here, I can't very well dress in all black and look like a ninja. The suit I wore to the wedding will have to do. On the plus side, it might make me blend in easier afterwards, in case there's a chase or something goes wrong.

"What are you talking about?" Avery gets up, wrapping herself in the robe. "You're leaving now? Where are you going?"

"Not very far. Just to the business center. I have to do something. It won't take long."

I put on my jacket, skip the tie. I slip on the shoes.

"But why do you have to do it now?" she asks.

I walk back to her and take her into my arms.

"I'm really, really sorry. You don't even know how sorry I am about this, but I really need to do this. I'm just going to be in the business center. I should be back in an hour or so. Get some sleep."

Her eyes twinkle in the moonlight. I hate the disappointment that I see in them.

"I can't sleep," she shakes her head.

"Well, then watch some TV. Order some room service. I'll be back soon," I press my lips onto hers. I feel her losing herself in the moment. I would to, if my mind wasn't on the mission. Ideally, this should look like an accident rather than an assassination. Assassinations always bring about the worst in rebels. They make the assassinated leader a martyr.

A legend. People start imagining that he was better than he was. We can't have that. Sanchez is an old man. He's also a very unhealthy man. Someone who could easily have a heart attack and die. The best way to handle this is sneaking into his room while he is sleeping and suffocating him with his pillow. That would be ideal, but might not be possible. I have to be prepared.

I pull away from Avery.

"Are you okay?" I ask. She nods.

I let go of her and go to the closet. I feel her watching me as I search my suitcase for the hidden compartment with my weapon. Luckily, all the lights in the room are off, and I'm able to slip the gun in the waist of my pants and the silencer into my pocket of my jacket without her noticing.

I walk back to Avery to give her one last kiss before I go. This time I don't embrace her; I don't want her to feel anything around my waist. Instead, I keep her at arm's length.

"Do you remember what I said when we were making love?" I ask. She looks at me.

"What?" she asks. I can tell that she isn't happy. Her arms are crossed at her chest and her lips are pursed.

"I love you."

She looks up at me as if she doesn't believe me.

"You don't have to say anything back. I just want you to know how I feel. I love you Avery, and I've never felt this way about anyone else before."

Suddenly, a warm, inviting smile sweeps over her face. I give her one last kiss and disappear.

CHAPTER 24 - AVERY

I don't know how I feel about Logan Davenport at this very moment. He has just told me that he loves me, and I could feel his love in the kiss and the way he held me. And the way he made love to me. But then he left. Off to somewhere mysterious in the middle of the night. After receiving a mysterious call from his other phone. What. The. Fuck?

Who the hell conducts business so late at night? What kind of business is this that requires him to have another phone? No, all of his perfect explanations are just that. Too perfect. I don't buy them. They're bullshit. But what else could it be?

I change out of the bathrobe and into my yoga pants and light t-shirt. Before I really know what I'm doing, I grab the key to the room and follow him out.

A million thoughts rush through my head. He isn't telling me the truth. And I want to – have to – find out what is really going on. If he's having an affair, then I need to know that so I can dump his sorry ass.

I walk passed the business center. I peek in through the little window on the door. It's completely empty.

Shit, I lean back against the wall. He's lying. Of course, he is. You know this already. So why are you so surprised?

Because a huge part of me, all of me, in fact, wants to believe him. Why can't he just be this wonderful guy who's in love with me? Why does he have to be a liar?

I take a deep breath. Suddenly, another thought enters my mind. What if he's not having an affair on me? What if I'm the affair? What if he's married and I'm the other woman?

No, he isn't married. Dolly would never set us up if he were married. Though, he could have a girlfriend, and he could be cheating on her with me. I mean, why else would he have another phone? And have it password protected?

I have to find him. But how? I have to see if he left the resort at least. Go to the parking lot and see if the car is there.

I head outside. The car we used earlier is there. But then again, he could've rented another car. Or maybe this isn't our car at all. We were in it for like a second and haven't used it since arriving at the resort.

I'm at a loss as to what to do, so I head around the building and toward the water. I don't want to walk past the business center again and not see him. I need time to reflect on this, and out by the water is probably the best spot.

I welcome the ocean breeze in my face, allowing it to cool off my scorching body. It's hot and humid, even at night, but my blood is boiling for other reasons.

I make my way past our suite and then another and another. By the time I reach the last suite, I'm pretty certain of the fact that Logan is cheating on me. It's hard to comprehend all of the conflicting emotions that I'm experiencing at the moment. I hate him. I'm angry with him. I want to punch him. And yet, I want him. I know that what we shared less than an hour ago wasn't a lie. It felt real. And, when he told me that he loved me…that couldn't be a lie as well? Why would he go out of his way and say that? I didn't bring it up. This is only our third date. There's no pressure on him at all. Why would he say that to me, if he didn't mean it? And why would he say it to me if he were cheating on me?

I trip on a piece of driftwood and fall down, head first into the sand. Shit. When I look around to get my bearings, I see the shadow of a man who looks a lot like Logan. Carefully, I get back on my feet. My ankle hurts a little, but it's not really injured. I limp toward the closest palm tree and hide in its shadow. From there, I squint to get a better view.

Yes, it's Logan. I'm certain. I don't see his face, but his deliberate way of walking is very familiar. I look around the patio and inside the suite. This isn't our place. What is he doing here?

The lights inside the suite are off, and the bed is illuminated only by the light of the television screen. As my eyes adjust a little more, I make out a large fat figure, probably a man, lying in bed. Logan walks through the open patio doors and toward the bed.

What the hell is he doing? I wonder. I need to get a better look. Quietly, I tiptoe toward a closer palm tree and again hide behind it.

Logan grabs a pillow off the sofa at the foot of the bed and takes it between his hands. He walks up to the man and puts it over his face.

What!?

I peer into the darkness just to make sure that I'm seeing what I think I'm seeing. The man's legs and arms flail around as he struggles for life. But Logan doesn't give in. He leans over him more and presses the pillow harder into him.

I need to yell out. Scream. But I'm frozen in time and space. I grasp onto the palm tree with all of my might, and I can't let go.

And then it just comes out. This blood-curling scream. It sounds so primal.

"Aghhh!" I scream at top of my lungs. It's so loud that when I do stop, my ears continue to buzz.

Logan stops and stares in my direction. Suddenly, the front door to the suite opens. Logan lets go of the pillow and pulls out a gun. He aims and shoots. It hardly makes a sound, but the man drops to the floor. He points the gun at the man he was suffocating with the pillow and shoots him as well.

He turns to head back toward me, but three more men come in through the front door. That's as much as I can handle. My body takes off before my mind even realizes what it is doing. I run back to the suite as fast as my legs can carry me. I fall a couple of times, landing with my legs and knees in the sand, get up and continue running. When I finally reach the suite, I lock all doors and windows and grab my suitcase. I don't dare to turn on the lights out of fear of being found. I throw every article of clothing that I see into it and zip it up as quickly as I can. I don't know what I'm doing. I don't have a plan. All I know is that I can't stay here.

Downstairs, I don't bother to wait for the cab. Instead, I ask the concierge to drive me two hours to the airport and pay him extra so that he doesn't tell anyone where he took me or that he saw me at all. At first, he's reluctant to take my $700, but I convince him that he has to. He promises to not tell anyone about my whereabouts and I believe him.

As I wait at the empty Cancun airport, I pace nervously near the gate. Please, let me get on this plane. Please, please, please. When I'm finally on the plane and the gate closes, I take a deep breath. I'm on my way home. But as the plane takes off, I realize that I'm not anywhere close to being safe. I just saw Logan murder someone. And not just someone, two people. He killed two men as if it was no big deal. And who knows what the hell happened with the other three who came in just as I left. Something tells me that either he is dead or they are all dead.

My hands go numb. My feet feel incredibly cold. I feel my forehead and there are sprinkles of cold sweat all along my brow-line. Who the hell is Logan? A serial killer? A murderer? Well, he is definitely that.

Oh my God. Suddenly, it occurs to me, he knows where I live! And he knows where I work! What am I going to do when I get home? I don't just live in an apartment. I can't just pick up and leave. What about my customers? How am I going to make a living? One thing's for sure, I can't go back home. He'll find me there for sure.

My worries about my ex, Cal, all of a sudden seem like a walk in the park. Yes, he tried to choke me, but Logan is a whole other deal. He's a murderer. And he knows that I've seen him kill someone. What the hell is he going to do to me to make sure that I don't tell anyone? There's probably nothing that he wouldn't do.

CHAPTER 25 - AVERY

After getting back from Tulum, I didn't know where else to go, so I spent the week at Cynthia's. Of course, I had to tell her something. I couldn't just invite myself over without so much as an explanation, but I don't tell her anything important. All I say is that we had a fight and I need some time away from my place. I don't think she fully believes me, but it's as good of an explanation as she going to get. I don't want to involve her. I've seen something that I had no business witnessing, and I have no idea what the fallout will be. What happens if you are a witness to a murder? Will the murderer come after you?

"Are you sure everything's okay?" Cynthia asks me coming home from work one day. I haven't been in the shop for five days. I took some of the days off earlier for the trip, but now I'm just avoiding it. At first, I thought that I needed time to get together a plan. But now, I'm not so sure. The more days that pass, the less of a plan I'm able to come up with.

"Yeah, fine," I nod, eating a bowl of cherries. "Why, did something happen at the shop?"

"No. Something happened to you. I've never seen you like this before."

I shrug, trying to pretend that everything's fine.

"You never skip work willingly. You have to tell me what's going on."

"Nothing's going on. Logan and I just had a very big fight, and I don't want to see him, in case he comes by."

"Did he hurt you?" she asks with a concerned look on her face.

I shrug. Shake my head. No. Not yet, I think to myself. She waits for me to say the words.

"No," I say, raising my eyebrows. "What?"

She doesn't believe me, but she lets it go.

Later that night, while we watch the People's Couch on Bravo, I get a call. I look at my phone. I let it go to voice mail.

"Who's that?" Cynthia asks.

"Cal," I whisper. My hands grown numb. Not this again. What the hell is going on?

I freeze, unable to move. She takes the phone from me and plays the voice message on speakerphone.

"Hey Avery. What's up? I was just thinking about you? You know that I love you, right? I'm sorry about everything. But we can't keep doing this to each other. I know that you love me too, no matter how much you try to deny it. I've made some mistakes. But you're not perfect either....Oh, who am I kidding. You are perfect. I miss you. I don't care about the restraining order. I need to see you again. And you better be there. You better act nice. Otherwise...I don't know, Avery. You just can't keep pushing me away like this. I want you. I need you back, honey. You have to take me back, honey."

I get up and walk toward the kitchen. Tears are building up within me.

"Are you okay?" Cynthia asks. Suddenly, they all flow out of me like a torrent. A rainstorm. I start sobbing. I can't stop. I can't breathe. I can't utter a word.

"Oh my God! Avery!" Cynthia runs over and puts her arms around me.

"I'm so, so scared," I manage to say through the sobs.

"You have to go back to the police."

I nod. I try to take a breath, to calm myself down, but I can't. Waves of pent up emotions continue to flow through me. After a few moments, I stop fighting them. Instead, I just let them go. I collapse onto the floor, wrap my hands around my knees and bury my head in my chest. I feel Cynthia's presence, but I don't really see her. I feel her rubbing my back and head, but she seems so far away that she might as well be on the other side of the country.

"I just don't know what to do," I finally say after the tears slow down a bit.

"You have to go to the police."

"But they don't do anything. They just give him citations and that's it. Nothing's different."

I take one deep breath after another, but despite how much air I inhale, I continue to suffocate.

"Maybe you should get a gun," Cynthia says quietly. I look up at her. She wipes my cheeks with her sleeves and fixes my eye makeup. I must look like a fright.

"What?"

"Maybe you should get a gun for protection. In case, he tries something."

"A gun? I can't get a gun. I don't know how to use a gun."

"You could learn. It might be helpful. I mean, what if, God forbid, Cal had a gun?"

My whole body gets covered in goosebumps at the thought of that. I take more breaths, but I start to choke.

"You're hyperventilating, Avery. Here, bury your head in your knees. Don't breathe so fast. Breathe in. And then out. In and out," Cynthia says calmly. I try to follow her instructions. At first, it is futile. But after a few breaths, it gets better.

It takes me close to half an hour to get myself under control. Eventually, my tears dry up. My breathing becomes more even, and I'm able to think a little more clearly. Cynthia helps me off the floor and makes me a cup of green tea. The steam coming from the cup puts me a little bit more at ease, but decisions still have to be made.

"Maybe, I should get a gun," I say looking directly at Cynthia. "No, I will."

She nods. Both of us know that getting a gun will be crossing some sort of line. Life is not like the movies where people shoot each other with little consequences. Owning a gun is a responsibility, and one that I should only take on if I'm really ready. I'm not ready, not today, but perhaps I will be in the coming days. The one thing I know for sure is that I can't just sit around and wait for Cal or Logan to come after me.

CHAPTER 26 - AVERY

A couple of days later I go back to my apartment. At first, I enter cautiously, terrified of my own shadow, but nothing seems amiss. Everything is exactly as I left it before my trip, only a little dustier. That night, sitting with the curtains drawn and the television on low, I realize that I've never been more grateful for the fact that I have a small, studio apartment. I can only imagine how I'd feel in a large spacious three-bedroom house all by myself. At least here I can see the whole place from my bed, and I know that no one is secretly climbing in through one of the other bedroom windows.

After a couple of days of coming home after work, I finally start to relax. Maybe Cal isn't going to come and surprise me. Maybe Logan will let me just be. Carrying a large bouquet of baby's breath and my groceries, I struggle to find my keys in my purse.

I really need a smaller purse, I say to myself. Everything in this one just falls to the bottom and it takes me forever to find it again.

Finally, I open the door and head straight to the kitchen.

"Hello Avery," I hear an unfamiliar voice coming from somewhere behind me. I think I have my purse on the counter, but I drop it to the floor with a large thump sound. All the contents spill out.

"What the hell do you want?" I ask, grabbing at my purse and pulling out my new gun. I just got it two days ago, and I just learned how to load it. Unfortunately, I hadn't loaded it yet.

"Hey, hey, hey, Avery. Please put that away," the man says. I peer into the darkness. The curtains are closed and I can't see his face very well.

I don't listen to him. Instead, I stand up straight and point the gun right at him, with my arms extended just like I've seen Detective Benson do hundreds of times on *Law and Order: SVU*. I'm bluffing, but he doesn't have to know that.

"Get the fuck out of here," I say. I hold the gun steady. I don't want him to know how terrified I am of it and of the very act of pointing it at him.

The man remains seated. He looks calm.

"Avery, I am Director Franklin Truman. I work for the CIA. I am happy to show you my credentials if you just promise to not shoot me."

He motions toward his jacket's breast pocket and waits for me to respond.

"Can I get it?" he asks.

I nod, but keep my arms extended. What the hell is the CIA doing in my apartment? He has to be lying, I decide. But I secretly hope that he isn't. My gun isn't loaded, and this is pretty much the extent of what I can do with it.

Slowly, he reaches into his pocket and retrieves a badge.

I take a few steps forward to get a better view. The picture looks like it was taken years ago, but it's him. Even if he is fifty pounds heavier now. For a second, I hesitate. Maybe it's not him after all, but I know that I have to take a chance. I don't have any bullets, and I'm not going to shoot him anyway.

I put down my gun. Director Truman lets out a sigh.

"Nice to meet you, Avery," he says, standing up and extending his hand. We shake hands.

"What are you doing here?" I ask. "What do you want?"

"Are you always this rude?"

"I am to strangers who barge into my place and scare me half to death."

"I am sorry about that," Director Truman says. "You are very good with a gun," he adds with a coy smile. I stare at him as if he had lost his mind.

"I hate guns. I have a lunatic after me. My ex-boyfriend and the cops aren't doing shit."

"Still, I'm impressed." He pulls out a pack of cigarettes.

I stare at him. He doesn't seem to notice and pulls out a lighter.

"You can't smoke here!" I shake my head. "This is my apartment. And if you hadn't noticed, it's not very big."

"Okay, I'm sorry," Director Truman puts everything away. "You just left me a little unnerved. Do you have a drink or something?"

I shake my head. "Aren't you not supposed to drink when you're working?"

"Do you know a lot about the CIA?" he asks, with an amused look on his face.

"I know enough. I watch TV."

"Oh yes, television. Television makes every Tom, Dick and Harry think that he knows about the inner workings of government organizations."

I shrug. "I still don't really understand why you have broken into my apartment?" I ask.

I need to get this guy out of here, one way or another.

"Okay, then let's get right to it," he says. "Where's Logan?"

"What?"

"Logan Davenport? You were with him last week in Tulum. Where is he?"

My heart drops to my feet. I feel my face lose all color. I feel like I'm going to faint right there and then. You didn't do anything wrong, I say to myself. Why are you so worried?

"I don't know. I left after the wedding, and I haven't seen him since," I say in my most confident tone.

I can't tell him what happened. He's the CIA. They arrest and detain people without fair trials! I saw Logan murder people. What does that make me? An accessory to murder? An accomplice. Various legal terms swirl around in my head. Homicide. Accessory. Death penalty. Fifth amendment.

"You had plans to leave the day after on his private plane. But instead, you took a 6 a.m. flight out of Cancun. Something must've happened."

He walks up to me. Stands too close. He's trying to intimidate me. And succeeding perfectly!

"We had a fight. I didn't want to stay with him any longer. I could take my own flight," I say. I meet his eyes, even though I'm terrified. I don't look away. I don't mumble, but inside, I'm trembling.

Director Truman takes a step back. He goes to my refrigerator and pours himself a glass of orange juice. These people don't really have a lot of respect for private property, do they? I wonder in disgust. I mean, who the hell does he think he is?

"Come sit here," he sits down at the dining room table in the kitchen. "I didn't want to do this, but I guess I have to. There are some things you don't know about Logan."

Reluctantly, I sit down across from him. I hate the way he's treating my apartment as if it's his. I wonder if it's a Truman thing or a CIA thing.

"This is top secret information. And if you were to ever tell anyone, you could be arrested and sent to jail. And we would deny it, of course."

I feel him studying my face. My heart beats so loud it feels like it's going to pop out of my chest. But I remain stoic, waiting for him to continue.

"Logan is a CIA agent. He works for a special unit with the CIA. He's one of our top agents. And we haven't heard from him since the night of the wedding."

"A CIA agent? What does that mean exactly?" I ask. Does that mean he's allowed to murder people? I want to ask, but I don't. I've seen the movies. I'm afraid that if I tell him too much, he won't tell me anything at all. We're locked in a game of who knows what, and neither of us are caving easily.

"It means that in addition to being in Tulum for his brother's wedding, he was also there on a mission. The mission was supposed to take place the night after the wedding, but we haven't heard from him since then. And we are worried. Very worried."

"Oh, wow," I mumble. I shake my head. "That's not good."

"No, it's not," Director Truman says. "I probably shouldn't tell you this, but it took a lot of convincing on my part to get permission to reveal to you these details. What we do is covert, and everything is on a need to know basis."

I nod.

"So, what can you tell me?"

I take a deep breath. I have to tell him everything.

"I didn't know he was there on a mission. He just left. Without an explanation. I didn't mean to do that."

"Do what?" Director Truman's eyes narrow.

"I followed him. And I saw him in that man's hotel room. He was trying to suffocate him. And then someone else came in and he shot him. And I screamed and ran away. I thought he was a murderer. I didn't know he worked for the CIA."

"Well, the line is very thin there," he smiles. "Did you see anything else?"

"I saw three men enter. But I don't know what happened. I never heard from Logan again."

Director Truman nods and gets up.

"So, what does this mean?" I ask. "Where's Logan?"

"I can't be sure," he shrugs. "You have been very helpful. Thank you."

Director Truman heads toward the door.

"Wait, where are you going? What's going on?"

"I don't know. But if it happened as you had described, it's not good."

"Are you saying..." I can't let myself go there. But I need to know the truth. "Are you saying that he's dead?"

Director Truman shrugs. "I don't know anything more than you do. Someone will be in touch with you in the near future. You will need to come into the office and get debriefed."

I nod. He waves good-bye and leaves. I close the door behind him and lean back against it. Suddenly, my knees grow weak and I slide down to the floor.

Logan isn't a murderer. He's a good guy. He was just doing his job. And now...he's dead. Is that what's really going on? I search my mind for any details from that night – all the details that only a few days ago I tried so hard to forget. Those three men were armed. And they came there for him. He had just killed someone very important to them. Oh no, this isn't good.

CHAPTER 27 - LOGAN

I open my eyes slowly. Every part of me aches and throbs. The sun is so bright, it's blinding me. I can't keep my eyes open for more than a few seconds at a time. Squinting helps a bit. After a few moments, I manage to lift up my head and look around. I'm in the middle of a thick jungle. Mosquitos and other insects are crawling all over my body. I'm experiencing everything in third-person, as if I'm watching myself onscreen and none of this is actually happening in real life.

I notice that I'm dressed in the same pants and dress shirt that I wore to the wedding.

Except that the dress shirt is drenched in blood. I reach my hand and place it on my stomach. When I pull my hand away, it's covered in blood. Suddenly, it's no longer a third-person experience. My stomach hurts like hell and so does my leg. I was in shock. My training tells me that I was in shock, but now I'm coming out of it, and everything's going to get a lot worse. Shit.

I look around again. The jungle is a flurry of activity. Insects and reptiles all around. People. I need people. I try to sit up, but I was shot in the stomach and curling up is pretty much out of the question. I try to check my body for other injuries. Both arms seem to move fine, but the left leg...something's wrong with my left leg. I reach down as far as I can and feel the wetness of my pant leg. More blood. The calf throbs, sending shooting pains up to my spine. I've been shot there too. Perfect.

And then, somewhere far away I hear voices. Little kids. Laughing and giggling. With great difficulty, I turn my head in the direction from which the sounds are coming.

"Hey! Hey!" I yell. The first one is barely audible. My voice cracks and I cough. I try again. I don't know how much time I have, but I'm pretty certain that they're my only chance.

I try again in Spanish. "Hola! Hola!"

Their laughter stops as they walk up to me. The kids are two boys, no older than seven or eight. They are very small for their age – must be Mayan rather than Mexican.

"Help," I whisper, first in English, then in Spanish. They stare at me and then talk amongst themselves. I can't understand them. They must be speaking Mayan, an indigenous language of the region, and I don't know any Mayan. Suddenly, one takes off. The other one stays with me. He rips some leaves off a nearby bush, cleans my leg wound and presses the leaf to it. He whispers something in Mayan. It has a calming effect on me. I lay my head back down on the ground and close my eyes.

I MUST'VE PASSED OUT, because the next thing I know, I wake up in a small wooden cabin with a beautiful old Mayan woman leaning over me and applying bandages to my body. She sings something quietly as she takes off one bandage and puts on another. When she sees that I'm awake, she smiles at me and continues her work without stopping. I look around the place. I'm lying on the floor in the main room. A few hammocks hang around me, attached to the walls. The cabin itself has a thin metal roof and no glass in the windows. Just shutters to keep the elements out. But most of the time, the windows and the door are wide open to let in the sunshine.

Somewhere near the front door, two boys sit on the floor, eating something wrapped in large green leaves. The place is filled with the most delicious aroma I've ever smelled – fresh tamales and spices. My mouth starts to water. As if she can read my mind, the woman finishes with my bandages and brings me a glass of water and a plate with an unwrapped tamale. My stomach throbs as I sit up a little against the wall, but it's definitely a lot better. I stuff some rice and beans into my mouth and thank her by nodding my head. She just smiles and walks away as if recuperating recently-shot CIA agents who were left for dead in the jungle is something she deals with every day.

As I sit there, I see a large cockroach crawling on the ceiling. I have already seen geckos and an assortment of other little creatures, but this is the first cockroach that I've seen this close up. This area is filled with them – and they are huge with wings. I move my index finger a little and point out the cockroach, expecting the woman to scream and let her two boys deal with it, but everything about this place is a surprise. Without so much as a change in her expression, she walks over to the front door, grabs a flip-flop, and knocks it down on the ground. The cockroach opens its wings, but she catches it between her palms and hands it to one of the boys. From what I understand, she tells him to go deep into the jungle and let him go. Until this very moment, I still had some doubts. But as soon as I saw her do this, all of my worries vanish and I drift back to sleep certain that I would make a full recovery.

Over the next few days, I keep getting stronger and stronger. The woman continues to give me doses of her medicine, which she grinds up with a mortar and pestle from dried plant ingredients. After each dose, I always fall asleep and wake up half a day later, but every time I wake up, I feel stronger. I eat more, drink more, and sometime later, I even start to move around on my own. My stomach's healing, and so is my leg. The woman seems pleased with my progress, nodding and smiling during each pivotal step in my recovery. Eventually, I start to make my way outside and walk more and more around the cabin. As I suspect, the woman lives all alone with the two kids in the middle of a thick jungle, with only a dirt road leading up to their house.

When it's finally time for me to go, the goodbye is bittersweet. For more than a few days, I actually debated whether or not I should stay here for good. Everyone thinks I'm dead, so what if I actually stayed dead? I could start a whole new life. I used to think that a simple life is nothing to want, but now I have my doubts. This family seems much more content than many middle class families that I've seen in the States. They're actually happy. Genuinely happy. Everything is simple here. Life is about all the little pleasures. Growing your own food. Going swimming under the waterfall. Playing with the chickens and the dogs. There are no worries about careers and mortgages. Those aren't really my concerns, but I would be lying if I said that I wasn't a little jealous about their way of existing in the world. And if I stayed here, then I definitely wouldn't have to fulfill the rest of my contract to Truman and that organization, which I've come to despise.

And I probably would stay here, were it not for one person. The person who I thought about day and night during my recovery.

Avery.

I should not have kept this secret from her, but how could I have known what would happen? What the hell was she doing there on the beach? Without context, I must've looked like a murderer to her.

I don't want to admit it, but I'm a little more than terrified of her not believing me. When I find her again, will she believe me? I mean, isn't being a CIA agent some perfect lie to cover up being an actual murderer? I think I heard that killers use that lie on more than one occasion in television shows and movies.

What if she asks for proof? I don't have any. That's the point of being covert. I'm not even on CIA's regular payroll. Only a handful of people within the CIA even know about Daffodil. Besides the extra phone, which is encrypted, I don't have any other paperwork or physical object proving that I work there and that I was authorized – no, forced – to do what I did. And of course, there's no way that Truman would ever corroborate anything I'm saying to a civilian. He's not the sentimental type. So, if she doesn't believe me…that's that. She'll be terrified of me, and I can't scare her more. She deserves better than that.

If she doesn't believe me, then I'll come back here, I decide. I'll build myself a little hut a little bit away from this one. I'll help the woman with her animals and the gardening. I'll play with the kids. I'll learn Mayan. I'll start a new life.

CHAPTER 28 - AVERY

Truman leaves and takes life as I know it with him. All of these thoughts that I thought about Logan over the last couple of weeks are completely false. He was completing a mission for this country and died on his mission. And I caused it. If I hadn't screamed, then none of those other men would've come in and killed him. The thought of that is devastating. I can't breathe. I start to cry, and I can't stop. Cynthia isn't here to help me. Not that she could anyway.

I sob and cry and sob for hours until my tear ducts run dry. And when twilight falls and the moon comes out, I cry some more. It starts like a wave, a tsunami, that I have no power of stopping. I cry myself to sleep and when I wake up, the first thing I do is cry again. The very thought of Logan breaks me down. Suddenly everything in the apartment reminds me of him.

There's a knock at the door. By the sound, I can tell that it's Cynthia. I mumble something and she comes in.

"Oh my God, Avery, what's wrong?" she asks. "What happened?"

I look at her and break down again. My eyes fill up with tears that I didn't know I still had and then roll down my face. My eyes are so dry that the salt in my tears feels like someone's cutting at my naked eyeball with razorblades.

She goes to the kitchen and comes back with something. I can't see very well. When she presses something cold and soft to my face, I feel a little better. If only you could die from crying, I think to myself. Then I'd be dead already, and maybe that's not such a bad thing.

After I calm down a bit, Cynthia asks me what's wrong again. I don't know what to say. I don't want to lie. I can't. Since Logan is dead, what does it matter anyway? So, I tell her. Everything. As it happened. She gasps and then doesn't say anything for a while. From what I can make out of her face, she's in shock.

"I can't believe this," she shakes her head.

"I know," I mumble. My throat is dry, and I cough. She hands me a bottle of water. I gulp it all down before either of us says anything else.

"So, all this time, you thought that he was a killer? That must've been so scary for you."

"That's why I stayed at your place."

"Oh wow, it all makes so much more sense now," Cynthia says. "And now he's dead?"

I nod. Something about her presence makes the pain not so acute anymore. I still feel it, but it's no longer like a knife through my chest. Suddenly, I feel a little numb to it.

"And all this time, I was fearing him. Terrified of seeing him again," I say calmly. "And now, all I want is just one more moment with him."

Cynthia puts her arm around me, and we stay in bed for the rest of the day.

A COUPLE OF DAYS LATER, things calm down a bit. The pain and the heartbreak aren't as intense. It doesn't mean that my world isn't full of regrets of all the things that I should've done or could've done that night on the beach. It just means that I'm able to go back to work and cut flowers. I'm able to answer the phone and explain our services to customers. I'm able to arrange bouquets and even design a few new ones.

Being back in my shop puts me a little bit at ease. The splashes of greens and colors swaddle me as if I'm wrapped in a tight blanket. Everything's going to be okay, eventually, they whisper to me. It might not be as you planned, it might be without Logan, but you will find love again.

Cynthia walks in with two coffees and a big smile. Her positivity has really played a big role in bringing me around these last few days. After I gained some control over my senses, I realized that I probably shouldn't have told her about Logan working for the CIA, but Director Truman never did explicitly tell me that I'm supposed to keep his identity a secret. Besides, someone was supposed to contact me for a debrief over what happened, but no one has yet.

If they do contact me, then I'll tell them that Cynthia knows, I decide, and that I didn't think it was a big deal to tell her, because he's dead.

The thought of Logan being dead sends shivers up my spine. Instead of breaking down, I bury my face in the daffodils that I'm holding in my hand and try to think of something else. Something more pleasant and not so hopeless.

The door to the shop opens.

"Well, hello, there!" the woman says. I can't make out her face because she's flooded with light from the outside, but I recognize that West Texas accent anywhere.

"Hi Dolly!" I say with a newfound pep. I'm not faking. I'm actually happy to see her.

Cynthia looks up as Dolly comes closer. She's dressed in a white Chanel suit, which has undoubtedly been tailored to accentuate some of her most prominent features.

"Oh, wow, are you Dolly Monroe? *The* Dolly Monroe?"

"It's a pleasure to make your acquaintance," Dolly extends her right hand. Cynthia's eyes focus for a second on a ten-carat diamond ring. I nudge her out of her trance.

"It's such a pleasure to meet you," Cynthia says. Dolly smiles. "I'm not sure if you know, but I'm the one who got the gift certificate for your services for Avery."

"Oh no, I had no idea. Well, isn't that swell?" Dolly asks. "So, this is your shop? It's very cozy in here."

I smile. She's being nice, but I know that cozy is just a euphemism for tiny. A bit too small, actually.

She walks around the shop as if she owns the place. Some people I'm sure find her arrogant and full of herself, but I love her confidence. I know that she's coming from a good place.

"I love your designs," she says, holding up one of my bouquets in front of her. "I wish the woman I hired to do my niece's wedding had half the talent you have."

"Thank you," I say. "I really appreciate you saying that."

"Can I get you anything? Coffee? Tea?" I ask. "We don't make it here, but there's a coffee shop right outside."

"Oh no, there's no need. I'm fine."

She explores the shop a little more, carefully examining the flowers and the bouquets. I get the feeling that she isn't just dropping by. I wait for her to talk about what actually brought her here.

"You have a beautiful place here, Avery," Dolly finally says. "I'm going to get all of my flowers from you in the future."

"Oh wow, thank you," I say, but she continues before I even finish.

"But I'm also here to talk to you about something else."

Here it goes. I take a deep breath. Logan.

"We are all wondering about Logan," she says, carefully choosing each individual word.

"We?" I ask.

"Mainly, Liam, Kora and I. We haven't heard from him for a while. Not since the wedding."

I nod. I don't know what to say.

"Have you heard from him? Kora said that you left the wedding without saying goodbye. Did something happen?"

Dolly's face has an earnest, eager expression on her face. She isn't accusing me of anything. She's just interested in finding Logan.

"I thought he was just not staying in touch with me. But then Kora called and we realized that none of us have heard from him since the wedding. Not even Marilyn."

"Who's Marilyn?" Cynthia asks.

"His housekeeper."

I nod. Take another deep breath. I had hoped that Director Truman would notify the family members, but I guess he didn't bother. I don't know what else to tell her, but the truth. I can't just string her along, making her believe that everything's fine when he's really missing. And not just missing. Dead.

"I'm not sure if I should be telling you this," I start. "But I think you deserve to know."

I tell her everything.

CHAPTER 29 - AVERY

Later that afternoon, after a very much distraught Dolly finally leaves, Cynthia also takes off. She has some errands to run and I'm left all alone to close up.

"Are you sure you're going to be okay?" Cynthia asks one last time. This is my first time alone here since I got back from Tulum. I nod, trying to be brave.

"I'm going to be fine."

"I don't believe you," she says. "But fine. If this is what you want, then I'll go."

"This is what I want. Thanks."

The shop is eerie at closing time. The buckets of flowers cast long shadows and make me feel uneasy. I'm not really afraid of anything. Logan is no longer after me. He's not a murderer, after all. But still, I have a strange premonition that something bad is going to happen.

For a second, I think that maybe I should text Cynthia and ask her to come back. I did have a hard day. Telling Dolly the truth has been one of the hardest things yet. The expression on her face. The sadness. The tears. All these things made my own feelings so difficult to keep at bay. And then, there are the regrets. One really major one. Logan told me that he loved me. And I didn't say it back. I was afraid. I wasn't sure if I loved him, but now looking back, I know that I did. I still do.

No, I say to myself. It's not a good idea to ask Cynthia to come back. Then she'll never leave me alone again. I need to be able to be here on my own and now is as good of a time as ever to start this process.

I cash out the register, count the money and put it in the safe. I make a mental note to drop all the money off at the bank tomorrow morning before work. Don't forget, I say to myself. I sweep the shop and toss away random pieces of paper that were left out on the counters. When I get home, I'm going to pour myself a big glass of wine, climb into bed and watch Netflix. I need a new show to binge-watch. I haven't seen *Mad Men* yet, maybe that's a good one to start with. Yes! That's exactly what I'll do.

Lost in my daydream of what's going to happen this evening, I don't hear the front door open. I continue to sweep all the leaves and stems into one pile in the middle of the shop. And then I feel a presence. Somewhere behind me. Shivers run down my spine, and my body gets covered in goosebumps. I know who it is without turning around.

"Hello Avery," he says slowly. Be strong. Be strong, I say to myself over and over like a mantra.

"What are you doing here, Cal?" I ask in the most authoritative voice that I can conjure up.

"I came to see you. Have you heard my messages?"

He had called a few times in the last couple of days, but I put them out of my mind. I didn't even listen to them.

"Yes," I lie. "You can't be here, Cal. The restraining order is still in effect."

Slowly, I inch my way back to the counter. I try to think where I had left my gun. It must still be in my purse. I don't think I've ever taken it out. But it's still not loaded! And I've only tried to load it a couple of times. I'm not sure I could do it on the fly. There's always bluffing. Truman believed you. And he's a CIA agent. Cal will have to believe you. I just have to get to my purse.

"I know. I'm very sorry about that," Cal whispers. Every inch that he gets closer to the front counter, Cal makes up by taking one big step closer to me.

"Where are you going Avery?" he asks, running his fingers over my arm. My skin feels like it turns into reptilian skin at his touch. I can't stand it.

"Cal, you can't be here," I turn to face him, shrugging his hands off me. "You need to leave."

"I don't want to, Avery."

I sense something different about him. He looks more menacing than before. Determined even. I smell alcohol on his breath. When I feel like I'm close enough, I reach for my purse, which is behind the counter. But it's too far away. Cal puts his hands on both of my shoulders and pushes my arms around his neck.

"Let go of me!" I say and push him away. He wobbles away and then reaches into the front pocket of his jacket.

"It's time that we stop playing games, Avery," Cal says, pulling out a handgun. I freeze. My eyes focus on the size of the gun – it's much bigger than mine. And I'm pretty certain that it's loaded. My heart starts to beat a mile a minute. I take one deep breath after another, trying to calm myself down. Think, I say to myself.

"What do you want, Cal?" I ask. Think. Think. But nothing comes to mind.

"I want you to come with me," he waves the gun toward the front door. I shake my head, no.

"Do you not see this gun, Avery?" Cal says louder. "Let's go."

I shake my head no, again. I remember what I heard a detective say on Dateline once. Never get into a car even if the perpetrator is waving a gun at you. It's much harder for anyone to find you once you get into the car.

"If you're going to shoot me, then you can do it here. I'm not going to get into any car with you."

Cal narrows his eyes.

"Why do you have to make everything so difficult, Avery? Don't you know that if you had just forgiven me for doing that and not gone to the cops everything would have been fine? But no, you have to be independent. You want to know another word for an independent woman that's much more applicable? Difficult. And you want to know another one? Bitch."

My mind races as he babbles on, trying to come up with some sort of plan. I can grab the gun out of my purse and bluff him. But if he shoots me…I can't very well shoot him back. I can try to make a run for it out of the front door, but he will most likely catch me. And I'll be that much closer to his car. Then it hits me. I should dial 911 and hope that they can figure out what's going on. In the meantime, I need to get him to continue talking. After I call 911, I can try to hit him with something.

"I'm not difficult, Cal. We just aren't right for each other. Why can't you see that?"

Questions always start him up on tirades, and this one is no different. As he goes into all the reasons as to why we are right for each other, I inch my way toward the back of the counter, reach into my purse and search around for my phone with my fingers. I turn it on. Slide off the lock screen. Click the button for making calls, which is in the lower left hand corner. Okay. Now, which one is the keypad? I try to remember what the screen looks like while maintaining eye contact with Cal so that he doesn't get suspicious. The fourth one over, I decide and press it. With one click glance, I look at my phone and then back at him. Yes! I'm on the right screen. Now, all I have to do is dial the right numbers. There are three across and four down. I carefully count until I reach the number 9. I quickly click the number 1 twice. The green send button is at the bottom of the screen. I press it and wait.

Cal continues to babble. I nod and agree with everything he says.

"911, what is your emergency?" I faintly hear someone say on the line.

"So you see what I mean, Avery?" Cal asks.

"Yes, I do Cal. And I agree with you. Just please put down the gun," I say as loudly as I can without drawing suspicion from him.

"Ma'am. Where are you?" the faint voice from phone asks. Please, don't hear it, I pray. Please, please, Cal. Don't hear the voice.

"Cal, I still don't understand why you're here. Waving a gun in my face. In my floral shop. In Topanga Canyon," I say. I debate whether I should say the name of my place and that it's on Topanga Boulevard, but I decide that it might draw too much attention from him. I'm the only floral shop here, hopefully they can find it. "You're going to be in trouble, Cal. You can't be here threatening me with a gun, asking me to go into your car with you. I have a restraining order against you."

"Someone's on their way, ma'am," the woman says.

Okay, now for the other part of the plan. I have to get that gun out of his hand somehow. What can I knock him out with?

Cal starts talking again. About how unfair I was in getting a restraining order against him. His keeps putting his hand down and holding up his elbow with the other for support.

"Cal, why don't you put that gun down?" I ask. "It's getting heavy holding it like that? Isn't it?"

"No!" He extends the gun toward me in defiance. Just at that moment, I grab the heavy three-hole punch from behind the counter and hit his hand with it. The gun comes flying out and lands on the other side of the shop.

He grabs his hand and winces in pain. I hit him with the hole-punch upside the head. He falls to the floor. I run to the other side of the shop to get the gun, but it's missing. It's not anywhere on the floor. It must've hit the wall and landed somewhere among the flowers. We keep all uncut flowers in big round metal vases. I search behind all the vases, but I still can't find the gun. What the hell is going on? How could it just disappear?

Thump.

I crash to the floor. It takes me a second to figure out what's going on. Cal pulled my ankles from under me and I fell straight to the ground. Another second later, he's on top of me. Blood from his head is dripping onto my face. He presses his body onto mine. I can't move. He has gained even more weight since the last time I saw him. I try to push him back, but he pins my arms behind me. He presses his lips onto mine. My stomach turns from the iron taste of his blood. When he pulls away from me, I spit into his face. He just laughs.

Finally, I break one of my legs free from under him. The other one moves over to the center of his body. I force my knee in between his legs and knee him as hard as I can in the balls. He winces in pain. I push him away, get up and get away, but he grabs me and pulls me back. Suddenly, he's on top of me again. This time, he has his hands around my throat. I can't breathe. His face gets more and more blurry. A few seconds later, the whole world starts to fade away.

Then he releases his hands. I struggle to breathe.

"I'm going to keep doing this, Avery. Over and over again. Until you agree to come with me like a good girl."

I barely hear him. I manage to catch some air in my lungs. Blood starts to flow through me again. Suddenly, I feel something that's digging into my front jean pocket. A pen!

Cal is lying on top of me and leaning to one side of me. Luckily, it's not the side with the pen.

"Well, what do you say?" Cal says showing me one of his hands. Threatening me with them again, but I don't even process the threat. Instead, I focus all of my mental energies in getting that pen out of my pocket. It's facing cap down. I knock the cap off and pull the pen out, hiding it in my hand.

"Fuck you," I say, wrapping my hand firmly around the pen. He pounces toward my neck again, grabbing it in both hands, but before he gets the chance to squeeze, I stick the pen into his neck. Blood squirts in all directions.

"You bitch!" Cal yells out and grabs at the pen. When he pulls it out, I get covered in a waterfall of blood. I close my eyes. When I open them again, Cal is off me. I pull myself up to my feet and rub my eyes. Someone is punching him in the stomach and the face. The man, whose shadow looks familiar, gets behind Cal and puts his head in a headlock. He twists it and Cal falls to the floor.

Somewhere in the distance, I hear sirens. The cops are finally here. When the man turns around, I take one look at his face and my legs refuse to hold me up anymore. I slide back down to the ground.

When I open my eyes again, paramedics are crowding around me.

"She's conscious!" one of them yells out. Suddenly, Logan appears above me.

"What are you…?" I try to ask. My voice is raspy. I cough and sit up.

"Careful," one of the paramedics advises me.

"I'm okay," I say to them. "Really."

"Where is the bleeding coming from?" Someone asks, checking me for holes.

"This isn't my blood," I say. "It's Cal's."

They don't believe me. They feel me up and down before they are satisfied.

One of the police officers pulls Logan away from me to ask him some questions. Another one talks to me. After the paramedics wrap me in a warm, grey blanket and give me a bottle of water to drink, I tell them what happened. Every single detail of what had happened this afternoon is burned into my mind. I'm pretty certain that it's going to stay there forever.

An hour later, one of the detectives brings me a cup of tea and I drink it, sitting on the stoop outside the shop. Since I refused to go to the hospital, the second ambulance leaves empty. The first one left almost immediately with Cal, who is apparently not dead but in critical condition. When he left, he was losing a lot of blood (thanks to me), and his neck was probably broken (thanks to Logan).

"Thank you very much for all of your help, Officer," Logan says walking outside with one of the detectives. This is the first time I get a very good look at him. I still can't believe that he's alive and actually standing here in front of me.

"Let me know if any of us can do anything else," Logan adds.

"We'll be in touch." The detectives give us their cards, and all four police cars leave the parking lot.

Logan and I watch them drive away.

"What are you doing here?" I ask as soon as they disappear out of sight. "How are you still alive?"

"Avery, I need to tell you something. What you saw on the beach that night—"

"Truman was here," I interrupt him. "He told me that you worked for him. He told me that you are an agent."

Logan takes a step back. It's almost as if he can't believe his ears.

"Truman told you that?"

"He was here. He was really worried about you. I'm so, so sorry that I screamed like that. I just saw what you were doing and I thought you were…" I can't bear to finish the sentence.

"A murderer?"

I nod.

"And I freaked out. I was so scared. And then when Truman came here and told me what you actually do…and that you were missing. He said that you were dead, Logan."

"I was, pretty much. They thought that I was when they dropped my body off in the jungle. But then these two kids found me, and their mom cared for my wounds, and brought me back to life. I would've died for sure if it weren't for her and those kids."

I nod, trying to process what he's saying, but it's all a bit too much.

"Would you mind doing me a favor?" Logan asks. I nod. "Would you mind driving me back to my house? My wounds aren't all entirely healed, and that was a little too much activity for me."

He lifts up his shirt a little and I see the stitches on his stomach.

"Oh my God," I gasp.

"Don't worry, I'll be okay," he says, taking me into his arms. "As long as I can kiss you again."

I nod and smile. He presses his lips against mine and the world fades away.

CHAPTER 30 - LOGAN

*O**ne Year Later.*

DRESSED in a little yellow polka dot bikini, Avery walks a little bit ahead of me, carrying her surfboard. This has become something of a tradition of ours ever since she moved in. Even though I've seen her dressed like this almost every single day, it takes all of my strength not to pull on those little strings holding up her top and wait for her to yelp and run into my arms. Though going surfing every morning has become something of a tradition, today is different. I have a surprise waiting for her at breakfast, and I'm a nervous wreck. My palms are sweaty. My breathing is sped up. As I make my way into the cold waves, I take a moment to reflect on everything that has happened since that fateful day.

When Avery drove me home that evening, she never really left. I asked her to stay the night and then another night and another. After hiring a staff of cleaning people to put her floral shop back in place, so that there was no sign of what had happened there, her friend Cynthia stepped up and ran the place until Avery was ready to go back. Within a week of her staying with me, I knew that I wanted her to stay with me forever. So I asked her to move in. She was shocked, of course, crinkling her nose in that cute way she does when she looks at me like I'm crazy.

"This won't be good for our relationship," she said. "We're moving too fast."

"There are no rules for our kind of relationship. I don't think we're moving too fast, but if you do, then we can stop."

"No, I don't want to," she said and kissed me. It didn't take much more coaxing after that before she brought all of her clothes over and took up one small dresser in my walk-in closet. That's when I knew that she'll definitely need more clothes.

Much to my dismay, Cal ended up living. He was in a coma for a few months as a result of Avery and her ingenious pen trick. Unfortunately, I was the one who had fucked up. I didn't have enough strength to actually break his neck, so I only managed to paralyze him. He'll be in a wheelchair for the rest of his life, and from what I've heard, he also has severe memory loss. My hope is that he has completely forgotten about Avery. Regardless, Avery has filed charges, and he'll stand trial as soon as he's a little better.

My own recovery is going pretty well. My leg has healed completely. The scar on my stomach is almost entirely gone. I only occasionally feel some pain around my stomach if I move too fast on my surfboard. I'm not sure that my injuries would've been enough to get me out of work for more than a month or two, but thanks to Avery and her big mouth, I'm out of the CIA. (She told Dolly that I was an agent and that I was dead and Dolly in turn told practically everyone else in my family). So, I'm finally a free man.

We surf most of the morning and then head back exhausted, but rejuvenated. Avery jumps into the shower while I chitchat with Marilyn in the kitchen. Sanchez is dead, and the elected president has returned from exile and is running the country again. After Sanchez's death, after the prisoners from all those illegal prison camps were released, the world learned about all the atrocities that he committed against his people. We didn't even know half of them. Marilyn couldn't be happier – she's practically skipping. She's no longer worried night and day about her family members, and it makes me feel good that I've done something to put that smile on her face again.

"So, are you ready?" Marilyn asks. She knows what I'm up to.

"Nervous," I say.

"Oh don't be. That girl loves you!" she waves her hand dismissively.

I go into the bedroom and change into a pair of linen pants. I dig through the top drawer for the box that I've hidden there and put it in my front pocket.

"Hey," Avery says coming out of the bathroom. She's dressed in a light summer dress. Her hair is dripping onto the floor and she looks radiant.

"Ready for breakfast?" I ask as casually as possible. She nods and follows me out onto the patio. As we walk, I finger the delicate clasp of the leather of the box in my pocket.

On the patio, we are greeted by a beautiful set table with a white tablecloth and a platter of cut up fruit. Another platter has toasted bagels, pastries and danishes.

"Wow, this looks amazing, Marilyn!" Avery yells back to the kitchen.

"I know," I mumble.

"What's the special occasion?" she asks rhetorically, sitting down. "A white table cloth even. Marilyn's definitely in a mood, isn't she?"

Avery flashes a smile and reaches for the cut up watermelon. I place my hand on her hand and stop her.

"Before we start, I want to say something to you."

"Okay," she says carefully.

"I was just reflecting the other day on how wonderful this year has been for us. I never thought that I would ever want to have anyone sleep in my bedroom night after night, let alone move in with me. Until I met you."

Avery's eyes twinkle in the sunlight.

"And then, after you moved in, I kept waiting for this bliss to wear off. It couldn't last, I said to myself. People can't actually be this happy all the time."

She smiles with her whole face. The sun wraps her in a warm glow, placing a halo around her head.

"I know, I'm pretty happy too," she says.

"But time passed. I kept waiting for things to get worse – for you to tire of me, for me to get bored with you – but it never happened. I love you, Avery. And now I know that I always will love you."

"I love you, too, Logan."

I get the box out of my pocket and get down on one knee in front of her. Her eyes get round and she gasps.

"Will you marry me?" I ask, opening the ring box before her.

"Yes, yes, yes!" she screams out. I barely get the ring on her ring finger before she wraps her arms around me.

When she pulls away, I see that she's crying. Happy tears.

"Well?" Marilyn asks, peaking around from the corner. "I can't wait any longer. Oh my God, Avery! Why are you crying, honey?"

"I'm not crying," she says through the tears. "I said yes!"

Marilyn pulls her into her bosom and when they pull away, I see that now they're both crying.

"For crying out loud," I joke. "This is supposed to be a happy time."

"Oh, men!" Marilyn shakes her hand at me, dismissively.

When the tears finally dry, Marilyn asks to see the ring. Avery extends her hand proudly like a proper bride-to-be.

"Oh wow," Marilyn gawks at the ring. It has a halo three-carat diamond with a diamond band.

"This ring is beautiful. But it's too big," Avery says shyly.

I shrug.

"That is what happens when you take Dolly to pick jewelry with you," I add.

"Oh nonsense! This ring is perfect! He did good. Real good!" Marilyn pipes in.

Avery and I both laugh.

When Marilyn disappears back inside, I look into Avery's eyes. She has never been so beautiful or happy as she is at this very moment. I pull her close to me and close my eyes. Pressing my lips onto hers, I know that my life will never be the same again. And that is exactly how I want it.

THE END

FREE EXCERPT: THE DEBT

R ead more about the Wild family!

ABOUT THE DEBT

THE LOVE STORY of Wyatt Wild, Gatsby's younger brother, and Brielle Thompson.

WHEN BRIELLE THOMPSON, a 25-year-old waitress, receives a mysterious check for $250,000, she uses the money to pay for her mother's very expensive cancer treatment, saving her life.

Two years later, she is called to pay back her debt. All she has to do is travel to an isolated mansion and work for one year as a personal assistant to an arrogant asshole whom she hates.

Wyatt Wild is **a gorgeous alpha billionaire playboy who's not used to girls saying no to him**. He has bedded models, actresses and socialites and then a waitress from some crappy roadside café dares reject him. Who does she think she is?

Wyatt always gets what he wants and his desires focus on the innocent and stubborn Brielle . Neither give in easily and they quickly get locked **in a game of seduction**.

HOT, Steamy and Romantic!

1

WYATT

I wanted to fuck her the first time I saw her. She wasn't my type. Not at all. A little plump with messy brown hair, and a sweaty forehead from taking too many orders and delivering food to strangers who left her fifty cent tips.

She was dressed in a plain white t-shirt and ratty jeans. The jeans dragged a bit on the floor, and the holes were definitely not made by a manufacturer. No respectable girl I knew would ever wear something like that and that made me want her even more.

Her jeans were tight at the waist, and she adjusted them periodically. Pulling them up over her hips while pulling down her shirt. She was trying to hide her figure as if she was embarrassed by her gorgeous thighs, hips, and breasts. Contemporary society is all fucked up. This girl's, this woman's body, was what every man wants. Every straight man of every race, ethnicity and creed. A tiny waist, shapely hips and legs, and breasts big enough to grab on to. Despite that, all the women's magazines try to do is to convince them that they're too fat because they're not shaped like 12-year-old boys!

The name tag on her shirt said, Brielle, which was a fancy French name to have for a girl who worked at a crappy roadside diner in the middle of the workday. It didn't take a genius to figure out that this was her full-time job. I would be surprised if she worked here to get through school. There wasn't a college for a hundred miles in any direction.

No, this Brielle was all wrong for me. And the worst part was that she didn't have any money!

I don't like girls without money. It's not because I'm shallow. It's because I'm practical. I don't fuck girls without money because it gets too complicated. It's much more likely to make things more complicated. Girls without money feel taken advantage of. They want to see me more. They think that a one night stand is unreasonable. And if it goes past one or two nights then they want me to save them. Rescue them from their pathetic little lives. But I'm not a prince. I'm not a white knight either. I don't have it in me even though I do own a white horse that I love to ride.

I don't like to rescue girls. I don't like needy girls. No, the girls I fuck have to have their own careers – a starring role in a TV show, a signed contract with a prominent modeling agency, or at the very least a reasonably-sized trust fund with one or two million from mommy and daddy. Oh hell, who are we kidding? It's always from daddy.

I established these rules long ago. And I abide by them religiously. They are there to keep both of us safe. To make sure that we both have fun, but not too much. I don't want the girls I fuck to have expectations about me. Expectations that I will never live up to.

And now, walking into this café, and seeing Brielle, I'm ready to toss them out of the window. I want her. I want to put my throbbing cock in her wet pussy and pull her hair until she moans.

I got hard in anticipation as I watch her take an order from an old trucker at the next table.

"Hey, what the hell do you think you're doing?" Brielle says, pushing his hand away from her ass.

I was too focused on her breasts that I hadn't even noticed the trucker's itchy hand reach out and grab her ass.

"Oh I'm so sorry," he says sarcastically and laughs to his friend.

"Not as sorry as you're going to be," she says, grabbing his uneaten plate of food.

"What the hell are you doing?"

"I don't know where you think you are, but this isn't *that* kind of establishment. You can't just go around touching women inappropriately here. And you'd better get the hell out."

"But I didn't finish eating," the trucker stands up dumbfounded. He reaches out for his plate, but she moves it away from him.

"You're done," she says with the kind of determination in her voice that makes me ever more hard.

"Please leave," Brielle says. "And don't come back."

"I'd like to see your manager, you little cunt. You're going to get fired."

"I'm the manager here. Now, get the fuck out!"

I get out of the booth and stand next to her. I'm thankful for my loose fitting jeans.

"You heard her, sir," I say. "The lady would like you to leave. So please leave."

People at the next booths start to clap, and cheer and my friends join in. The trucker and his friend curse her out, but head toward the door.

"You're a real cunt. You know that? You're going to be sorry for this!"

I'm standing right next to her and, though, she's trying to stay strong, I can see that she's really shaken. Her chest is flushed, and the trucker's plate is rattling slightly in her hand.

"That was really impressive," I say.

She turns to me.

"I'm probably going to get fired over it."

"I thought you were the manager?"

"No," she shakes her head and starts to gather the plates and cutlery from the trucker's booth. "The manager's coming in later tonight. I'm just the waitress."

"Well, I don't see why you'd get fired. He had no right to grab your ass like that. He was a real asshole."

"Thanks," she smiles. Her smile lights up the room. "Can I get that in writing from you?"

"Yes, of course."

I startle her. Catch her off- guard, in a good way. I like that.

"I'm just kidding," she finally says. "Let me just get all this stuff to the kitchen and I'll come back and take your order."

When I return to the booth, the guys laugh and slap me on the shoulders. They know she's not my type, they know that I'm breaking my rules.

"I don't know, Tyler. Looks like Wyatt's in love," Logan laughs.

"With a waitress!" Tyler chimes in.

"What happened to only dating girls with jobs or rich girls? Preferably both?" Ryan asks.

"She's got a job," I say. "We're at her job."

"Oh, please. A waitress? That's not a real job. You're breaking your rules, and you know it," Logan jokes.

It's all in good fun, but right now I hate their teasing. They're right of course, and still I want her.

"Nothing's happening. I don't know what you're talking about," I say as assertively as possible.

"We see the way you're looking at her," Ryan says. "We're not blind."

"I was just impressed with what she did. Brielle's got spunk."

"Oh, Brielle, is it? You two are on first names basis already?" Tyler chuckles. Dammit. I shouldn't have let that slip.

"It's on her fuckin' name tag, idiot," I try to save myself. But they're not buying it.

Brielle comes back to our table to take our order. After writing down everyone else's orders, she looks up at me from her notepad. My cock gets hard again, and I push it back down, under the table.

"You know, you made quite an impression on our friend, Wyatt, here," Logan suddenly says.

"Is that so?"

"I really liked how you handled that trucker," I say. I feel like I'm on my back foot. I don't like coming on to girls in this manner. I glare at Logan, but he doesn't stop.

"Wyatt was just telling us that you're not at all like the girls we're used to," Logan continues.

"Well, working for a living would do that to you," she says with a smile. I hate how she mocks me for having money. I want her even more now. I want to push her down on the bed, and I want her to let me tie her hands to the bedpost. I want to tease her until she screams my name.

"So what would you like? Wyatt, is it?" she turns to me.

I had picked out something on the menu, but now I couldn't remember what it was.

"What would you recommend, Brielle?" I say reading her name tag. Her name is burned on my cock, but I can't let her know that. Not yet.

"Our spinach omelet with feta cheese is quite good."

"Okay, I'll take that."

~

THE CAFÉ CLEARS OUT A BIT. While my friends continue to pick at their food, I excuse myself and head toward the bathroom. Before I get there, I pop into the back and find Brielle sitting on a crate reading a book. She quickly puts it away, but not before I catch the title. Jane Eyre. My sister's favorite.

"Can I help you with something?"

"No, not really."

She stares at me. I know I need a reason for being here.

"Yes, actually. I was just wondering if I can take you out for a drink sometime."

I catch her off guard. Her face lights up, and a brief smile crosses her face.

"That's probably not a good idea," she says with a forlorn sigh.

"Why's that?"

"Well, for one thing, you don't even live here."

"How do you know?" I ask.

She furrows her brows and folds her arms across her chest, pressing her breasts together in front of me. They look as if they are on a platter, and it requires all the strength within me not to reach out and touch them.

"People who drive Bentleys don't live around here."

She's right, of course.

"And the other thing?"

She takes a deep breath.

"I'm not looking for a relationship."

"Who said anything about a relationship?" I ask and immediately regret my choice of words.

"And I'm definitely not looking for anything casual."

"Why's that?" I ask.

I should just drop it, but I can't. No one, and I mean, *no one* has ever turned me down. I can't even believe that this is really happening. Maybe she's just toying with me. Maybe she's just flirting.

"Because I'm not into one night stands, Wyatt," she says and walks away. I love the sound of my name in her mouth. I want to put more of me there.

BRIELLE AVOIDED eye contact with me the rest of the time that we were there. That made me want her even more. She was feisty, and hot and she didn't take shit from anyone. An unusual girl. I wanted her so much I thought I was going to explode.

When she came over with the check, I purposely extended my hand. She tried to place the plastic cover with the check into my hand, but I took the opportunity to reach out and touch her. Her touch was electric. It sent shivers through my body.

Suddenly, Brielle let go of the plastic cover, and it dropped to the floor.

"I'm sorry," she said. "I'm so clumsy."

"No, I'm the one who's sorry." I apologized.

I could hear Logan, Tyler and Ryan smirking at me from around the table. But my eyes remained fixed on Brielle. When she bent over, her cleavage expanded, and her breasts looked like they were going to spill out of her t-shirt.

"Thank you," I say and hand Logan the check.

It was Logan's turn to cover the bill. We never split the bill, unless it was a VIP table at a Vegas nightclub or something extravagant like that. The bill at this roadside café hardly registered as real money. Logan's family was equally wealthy, but he was cheap on tips. If the girl didn't flirt with him or go really out of her way to impress him, he didn't like to leave her more than fifteen percent.

I made sure that I was the last one out of the booth and quickly slipped a $100 bill under the check.

2

BRIELLE

I notice him just as he pulled into our little dusty parking lot with his Bentley. That car costs more money than I'll make in a decade. There are five guys in it, all equally attractive and cocky, but he was the only one who caught my attention.

Tall, handsome, tan. Blue eyes and dark sandy hair that made him look like a brooding dark stranger and a surfer boy depending on the light.

He strolled into my café with a confident and laid back swagger that would make male models jealous. There's a carefree nature to his demeanor and yet, at the same time, there's something very intense about him.

I like the way that he says my name. I like the way that he's impressed with my ability to deal with annoying pestering old men. What he doesn't know is that, unfortunately, I'm used to unwanted sexual advances from gross strangers. What that trucker did was one of the least offensive things, frankly. The men who come in the middle of the night try worse things.

Wyatt wants to take me out for a drink. Yes, yes, yes, I say to myself. Say yes. You deserve this. But I reject him. I want to say yes, more than anything, but I can't. I'm too fragile to have my heart broken by the likes of him. And, of course, it would happen. He's cocky and rich and arrogant, and guys like that only want one thing. The thing that I certainly want to have with him, but not now. Not considering everything else I have that's going on.

~

THE FOLLOWING DAY, just as the sun throws its harshest rays on our dusty part of the world, my mind drifts back to Wyatt. If only he would walk back into this place. If only he would ask me again. Then maybe I would say yes. But it's all a daydream.

My mind drifts from one part of his body to another. He's got the kind of veins lining his forearms that make me wet in my panties. I want to pull off that $200 t-shirt and run my fingers over his chiseled abs. I want to grab both of his butt cheeks at the same time and get down on my knees before him.

"Brielle?"

A familiar voice startles me and brings me back down to earth. It's Wyatt. He's casually leaning on the countertop and tapping his fingers.

"Hey," he says.

"Hey."

I'm at a loss for words. My mouth gets parched.

"So I was in the neighborhood, and I thought I'd stop by."

"Oh, okay," I smile. "Can I get you a menu."

"You can, but I'll just get whatever you recommend anyway."

His cockiness is oozing out of him. I look around. His friends are nowhere to be found. But the Bentley is parked in the first available non-handicapped parking spot.

"Where are your friends?" I ask.

"Not here," he smiles.

"Why are you?"

He takes a breath. "Like I said, I was passing through the neighborhood."

I roll my eyes.

"You don't believe me?"

"No," I shake my head. This guy is dangerous. In a good way. No, in a bad way.

"Well, take a seat. Anywhere you want," I say.

He looks around the café. There are three other people here. The lunch 'rush' just left, meaning the four other people who typically pop in for lunch. Wyatt chooses the seat at the counter. Right in front of me.

I grab a rag to pick up the few crumbs left over by the last customer and notice that my book is still in my hand.

"Jane Eyre," he nods. I hide the book behind the counter and wipe the counter around him. He doesn't move his arms, and I stop to see if he will. He takes a moment before lifting his arms.

"You were reading that yesterday," he says. I nod and get my pad out. I can't find my pen and frantically look for it at the cash register. I can feel his gazing burning a hole in the back of my jeans. He's checking out my ass. I don't want to admit it, but I like it. A lot.

"Yes, I'm not done yet. Have you read it?"

"Yes, in school. It's got a good story. Love and tension. Lots of awkward situations,

It just needs something."

"You think a classic of English literature needs something? Seriously?" My tongue often gets away from me, but this is one of those situations where I don't really care. I love talking about literature, and he was the one who brought it up.

"Yes, so what?" he shrugs.

I shake my head at his arrogance. He's an asshole, and he knows it. He also knows that in some situations, like this one, it's ridiculously hot.

"So what does Jane Eyre need? How would you improve on Emily Bronte's masterpiece?"

"Hey, I'm not saying it's bad. I'm just saying that it's missing something that would really make it complete."

I cross my arms over my chest and wait for him to answer my question. This should be good!

"It needs sex. Lots of sex."

I stare at him.

"They have so much sexual tension. They are cooped up in this house together. They have all of these feelings developing for one another. We as the audience need a release. We need them to have sex. And lots of it."

I can hardly believe what I'm hearing.

"That's crazy," I shake my head. "Jane Eyre doesn't need sex."

"Oh yes, she does. C'mon, aren't you just aching to read about them doing it?"

"Doing it? In Jane Eyre? Tempting, but no," I say definitively. How crude and vulgar and insulting can he be?

"Okay, it doesn't have to actually use those words. It can be much more poetic than that. But still as graphic."

"Like what, for example?"

He takes a moment to think about it. I wonder if he's going to choose a metaphor or go straight for a direct and honest description.

"How about this?" Wyatt leans back from the counter tilting his head back. He lifts up his hand in the pose I've only seen professors do in movies.

"He slid his big cock into that heavenly place between her legs."

The words dangle in the air between us as if they are suspended by a string. I don't say anything for a moment. I'm speechless. I want to be embarrassed, but I'm more turned on than anything.

"So both graphic and romantic is your suggestion?" I finally say.

He nods. "I thought that struck an interesting tension between the two depicting both his masculinity and her femininity in just the right way."

I smile and blush. I think so, too.

"You know you can't really talk like this in a public place," I say.

"Well, I'd love to go somewhere private," he leans closer to me.

His confidence is exuberant. I want to say yes. More than anything I want to say, yes. I want him to take me somewhere private and have his way with me.

"I'm sorry," I start.

"Awe, why?" he leans even closer and runs his fingers over my hand. I want to grab it and pull him close to me. I want to kiss his luscious lips and suck his tongue into my mouth.

But I pull my hand away.

"I just can't, not now."

"When? Why?" At that moment, Wyatt's deep set eyes resemble those I've seen in photographs of the Great Depression. Lost. Forgotten. Broken.

I can't explain. He's a stranger. And I feel like if I say *it* out loud to someone, I will burst out crying and never stop.

3

WYATT

Her words pierce through my heart. Now, I want her even more. I thought that things would be different since I came alone. I left my friends back home and drove two hours back to this god-forsaken town to see her again. She doesn't know this, of course. I hate the feelings of helplessness that she evokes in me. Why? Why didn't she say yes this time?

I have to have her. Not against her will. I have to make her beg for me.

I look at Brielle. She stares at me with a blank stare that's impossible to read. She brings me my food and disappears back into the kitchen. She's not staying around to talk. I have no reason to eat at this shitty place without her presence.

"Don't take it personally," an older woman with a lifelong smoker's voice says.

She has been sitting at the far end of the counter all this time, but I didn't notice her until now. The woman came closer. She smells of cigarettes and wears a small white apron with pockets, just like Brielle. There's no dress code here, but I know she's a waitress. Her name tag is old, and worn and I can't read her name.

"Brielle's going through a lot right now."

I nod as if I understand. The old woman is thin but looks as strong as an ox. She leans over the counter.

"Brielle just doesn't want more complications in her life right now," she whispers.

"What do you mean?"

"You know about her mom, right?"

"Yes," I lie.

"Well, she's getting worse. Neither of them can afford the chemo treatments anymore, and the insurance ran out a few months ago. It's looking really grim."

I nod. Her mom's dying of cancer.

"There's some experimental procedure that's available and looks like it could be an excellent option for her."

"That's good," I say.

"Yeah, except that Brielle can't afford it. She can't even come close."

"How much does it cost?"

"Not sure. Thousands. A couple hundred or so, I heard. And who's got that kind of money?"

I look away. My gaze drifts outside to my Bentley. That car costs as much as a cancer treatment to save someone's life. I've never put it in that perspective before.

The old woman startles me when she puts her long shriveled up fingers on my face and turns it toward her.

"So don't take it personally, kid. She's got a lot on her mind. But I know she likes you. I saw the way she was looking at you. In the seven years that I've known her, I've never seen her look like that at a guy before."

4

BRIELLE

I've entered the double- wide trailer, which has been my home since I was six, with a sense of dread. My Momma's hospital bed barely fits into the back room and ever since we had that installed everything else had to be moved around and put into every which crevice throughout the house it would fit in. Clothes and boxes and shoes and magazines are everywhere. Now that Momma's not working at the bar, I have to work twice as many hours just to make the same amount of money. And it's never enough.

She has to take more and more pills, and the prices are constantly changing. Last month, one of her pills costs $40 for a week supply, and now it's

$325 for the same amount, without much of explanation as to why. I empty my pockets. The tips from the regulars after an 8-hour shift are a little over $12. I don't blame them. They don't have much to spare themselves. But it's not enough. Not nearly enough.

I reach into my other pocket and pull out a crisp $100 bill. Wyatt left it before I could come back and stop him. He left me a $100 tip yesterday, too. I'm eternally grateful. These $200 will go a long way in paying this month's rent and the rest of the bills. Might even let me get some of my mom's jewelry from that pawn shop. No, I can't think like that. Medication is more important than heirlooms.

"Is that you, Brielle?" I hate how faint my Momma's voice is. She used to be such a tough and strong woman. She never took shit from anyone, especially not the men. I'm much shyer and unsure of myself than she is. Not as confident. Not as strong. But now, my Momma is weak and tired.

"Don't come in yet," she says when I approach the door.

"Momma, it's okay," I say through the door. I hear her moving around in the bed and making a ruckus. Things are falling over and a glass shatters.

"Shit, shit, shit," she says. I'm about to open the door.

"Don't you dare open that door, Brielle Elizabeth Cole."

When Momma uses my full name, I know she really means it.

After a couple more minutes, she shouts, "Okay, I'm ready."

I walk in. She's looking into her compact and adjusting her wig. Her face is made up to the ten. Her eyebrows are penciled in, and she's even wearing fake eyelashes. She finishes off the look with a generous slather of lipstick and smiles at me.

"You look beautiful," I say trying to hold back tears.

"Oh, C'mon, don't start now. If you cry, you'll make me cry and then all this work will go to hell."

I smile. I love my Momma's soft Southern accent. She was born in Kentucky and moved to California when she was sixteen with her first husband, but her accent never went away.

"What would you like for dinner?" I ask trying to change the subject. Momma looks like she's ready to go to a ball, but all we will be doing is sitting around the television with tray tables and eating whatever concoction I dream up.

"Macaroni and cheese?" she asks.

"Again?" We've had it for a week straight.

"I'm afraid it's the only thing I can keep down nowadays."

I nod and head to the kitchen. When I get the butter out, tears are flowing out of my eyes uncontrollably, and I can't stop them.

Momma worked hard all of her life. She's worked since the age of fourteen, and she deserves better than this. She's only 44 years old, for goodness sake! And now she's dying a slow and horrible death. She can't eat anything without throwing it up again. The chemo is poisoning her, and we can't even afford the poison anymore. And there's nothing I can do to stop any of this.

A WEEK later

I AM DRIVING home from work on a beautiful, sunny day, thinking that the sky is so blue and, there's not a single cloud as far as the eye can see. My legs are cramping up, and I can't wait to get home to climb into bed. I'm not much of a morning person and these morning shifts are killing me.

I worked from 4 am until noon, and this eight-hour shift was harder than the busy evenings shifts any day. Barely anyone comes in after ten and breakfast customers don't like to tips as much as dinner customers.

I finally pull onto our street and see the house in the distance. The paint is peeling on the side, and the porch is cluttered with junk, which we no longer have room for inside the house. I need to take care of that one of these days. Just don't know how or when. Paint costs money. Putting junk away doesn't, but I don't know where to put it. A shed is close to $1000 and I'm not going to have that kind of money anytime soon. Cardboard boxes? Perhaps. But boxes full of junk are easier to steal than loose junk.

The street leading up to the house isn't really a street, but a dirt road. When we first moved here and Momma's second husband, my father, was still around, we would wash the car every week. Within a day, the desert's dry climate and our dirt road would deposit a thin layer of dust on the car making the exercise fruitless. My father insisted that we had to do it because of pride. But he left by the time I turned eight and took the car. I guess his pride extended only to the car, not to his family. We didn't have another car for more than a year after that.

I pull up to the chain linked gate and get out. The neighbor's pit bull and Rottweiler are already going nuts. They welcome me home from work multiple times a day with the excitement of a full marching band and always put a smile on my face.

"Hey, Bella. Boomer," I wave to them. "I'll be right over."

I put the car in park, get out and pull the gate open. I get back in the car, park and head over to the dogs. The other neighbors are afraid of them, but they are the sweetest dogs I've ever met. I stick my hands through the chain linked fence and pet them each on their heads.

After the brief hello, which is honestly, the highlight of my day, I try to pull the gate closed before heading in. Usually, this is barely a process at all. But today, the wheels on the bottom, which squeak so loudly they send shivers up my spine, get stuck. When I pull them harder, they take off and run over my foot.

"Shit, shit, shit," I curse hopping on one foot. "Dammit."

The gate needs to be oiled, but I don't really have any extra money to spend on WD-40 or the time to drive out to Home Depot to get it.

"Stupid gate!" I kick it, instead. Not a great solution.

I'm about to head inside when, out of the corner of my eye, I see the mail truck. I am about to turn back, but something keeps me there. Getting the mail is not as exciting of an event as it once was. A long time ago, I remembered looking forward to getting cards in the mail from my grandparents and tearing through envelopes with the words "Sweepstakes" and "Winner" on the cover. But nowadays, the only thing that comes in the mail is medical bills.

Despite that, something is holding me back. I wait for the mail truck to pull next to the house. The mailman is a sweet old man who has been delivering mail for close to thirty years or so. Whenever we are short on money, and I have to say that the check is in the mail, even though it isn't, I've always felt bad about it because I know that I'm blaming it on him.

"How's your mom?" he asks. There's no way to really answer that question. Throwing up every morning, afternoon and night. Staying in bed all day long. People don't want to hear these things.

"Hanging in there," I say. It's the best way to describe the teetering that she's doing between this world and the next.

The mailman hands me a thick stack of envelopes. All are approximately the same size, and I know they're all bills. I sigh and head to the house.

I don't have any money to pay any of the bills I will have to spend days in the coming week on the phone talking with various administrators at the hospital and Momma's different doctors' offices all with the hopes of getting some of the bills reduced.

~

I TOSS the pile of bills on the kitchen table and open the refrigerator door looking for something to eat. I've been up since 3:30 am so a simple grilled cheese sandwich is a no- brainer. While the skillet is heating up, I check on Momma, who's fast asleep with the blinds still down.

When I sit down at the kitchen table, I reach for the remote to flip on the TV and accidentally knock the stack of bills onto the floor.

"Dammit," I say. I gather all the envelopes, but one stands out. It's different than the rest, and my name is written on it in a beautiful cursive script.

Ms. Brielle Elizabeth Cole

I look at the envelope closer. The paper is fancier than the others. And the stamp is unusual not the standard issue stamps that they sell at the post office. It has a detailed painting of a buffalo in a field of grass.

There's no return address in the upper left- hand corner. When I turn the envelope around, I see that it's from The Wild Foundation. Something about that name sounds familiar. Wild. What's Wild? Is it Wild International, the pharmaceutical company?

Instead of tearing the envelope open like I usually do, I get a knife and carefully slice open the top.

DEAR MS. BRIELLE ELIZABETH COLE,

It has come to our attention that your mother is gravely ill. Please use the following check to pay for her treatment.

THERE'S MORE to the letter, but that's the only part I see. I read it over and over, not believing my eyes. I look into the envelope again and pull out a check.

$250,000

THE CHECK IS for a quarter of a million dollars! I don't believe it. This must be some sort of fake. A joke. But why? Who would do this? Why would someone play a joke on me like this?

WHEN MOMMA WAKES UP, I show her the check and the letter.

"I've seen this on Dr. Phil, Brielle. Don't cash it. It's from some scammer. A love scam."

"But you gotta be talking to someone for them to send you a check like this, don't you?"

"Who have you been talking to?" she asks furrowing her brows.

"No one! All I do is go to work and take you to doctors appointments. I don't have any time to waste talking to strangers."

MOMMA TELLS me to throw the check away, but I don't listen. Instead, I stay up late after my evening shift and go online. I look up Wild International. It's a big pharmaceutical company, which has just gone public. It's owned by some cute young guy named Gatsby Wild. Why the hell his parents would name him after someone so tragic is beyond me!

The next morning, I look up the Wild Foundation on my phone and call them. A pleasant young woman answers and confirms that the foundation does indeed exist, and they're located in Los Angeles.

"So are you in the habit of mailing out large checks to strangers?" I ask. I don't mean to be rude or direct, but I don't know how else to go about finding out if this is indeed a real check.

"Ms. Cole, that's primarily all we do," she says.

I'm dumbfounded. I explain my situation to her and wait for her laugh at me in my face. But she doesn't.

"I can always check your name in our database. And make sure that this is a legit check that came from us."

"Yes, please, do that."

She asks me to wait on the phone and puts me on hold. I don't wait too long, but the few minutes that do pass feels like it takes a century to expire.

I put on the teapot to pass the time. I also find one of the last tea bags at the back of the cupboard and make a note to buy more.

"Ms. Cole?" she says. I can barely hear her over the boiling water in the teapot, and I quickly shut it off.

"Yes, I'm here."

"I've got good news for you. Your name is on the list of approved donations and I also double checked whether a check was actually issued to you and I see that it was issued five days ago."

I can't respond. I've lost the ability to speak.

"Ms. Cole? Are you there?" she asks. Louder this time.

"Yes, yes, I'm here," I mumble. "So it's okay? I can cash the check?"

"Yes, please do. And if the bank gives you any trouble, just tell them to call this number."

She dictates the number of her boss, and I write it down on the back of the envelope.

WHEN I GET off the phone, I don't know if I'm going to cry or laugh. I feel like I could do either. Tears start streaming down my face, and I call for Momma. She's still asleep, but I don't care. We have the money to pay for her treatment. Whatever treatment she needs. My whole body begins to shake, and both my hands and feet go numb.

"Oh my god, Brielle? What's wrong?" Momma comes out of her room and slowly makes her way to me.

"What happened? What's wrong?"

She wraps her arms around me and begins to rock me from side to side. Tears continue to run down my face, but they are not tears of sorrow. I just can't catch my breath long enough to tell her.

"It's going to be okay, baby girl. Whatever it is, we'll get through it."

Suddenly, I start to laugh. "Yes, yes, it is," I say hugging her back.

"It's going to be more than okay, Momma."

"What are you talking about?"

"I just got off the phone with the Wild Foundation and the check's legit. They're paying for your treatment. You're going to get some real help now, Momma. And we're going to be okay."

"What are you talking about?" Momma stares at me. I explain, but she just keeps asking me that same question over and over again. Eventually, it sinks in, and I get up and jump around the house shaking it so hard it feels like it's going to fall over. Momma's too weak to jump around, but she does nod along.

5

BRIELLE

*T*wo Years Later

IT HAS BEEN two years since I got that check from the Wild Foundation and it has been one and a half years since Momma went into remission. Every three months she goes for a checkup, and the more checkups that come and go without a resurgence of cancer the better her luck is in surviving in the long run.

Every day, I am thankful for that check from that mysterious benefactor. I don't know why we were chosen, but I want more than anything to thank him or her in person. But even that won't do it justice. It's impossible to explain how I really feel about this. Because it's not just my Momma's life that that check saved. It also saved my life.

When Momma was dying, I was living my life day to day, week to week. I made no plans for the future. The future didn't really exist. I barely knew how I was going to get through the week. But now, the future is open and bright.

I even moved out!

I don't live too far now, only a few streets over, but Momma insisted on it.

"A young woman such as yourself needs her own space," she said. "What if you want to bring a guy over? Where are you guys going to hang out? In the living room, while I'm snoring in the back room?"

"Momma," I rolled my eyes. "I don't want to bring a guy over."

"Well, I want you too," she looked straight at me. "You're twenty-seven- years- old now. You've been taking care of me for almost seven years. That's a big burden. You should've been living your own life."

She's right, of course. But I can't say that. I don't regret a moment that I spent caring for her. But a small part of me does wonder how different my life could be.

"Besides," I remember Momma saying. "You need your own place so you can find a guy so you can finally give me grandchildren!"

Grandchildren! I've been caring for her for so long, I can't even imagine having the time in the day to care for children! Let alone a husband.

AND SO, with her insistence, I moved out. I got my own trailer a couple of streets away from hers. It's definitely nice to come home to my own place with everything put away neatly in its place. No boxes here. No clothes all over the floor. I have more time to focus on this now. And now, I even have time to focus on other things. Like my future.

My gaze goes to the course catalog laying on my brand-new kitchen table. Well, it's not brand-new, it's from the thrift store down the street, but it's nevertheless my kitchen table. All mine. I leaf through the course catalog. I wonder what else could be mine? Perhaps, I could have my own career. A nurse, maybe? I have a lot of experience now. The pay is really good, in comparison to a waitress, anyway. But I don't know if I can care for anyone anymore. Momma's cancer has really worn me out.

"Ding Dong! Ding Dong!" My new door bell goes off startling me. Who could that be?

"Yes, may I help you?" I open the door.

There's a mailman at the door. I've never seen him before, so he must be new.

"I've got a certified letter here for you, Miss," he says. He doesn't know my name.

"Where's Mr. Thompson, isn't he still working?"

He looks surprised that I know the other mailman's name.

"Yes, but he's transitioning to an internal role. So I'm going to be filling in for him sometimes."

I nod and sign for the letter.

THE ENVELOPE LOOKS FAMILIAR. The same fancy paper and the same elegant script which has saved Momma's life.

After he pulls away, I turn the envelope over. This time, it's not from the Wild Foundation. It's from someone named Mr. Francis Thompson. I open the envelope and take a deep breath. If they're asking for all the money back, I have no way of paying. We've spent it all!

Dear Ms. Brielle Elizabeth Cole,

WE HAVE RECENTLY LEARNED *that your mother has made quite a recovery, and her cancer is now in remission. What great news!*

We are pleased that you were able to put the money to such good use. And we are very happy for you.

However, we are now in need of your help. It is my pleasure to invite you to the Wild House for a brief residency, lasting no longer than a year. We hope you accept the invitation so that the process of you paying the debt back goes smoothly.

SINCERELY,
  Mr. Francis Whitewater

CERTAIN WORDS and phrases stand out. I read them over and over again, but they don't make any more sense.
  Residency.
  No longer than a year.
  Debt.

WHAT DOES THAT MEAN? What is he talking about? What debt?

"WELL, you didn't think you got that money for nothing, did you?" Dottie asks when I show her the letter at work.

She's close to 90-years-old, and she's the only one who I trusted enough to tell her about the check. And

I didn't even tell her anything until after half the money was spent and Momma was on her way to recovery.

"I don't know," I shake my head. "I guess I did."

Dottie laughs. "I've seen a lot in my long life, but this is a new one for me."

"What should I do?"

"I don't know what to do, child," she shakes her head. "But from the looks of this, the letter doesn't seem menacing at all. Maybe they just want you to work there until you pay off your debt."

"Work there? Where?"

"At the Wild House. Whatever the hell that is."

"But I didn't even know this was a debt. Don't they have the obligation to tell me? Shouldn't I sign for something if it was going to be a debt?"

"Perhaps, but I don't think this is any normal kind of debt. This isn't the bank. They would've never given you the money."

I know she's right, of course. No one gave us any money when we needed it. They all turned their backs on us.

"Well, do you think it's something sinister? Like some sort of brothel? Or prostitution ring?" I ask.

I don't know why my mind went there, except that I watch a lot of crime investigation shows on my days off.

Dottie thinks about it for a moment.

"I doubt it," she finally says.

"Those kinds of places usually promise you lots of money first and then use you up and toss you out. These people gave you a quarter of a million dollars first without even getting you to sign anything for it."

"And since I didn't sign anything for it, I technically don't have to do anything they say," I say. I feel my eyes lighting up with excitement.

"Well, technically, no," Dottie nods. "But I wouldn't want to play with Karma like that, honey. That might bring a whole lot of bad luck on you."

She's right, of course. I had to go. I owed a debt and if there was some reasonable and honest way that I could pay it back then I owed it to them to try.

6

BRIELLE

*T*wo weeks later

WITHIN A WEEK of receiving the letter, I quit my job at the café. I had worked there for many years and I promised to come back, but I couldn't leave them hanging, I didn't know how long I would be away.

Before I quit my job, I called Wild House and spoke to Mr. Francis Whitewater, who came off quite polite and well spoken. He said that my duties at the Wild House would consist of acting as a personal assistant, answering emails and phone calls, and maybe participating in light cleaning and nursing. When I asked about the nursing aspect, he was very brief and practically refused to give out details, but said that someone had to be taken care of, but the nursing duties are mild. Nothing like the ones I had to perform for my mother.

After I had agreed to go on the phone, he sent me an email with the work contract, which I had to sign and return before I could go. I read through the contract carefully, and was surprised to learn that I was actually going to get paid for this job. Four times more money than I made at the café and I would also be provided with a one bedroom apartment in which to live on the property.

After all the details were ironed out, I finally told Momma what I was going to do. I didn't tell her about the initial letter, but I did say that I got a new job and it was more than five hours away from her, somewhere in central California. Without missing a beat, she wrapped her arms around me and gave me a warm and encouraging hug.

"I'm so so happy for you, Brielle," she whispered into my ear, her voice cracking. "I'm so happy that you're finally starting your life out. Going somewhere new. I will definitely come visit you soon!"

Come visit me? I had no idea if this was allowed or proper or acceptable. I didn't know anything about this place, but I agree.

"Yes, that will be great."

I still had a few months until then to figure things out.

~

TO GET to the Wild House, I had to take a plane to Chino, California and then a car. I was planning on driving, but Mr. Thompson insisted that I did not need a car there. I didn't believe him of course. There's no place in California that doesn't require a car, except maybe the city of San Francisco, but I eventually and reluctantly agreed. Momma and I had only one car and we share it. I can't take it away from her.

In the baggage claim area of the small local airport, I meet my driver. We drive for some time down a lonely two-lane road leading somewhere into the desert. Desert mountains rise on either side of us, far near the horizon. This isn't an unfamiliar sight. I'm used to the nature that far-flung places in the wilds of California have to offer.

During the drive, I try to talk to the driver, but he offers very little in way of information.

"I don't know, miss. You'll find out when you get there," he says over and over again. That's his canned response to almost every question I have about this whole experience.

We turn off the main highway and onto a lonely desert road. My heart starts to pound and matches the bumps in the road that we drive over. The car isn't your typical sedan. It's a tall Jeep, which is meant for off road. Just as I thought that the road couldn't be any more off road, we turn onto an actual off-road road. There are no signs, but the driver turns to the left at the sandy fork in the road. Now we're driving through the desert. Across its wide expanse and over little shrubs and around tall creosote bushes that dot the area.

Finally, somewhere in the distance, I see a large house. It's actually in the middle of nowhere. As we get closer, I make out the beautiful tall white columns that give it grandeur and stature. There are two large white lion statues at the gate. The driver pulls to the intercom and pushes the button.

"We're here," he says. The iron-wrought gates open and let us in. The Lions don't move but continue to stare somewhere into the distance, probably wondering the same thing that I am at this moment: how the hell did we get here.

The driveway is expansive and circular and the driver pulls up right to the steps of the mansion. I've never been to the White House, but this house looks just like it. The columns are a pristine ivory color. How the hell they keep them so white in the middle of this dusty desert is beyond me.

"Go on up," the driver says when he comes around and opens my door.

"What about you?" I ask. I don't know him, but I don't want him to leave. I have no idea what awaits me inside. I look at my phone and see that I don't even have one bar! There's absolutely no reception here.

"Oh, I'm not going in there, miss."

There? Why did he say it like that? My heart starts to pound harder. It's so loud, I can barely hear my own thoughts in my head.

The driver gets my two modest suitcases out of the trunk and takes them up the few steps to the porch. The porch is made of beautiful polished wooden slats and it seems to wrap all the way around the building.

There are two imposing double doors before me. The driver picks up the large metal door knocker and slams it into the door. After two knocks, the door finally opens.

"Ms. Brielle Cole," a small older gentleman says. He's dressed up like a butler from Downtown Abbey.

"My name is Mr. Francis Whitewater, it's my pleasure to meet you."

I shake his extended hand.

"May I help you with your bags?"

I nod, leave one bag on the porch and go inside with the other one.

"Let me show you to your room," he says walking past me.

When I enter the lobby, my mouth drops open. The ceilings are close to 20 feet high and gorgeous natural light permeates the space. The desert sun is rather harsh outside, but in here the temperature is a cool and comfortable 75 degrees, without a whiff of central air. There's a beautiful round marble entry table with a bouquet of flowers in the middle of the entry room the size of a ballroom and two winding staircases frame the table on either side, leading up to the second floor.

"What a beautiful...house?" I say. House doesn't seem like the right word. Mansion? Castle?

"Thank you. I'll let, Mr. Wild know that you approve."

"So, Mr. Wild? Is that who requested my presence here," I take the opportunity to ask.

"Yes, of course. I thought that was clear from the letter."

"No," I shake my head. "The letter wasn't very clear about much. The thing is, Mr. Whitewater, I don't even know who Mr. Wild is. I have no idea why he wants me here. Or what he expects me to do."

Mr. Whitewater turns to face me. "I'm not sure what you're trying to insinuate by that, Ms. Cole, but you are not expected to do anything that you are not 100% willing and interested in doing. Mr. Wild invited you here as a guest. There is nothing sinister about his intentions."

I nod politely. I'm trying to understand, but rich people have a way of saying things that don't make sense. Supposedly, I'm only here as a guest, but the letter was also quite clear about a certain debt that had to be paid. So what would happen if I didn't pay it?

Mr. Whitewater led me through the foyer, the gigantic living room with even taller windows, which looked out to the expanse of the desert in the background. The windows were so large, floor to ceiling, and clear that I felt like I was walking outside.

"You probably have some problems with birds here," I say. I don't know why I bring this up, but large floor to ceiling windows always make me wonder about birds.

"How do you mean?" Mr. Whitewater asks with a grave expression of concern on his face.

Now, I'm totally regretting bringing anything up at all. Me and my stupid mouth!

"Well, it's just that, the windows are so big and crystal clear..."

He stares at me, waiting to continue.

"I just think that you probably have a lot of birds flying into it."

Mr. Whitewater takes a moment to consider the situation. "You know, come to think of it, yes, we do. It's almost every morning or so that I find one or two dead birds laying on the back porch."

"Oh, how sad," I say. "Well, I guess that's something I can try to fix."

Mr. Whitewater smiles at me. "Perhaps, perhaps."

"You don't think so?" I ask. I'm usually quite good at reading people. Waitressing for seven years has taught me that if nothing else. But I find Mr. Whitewater difficult to read and analyze. Perhaps, it's his English accent that's throwing me off.

"No, not at all. I just wasn't sure that would be part of your job description."

"I'm not sure either. But I was told that I am here to be a personal assistant and caregiver of the place. Perhaps, within the scope of those duties, I can make some time to try to prevent the deaths of one or two birds per day."

I don't mean to be smug and condescending, but as soon as these words come out of my mouth, I realize that I am. Luckily, Mr. Whitewater lets it slide.

I follow him to the left wing of the house, past the kitchen the size of three doublewide trailers, without another word.

"Well, here we are," Mr. Whitewater reaches into his pocket and gets a keycard. He slides it into an opening on the card reader and then hands it to me.

"This is your room. And this is your card."

We walk into a spacious one-bedroom suite with a full entry way leading to the living room and a large bedroom. The living room and bedroom are separated by French doors and there's also another pair of French doors leading to the private patio outside of the bedroom.

"Wow, this is beautiful."

Mr. Whitewater puts down my bag.

"I'm glad that it's too your liking."

"Yes, definitely. Thank you."

Mr. Whitewater starts to leave but then turns around.

"Oh yes, I almost forgot. Mr. Wild is expecting you for dinner at 6 pm. There are dresses and shoes in the closet. And you are of course welcome to wear your own clothes as well."

I nod. But he doesn't let me off the hook that easily.

"Can I tell him that you are coming?"

"Yes, of course," I mumble.

OF COURSE, I know that I'm supposed to meet this Mr. Wild at some point. I just didn't think it would be so soon. No, not so soon. It's not soon. It's in a few hours, and I thought I'd meet him right away. I just didn't think that it would be so formal. Dinner? Why doesn't he just come up here? Or I could come to his office? I don't know if I can manage a whole dinner.

After Mr. Whitewater excuses himself, I open the closet. The closet is almost as big as the bedroom!

I've seen these closets before. Walk-in closet with shelves lining all three walls and a large island in the middle. On elegant, real wooden hangers, I find five dresses. Pink, red, black, blue and green. Each one is more beautiful than the others. One is knee-length made of chiffon. One is short and tight with built in bra cups. I run my fingers over the dresses and inhale the luxury.

Below the dresses, I find 10 pairs of different kinds of shoes. All pristine, never worn, without one scuffed up bottom. The heels vary in size and I quickly try on each one. The flats are the most comfortable, but the high heeled five inch heels with red bottoms make me feel most like a woman.

"Oh my God! What am I doing here?" I say out loud walking out of the walk-in closet. "People don't do this for nothing. Why does he want me here? To live here?"

Crazy, anti-social thoughts flooded my mind. He wants something from me and whatever he wants isn't easy to get. But what? I shake my head. I don't know.

I sit on the couch and put my feet up on the soft upholstered coffee table. I need to decide what to do. Hours crawl by, but I am still at an impasse. Finally close to 5:45, I decide that I will go downstairs and find out what this is all about. I'm a guest here, at least so far, and I will act like a guest. But I won't do anything that I don't feel comfortable with.

I look at the dresses hanging in the closet. They are beautiful, of course. But I'm not a charity case. I don't know who this man is and I need to retain some power in this relationship. I open my suitcase and look for the best thing that I have. Jeans are too casual. Besides, I don't really have any without any holes in them. T-shirts are also too casual. Aha! A button-down shirt and a pair of khakis. Practical. Professional. Not too sexy. Not sexy at all, actually.

7

BRIELLE

I still had some time to kill before dinner. There was no television in the room. A part of me was relieved, yet another was horrified. My phone didn't work and, though I brought my laptop, there was also no internet connection to be found. What the hell did people do here? I wish that I brought some paperbacks from home. My mom has an extensive collection of romance books and a handful of those would at least keep me entertained in the evenings.

I walk over to the window. The sun is setting and hugging the whole world outside with a warm, comforting hue. This is the color of possibility. Nothing can go wrong in a world bathed in this color. I feel like that's true, but I'm afraid it's not. I look out of the window and see horses grazing in the distance. There's no grass to speak off, but hay is scattered for them on the ground and they stand with steadfast calmness, which puts me to ease.

I've never ridden a horse, but I've always wanted to. There were only a few girls from my high school who rode horses and both of their families were quite wealthy and owned many acres of ranch land. I always found the idea of living on a ranch very romantic, but now that I was on one, I wasn't so sure. The idea of Mr. Wild freaks me out. What kind of elusive and crazy millionaire would ask a stranger to come and live and work in his house for a year? What did he want from me? My mind immediately went somewhere dark and scary and I wouldn't let it wander too much. Too much thinking, too many scary thoughts, are not good. Especially, since I have to be here for some time.

On the other hand, my mind continues wandering without my permission, this isn't mandatory. Of course, he could keep me here without my permission, but I have no indication that it's what he means to do. So far, everyone has been nothing but nice and professional. Maybe, there's nothing sinister about this place at all!

∽

I LOOK at the clock again. I have ten minutes until dinner. Most girls would need more time, but I don't. I slowly change into my khakis and a pink button down shirt. Something about the pink shirt makes it clash with the khakis so I try on the blue polka dot button down shirt.

"Yes, this looks much better," I say out loud into the mirror. There's no one around. I'm not used to having so much privacy given that I grew up in a double-wide with my mom. And I'm kind of enjoying the space and the solitude.

"This looks great," I say to myself. I take out my hair tie and flip my head over. When I bring my head back up, my hair falls with much more volume than before. Though it's usually as straight as straw, today it's all in waves around my face.

"Not bad," I smile and run my fingers through it. "Not bad at all."

Makeup. The heat from the long ride from the airport has all, but melted off whatever little amount of eyeliner and mascara I'd applied earlier this morning.

I apply a generous amount of eyeliner with my mouth open. I'm not sure what opening my mouth does for eyeliner application, but it's been a habit since I was 13. I've also seen girls do it on television, so it must be how it's done.

When all of my makeup, hair and clothes were done, I again look in the mirror. And then at the clock. I still have 9 minutes left! How's that possible? Should I go down early? No, I decide. I can't go down early.

My eyes drift back to the closet. I open it again and look at the dresses. I run my fingers over the different fabrics. Each is different from the next. All are much more expensive than any fabric I've ever owned.

I start to unbutton my shirt and pulling off my pants before I even realize what I'm doing. Suddenly, I'm pulling on the dress with the thick taffeta skirt on the button. The dress poofs out at my hips and I love how small it makes my legs and waist look.

"Amazing."

I twirl and the dress continues without me. I try on the pair of high heels that are placed right underneath the dress. I've never heard of the company, but I love how pointy the front is and how high the heels are.

I twirl again in front of the window.

I feel like I'm a princess. The fabric feels amazing next to my skin. The taffeta skirt hides my hips and emphasizes my breasts. The polka dots make me feel young, friendly and alive.

I look back at the clock. I still have a few minutes before dinner. If I want to change.

"You should change," I say to myself in the mirror. But the girl who looks back at me doesn't want to.

"If I don't ever see Mr. Wild again, if I leave tonight after dinner, then at least I got to wear this beautiful dress once," I reason.

I'm rationalizing. Justifying. Trying to give myself reasons to wear it. But I don't need to. I want to wear it. That should be enough.

"Okay," I look in the mirror. "Okay, this is it."

I WALK down the elaborate and ornate staircase in my taffeta polka dot dress and high heels. My steps are cautious and deliberate. All I hear is the sound my shoes make when they hit the marble and echo off the walls. The walls are lined with beautiful ornate rugs I've only seen in expensive stores on Rodeo Drive. The stairs are a little slippery and I hold on to the railing. Why they don't put some of those rugs on the staircase is beyond me.

I remember where the kitchen is and I see Mr. Whitewater in the distance. Near the dining room. I take a deep breath and nearly float the rest of the way over.

"Ms. Brielle Cole, thank you for coming," Mr. Whitewater says to me. He's holding a tray and one tall glass with something in it.

"Would you care for some champagne with strawberries?"

I nod and he hands me the glass.

"Mr. Wild is waiting for you in the library."

Library? I wasn't shown a library before! My heart skips a beat. I'm not sure who I'm more excited to see. Mr. Wild or the library. The presence of a library solves the entire problem of what the hell I'm going to do in my room when I'm not working.

Mr. Whitewater takes me down a hallway which was not part of today's tour. In the end, he turns off to the right into a large spacious room entirely covered in books. Books line every imaginable part of it, from floor to ceiling. The ceiling is about twenty feet, just like in the rest of the house. What really makes the place special is the large bay window overlooking an orange grove.

There's a man sitting there in the shadows. I can't see his face, but I can see his well fitted suit and handsome profile. His hair is brushed back and his nose reminds me a Roman emperor.

"Mr. Wild. May I present, Ms. Brielle Elizabeth Cole," Mr. Whitewater announces.

I've never been presented before! I don't know what to do. Mr. Wild gets up and approaches me. His walk is deliberate and considerate. His shoes are so shiny they are bouncing light into my eyes even though it's relatively dark in the library. So dark, in fact, that I can barely make out his face.

"Ms. Brielle Cole," Mr. Wild says. Immediately, his voice sounds incredibly familiar. But I can't place it. Do I know him? How in the world would I know him?

Finally, Mr. Wild steps into the light and I see his face.

It's him!

No, it can't be! Can it?

My mouth runs dry. I can't speak.

It's the guy from the café. The one who drives the Bentley. The one who asked me out twice!

"It's very nice of you to join me," Mr. Wild says extending his hand. I don't know what to do. I take his hand and bend down at the knees before him. Just a bit, but enough for him to notice.

"What are you doing?" Wyatt smiles. "Did you just curtsy?"

Wyatt tilts his head back and laughs. His laugh is deep and strong and the sounds of which echo around the books in the library.

"Don't laugh," I finally say. My mouth is still entirely dry, but I manage to get the words out without a crack.

"Why are you laughing?" I ask. I'm so embarrassed. I don't know what came over me. I didn't mean to curtsy. But I've never been presented before. For some reason, it seemed to be like the right thing to do. Agh, I'm so stupid! I feel my cheeks growing hot. But Wyatt doesn't stop laughing.

"Why are you laughing?" I ask again. Now, my embarrassment is turning into anger. I make a fist and I get ready to punch him. Maybe not in that beautiful face of his, but at least in the shoulder, or chest or stomach, at the very least.

"I'm sorry," Wyatt says, still chuckling. "I just never had anyone curtsy for me before. I gotta say, I kinda liked it. Maybe you can do it again later tonight."

"It was an accident. I'm definitely not going to do it again later tonight."

"Okay, okay. Sorry!" he says sarcastically. "I'm just having a good time with you Brielle. Lighten up."

I take a moment to collect my thoughts. The curtsy has definitely broken the ice, but it got us nowhere closer to where we needed to be. I have so many questions for this man. The last man on earth, I thought I would see.

"Why am I here, Wyatt?" I ask.

I'm trying to be as serious as I can be. Even though, a huge part of me is relieved that Mr. Wild is NOT some 70-year-old man with hemorrhoids.

"What do you mean?" he asks, nonchalantly. As if he has nothing to explain. Nothing to hide.

"Why am I here?" I shrug. "What do you want from me?"

He shifts his weight from one foot to another and looks down.

"I don't know. I don't really have an answer," he finally says.

"You don't? You brought me all the way over here and you don't have an answer?"

"No, not really," he shakes his head. "I just wanted you to come. You didn't want to go out with me..."

He doesn't finish his sentence. I wait for him to complete it.

"I didn't want to go out with you so you decided to bring me here for a year. Force me to work for you?"

That gets his attention. And insults him, judging from how red his face gets.

"You are free to leave anytime, Ms. Cole," Wyatt looks straight at me. "You're not my slave or anything like that. Who do you think I am?"

I shake my head. Now, it's my turn to get incensed. "No, I can't. Not really, though," I say.

"Yes, you can."

"You paid for my Momma's very expensive treatment, Wyatt. I really appreciate it. Why? Why did you do that?"

"Because I heard that she needed help. You needed help."

"But there are millions of people in the world to help. Why me?"

"Okay, there you got me," he shrugs. "I did it because I like you. I wanted to help you. I didn't want you to lose her. I heard she's doing really good."

"Yes, she is. And I'm very grateful for that. I want you to know that I am."

"Great, that's what I wanted to hear."

"But I still don't understand this," I wave my hands in between both of our chests. He grabs my hand and wraps his warm, strong fingers around each wrist. My heart skips a beat. I feel a surge of electricity pass through him to me. It's just a spark. But it makes me feel warm all over. All shivers and uncertainty that I'd felt before dissipates. Now, I just want him to kiss me. I want him to keep holding my wrists and for him to slam his body into mine.

"What are you doing?" I whisper. I don't know how long he's been holding my wrists, but I never want him to stop.

"I wanted you..." he whispers. Wyatt takes a beat and looks straight into my eyes. "I want you."

That's it. The words just hang there in between us. I don't want to breath in or out for fear that I will make them dissipate.

"You want me?" I whisper. He stares at me.

"You want me to do what?" I ask.

"Nothing," he shrugs. "Nothing you don't want to do. I just want you here."

I nod. I don't understand. But I don't really need to right now.

There's a knock at the door.

"Mr. Wild? Ms. Cole?" Mr. Whitewater says. "Dinner is ready."

Wyatt hands me my glass of champagne. At some point, I had put it down on the coffee table. But I have no memory of doing that.

"This is delicious," I whisper.

"Yes, it's quite lovely," Wyatt smiles. "We grow the strawberries ourselves. Fresh from the garden."

I bite into a strawberry. Its flavor explodes in my mouth and fills my nose and mouth of the most luxurious aroma I've ever experienced.

"Thank you for wearing one of the dresses," Wyatt whispers over my shoulder as I follow Mr.

Whitewater down the hallway. "I know it wasn't easy for you."

I turn back. How does he know that? What the hell do you know about me? I want to ask. But I know he's right.

"I don't want to make you mad. I just want to say, thank you. You look stunning."

"You're welcome," I say. Though I have no idea why he's thanking me for it.

"It's just such a treat for me," Wyatt explains as if he knows what I was thinking.

His words send shivers up my spine.

The large 12-person table that I had seen in the dining room earlier that day is gone. Now, there's a small table there instead. It's elegantly appointed with sparkling silverware and crystal glasses. The plates are ivory white and the pottery is so magnificent I can't help but touch it.

"I love these plates," I say running my fingers over the middle of my plate. Then I realize that this is probably really not polite.

"I'm sorry, I shouldn't have done that," I say, embarrassed.

"No, it's okay," Wyatt laughs. "I didn't know someone could love plates."

I stare at him as if he was speaking a foreign language. "What are you talking about? These are magnificent! Look at how many little man-made imperfections there are in the middle. These are not factory made. They are crafted by an artisan. A very special artist."

He smiles at me. "You know, you're quite a surprise Brielle."

8

WYATT

She sits across from me staring at my mother's Mexican plates. She is doe-eyed and I want nothing more than to grab her and kiss her. Her innocence is enchanting and contagious. She's making me look at the plates my mother has bragged about for ages in a completely new way.

"You know, these plates are from Mexico," I say. "My mother brought them back with her many years ago. Apparently, they are quite unique and expensive because they are so plain. Mexican pottery isn't known for that."

Brielle's eyes open even wider than before. Now, I have her full attention. I just wish we weren't talking about fuckin' plates.

"Oh wow," she says running her fingers lightly against the grain of her plate. I want more than anything to be that plate. No, I want my cock to be that plate. I want her to run her fingers so carefully and lovingly along the curve of my erect cock.

"Wyatt?"

"Huh?" I come back to reality. Unfortunately.

"I just asked if you know what time period these are from."

"Oh, before the revolution. Mexican revolution. So at least at the beginning of last century."

When can we stop talking about the goddamn plates?

Finally, Mr. Whitewater emerges with two servants. They are carrying two plates.

"Pine nuts and kale salad with strawberries," Mr. Whitewater presents the food.

Brielle smiles and the world lights up.

"This looks delicious," she whispers and smiles at me and then back at Mr. Whitewater.

I pick up my glass to make a toast, but she has already dug into her salad.

"Oh, I'm so sorry," she swallows quickly and drops her fork. Her crudeness makes me horny.

"No, it's okay. I just wanted to say thank you for joining me here. It's a pleasure."

I have a whole speech planned out, but I leave it at that. She waits for me to continue, but I don't.

Something is making me tongue- tied. And I'm never tongue-tied.

"Thank you," she smiles. We clink glasses.

THE REST of dinner goes without a hitch. We don't speak much and when we do we are consumed with formalities. By the time, the dessert comes, I realize that this wasn't the best idea. I shouldn't have made this dinner so formal. She feels awkward and her awkwardness is making me feel uncomfortable. This place, this formality, isn't her. It's not me either. I just thought that it would be impressive. It worked on so many other girls that I'm lost as to what I should've done.

After dinner, I walk her back to her room. She walks a few steps ahead of me and I watch the way the taffeta under the dress bounces as she walks. I want to push it up and wrap my fingers around her ass.

"Did you have a good time?" I ask when we reach her door.

"Yes, very much so," Brielle smiles at me. "Dinner was delicious."

"And besides dinner?"

"You mean with you?"

I nod.

"Yes, I had a good time. To tell you the truth, I'm really glad you didn't end up being some 70-year-old creep. I had no idea who Mr. Wild was when I got here."

"Well, I'm not 70-years-old. Whether or not, I'm a creep is for you to decide."

I take a step forward, and she takes a step back. Suddenly, there's nowhere to go. Her head hits the back of the wall. I take another step forward.

I take her chin and tilt her head toward mine. Our lips touch, and I run my tongue on the side of her lips. She tastes like honey and lavender. She smells like the cheesecake, which we just ate for dinner. I pull her face closer to mine, and she wraps her hands around my shoulders. My cock grows large and pushes into her taffeta. She steps up on her tip toes, and my cock slides just a bit in between her legs.

Our kisses grow stronger and more powerful. I am thrust into a passion the kind of which I had never felt before. I grab her breasts and pull on the straps of her dress.

"Wyatt," Brielle whispers.

"Brielle," I manage to say. I kiss her neck. The urgency in my kisses intensifies, and I run my fingers up her naked leg.

"Wyatt," she pushes on me. I push back on her and continue to kiss her.

"Wyatt, stop!" her voice is powerful and needy. But I continue to kiss her. She's feeling just like I am. She must be!

"No, no, no, I can't," I whisper.

"Wyatt, stop!" she knees me in the balls. Shooting pain surges through my body and I drop to the floor.

"What the hell, Wyatt?"

"I'm sorry..." I whisper. I can't say it any louder. I'm laying on my back in the fetal position on the floor. I hear Brielle go into her room and lock the door. After a few minutes, the pain subsides. And I manage to scramble up to my feet.

I knock on her door. No one answers. I knock again, and for some reason try the door knob.

"It's locked, you asshole!" Brielle says.

"I'm sorry. I'm really really sorry, Brielle."

"Go away!"

"Please, Brielle. I'm really sorry. You don't have to let me in..."

"I know that! I mean, what did you think? You invite me here, get me a pretty dress, wine and dine me, and I'll just do whatever you want? I'm not a whore, Wyatt."

"I know," I say. "I never meant for it look like that. I just got carried away. I thought we were both feeling something, Brielle. I didn't mean to take it too far."

"Well, you did. And you're an asshole. When a girl says no, it means no. Keep that in mind for the future."

I'm so embarrassed. I can't believe this happened. I can't believe I did that.

"I honestly thought that we were both into it, Brielle. Please. You've got to believe me." My voice cracks a bit at the end.

"Fuck you!" Brielle says. "Oh yeah, and I'm leaving tomorrow morning."

She can't! I will stop her! She has no right! "You are?" I ask. Please, don't.

"I've decided that I'm not in debt to you," she says. "You paid for my Momma's treatment knowing that full well. And I'm not going to sleep with you. Not for any amount of money. Not even for a quarter of a million dollars."

She's right, of course. I did all that knowing that. I just thought that maybe as a thank you. No, that's not right. I wanted her to want me. I didn't want her to just sleep with me once. There's something about her that makes me want more. It's like she has some sort of spell on me.

"Okay," I finally say. "I understand. I'm leaving now."

I WALK BACK to the library. I don't know where I'm headed. I'm just lost. Distraught. Ashamed. Who was that person back there? Not me, for sure. Brielle's right. I was an asshole. Am an asshole. She deserves much better than that. Who knows how far I would've taken it if she hadn't kneed me in the balls.

"Agh, I'm such an idiot!" I say out loud. The words echo across the library chamber.

I hit my fist on the built-in bookshelves.

"Dammit!" I say. Now, my hand is hurting, and my heart is pounding even faster than before. I take a deep breath and look up.

The bookshelves are stacked three high with old books, but only one stands out. Charlotte Bronte's Jane Eyer. The library is poorly lit, but this book seems to have a spotlight on it. I look out of the window and see the bright yellow moon looming high in the sky.

She'll like this, I decide. I pick up the first edition and flip through the pages. She won't be able to throw this gift away, I decide.

There's my grandfather's old writing desk in the corner. I sit down and open the top. I take a small piece of decorative paper from the top shelf and pick up the old ink pen, which miraculously still writes.

BRIELLE,

This is a first edition of Jane Eyer. I hope you like it. I hope you accept this gift as my apology. I'm sorry.

Love,
Wyatt

I READ THE NOTE OVER. Of course, she will know it's a first edition. It says so in the front! I ball up the piece of paper and toss it in the trash can.

BRIELLE,
    I'm sorry. I didn't mean to do any of that this evening. Well, that's not true. I did mean to kiss you. I loved kissing you. I loved tasting you on my lips – I want to taste your sweet cunt.

I READ this note over again and again then crumple it up. This is supposed to be an apology. And like all apologies, it will have to be partly true and partly untrue. I can't say everything I want to say. Otherwise, she won't accept it.

I WRITE ANOTHER NOTE. My final note. When I'm finished, I wait for the ink to dry before carefully folding it and place it in front of the title page. In the back of the writing desk, I find a small box, which ends up being the perfect fit for the book. Now it really looks like a gift.

I WALK BACK to Brielle's room and knock on the door. She doesn't answer. I don't know if she can hear me, but I decide to leave the box right outside. After trying one last time, I finally give up and walk away.

I've done all I could. At this point, I have no choice but to accept her decision. Whatever it might be. No matter how much I hate it.

9

BRIELLE

I spent the night crying into my pillow. How dare he do that to me? I sob. My pillow is damp from all the tears I shed. I'm not just crying over what happened. I'm crying over what it means. He was such an asshole and now I can never trust him again. I had to physically push him off me. Who the hell does that? How far would he have gone if I wasn't strong to push him away? To knee him in his balls?

Millions of thoughts swirl in my head. I hate him. And I love him. I want to kiss him. And I want to punch him. I want him to knock harder on my door and knock it down. And I want him to go away and leave me alone. My makeup is running down my face and my eyes burn from all the cheap mascara getting into them. Finally, when they start to burn so much that it becomes unbearable, I force myself to go to the bathroom and wash my face.

"Why do you have to be such an asshole?" I say to myself in the mirror as if I'm talking to Wyatt. "We had such a great dinner. You were lovely. Polite. I was kind of a mess, but you weren't. You were...a gentleman. And then that. That happened. How can I forgive that?"

I shake my head. No, I can't forgive that. Because next time it might be much worse. I sigh.

I tried. I really tried. I came here. I had dinner. I even kissed him. This is all that he could've expected from me. It's okay if I go now. I've tried to repay my debt. It didn't work out. Because of *him*. So it's not my fault, right? Right.

THERE'S a knock at the door. Then another. And another. I don't answer. I've said enough. I don't want to argue anymore. My mind is made up. In the morning, Mr. Whitewater is ordering me a cab or a driver and I'm getting out of here.

THE FOLLOWING MORNING, I sleep in late. I'm still in bed at eight am. The bed is made of feathers and softness beyond my imagination. I feel like I've slept on a cloud and I'm not looking forward to going home to my thin, uncomfortable mattress at home. I got for $99 on sale, and it feels like it.

I pull on the most comfortable pair of jeans I own and my favorite turquoise tank top. Someone once told me that I looked great in turquoise, and I've stocked my closet with turquoise tops ever since. I always thought they were right, but this morning, I'm not so sure. I look pale and tired. A big part of me is regretting the fact that I'm leaving. But I'm not sure I have the courage to go back on my word.

There's a light knock on the door.

"Who is it?"

"Good morning, Ms. Cole," Mr. Whitewater says after I open the door.

"Good morning, Mr. Whitewater," I say with a yawn.

He looks like he has been awake for hours. His hair is perfectly groomed and coiffed, and his suit is starched and ironed, or whatever one does to suits to keep them wrinkle-free.

"Mr. Wild told me that you will be leaving this morning. I'm sorry to hear that."

"Yes, me too," I nod. I am sorry. I wish this weren't happening.

He doesn't say another word, doesn't make a move either. I stare at him. What's wrong? Slowly, his eyes tilt down. I follow them to the floor and see a light pink box.

"Oh, what's this?" I ask.

"I'm not sure. But it's for you," Mr. Whitewater says. He quickly takes a step back and turns away from me to give me some privacy.

I EXAMINE the box carefully in my hand. The cardboard looks old and smells a bit like cake. I carefully open the flap and peek in. It's a book! A book?

I pull out the book and let the box drop to the ground. Oh, my God. My heart starts to pound. Is this really what I think it is?

A first edition of Jane Eyer!?!?

The book is rather small and weathered, but otherwise it's in excellent condition. I flip through the pages. The pages are thicker near the front. Carefully, I flip the pages one at a time until I get to the title page and discover a note. It's written on perfumed paper, the kind that you see in expensive paper stores. There's a delicate floral design gracing each of the ends.

I open the note.

It's from Wyatt. I see his name written in beautiful, careful script on the bottom. The W is elongated and flowery, the y is elegant and the two sets of t's are defiant and proud.

Dear Brielle,
   I'm sorry. For everything.
   You deserve a lot better than me, of course. But please give me another chance.

Yours,
   Wyatt

Yours. I like the sound of that. I've never had anyone who was mine, in that way. My heart skips a beat again. And then another.

Mr. Whitewater clears his throat and I remember that he's still here.

"I think I need a moment, Mr. Whitewater," I finally manage to utter. I go back into my room and close the door.

"Oh my God," I whisper. "A first edition of Jane Eyer!"

I press the hardback book to my breasts and inhale its beautiful musty smell. This book has been around for hundreds of years and now it's mine. It belongs to me.

But can I accept it if I decide not to stay here? I want to. He owes me an apology and this was a marvelous apology.

My thoughts drift back to Wyatt. Suddenly, I remember the softness of his lips. And how they danced with mine to a tune that only we heard. I remember how hot I felt in between my legs and how much I wanted him to push up my taffeta skirt and let me wrap my legs around his strong, powerful torso.

He wasn't alone in feeling what he was feeling. I was there right along with him. We shared a chemical and electric connection. I was drawn to him as if he were a magnet and I had trouble pulling away as well. I loved how hard his cock felt pushing into me, pressing me to the wall. I wanted to rip off his clothes. I wanted him to rip off mine. And then it was just too much. In a split second, it was suddenly too much.

I don't know what I should do. I want to stay, but I also want to go. I want to stay to get to know Wyatt more. And I want to run away from this place and it's games.

The sound of a startled horse scares me and I walk over to the window. I lift the window and open the shutters. I didn't notice it last night, but there are stables to the right of me. The horse makes another piercing cry sending shivers over my body.

"It's okay, Sebastian. It's okay, guy," Wyatt says. I can't see him, but his voice is firm and commanding and I really believe that it's going to be okay.

Suddenly, they emerge. Wyatt is dressed in jeans, a pair of brown boots, and a simple white t-shirt. He's tan and his sweaty body glistens in the sun. His hair looks wet, either from sweat or water. He's riding a tall black horse with a thick black mane that flies up with each gallop. They are moving as one. I look closer, and I see that the horse is not wearing a saddle. Wyatt is riding bareback!

The horse and the rider dance together for a few moments in a circle. The horse kicks up swirls of dust, which in the sunlight look like periwinkle. And then suddenly, the horse shifts his weight and raises his front legs in the air.

"Oh wow," I whisper in awe. Wyatt remains in place on his back holding on by nothing but his powerful thighs. It looks like the horse is going to land on his front legs and then morph into a trot, but he doesn't. Instead, he lands hard on his front hooves and lifts his back hooves up high in the air. And then he does it all again.

My smile fades quickly after I realize that something's going wrong.

"Oh my God," I whisper and bring my hands to my face. "No, no, no…"

But it's too late. The horse bucks one last time, and this time, Wyatt doesn't hold on. I see him flying through the air. He misses the chain-link fence by less than a foot and lands flat on his back.

"Oh my God!" I scream. My voice echoes around the room, but Wyatt doesn't get up.

"Get up! Please get up," I scream, but he doesn't.

For a brief second, I consider running to the back of the room, down the long hallway, down the winding staircase, out of the front door, and around the entire 10,000 square foot house. But then I see a simpler way down.

"What are you doing?" Mr. Whitewater enters my room.

I'm already hanging out of the window, half of my body is on the roof of the patio.

"Wyatt is hurt, call 911!"

I climb down the post of the patio, jump into the orange grove below and run toward Wyatt.

I finally reach him. His face is so pale that it's the color of those white Mexican plates from dinner. All blood has drained from his face, and his lips are blue.

"Wyatt? Wyatt?" I scream. I want to shake him and bring him back to life. But I'm afraid he has broken something in his body, and that will make it worse.

"Wyatt? Wyatt? Please wake up. Please, please, please," I shout cradling my arms around him.

Mr. Whitewater runs over.

"How is he? Oh my God. He's unconscious."

I nod. I don't know what else to do.

"I just called 911, but they won't be here for some time."

"What, why?" I demand to know.

"Twenty minutes at the earliest," he says and puts the receiver back to his ear. "They say that we shouldn't move him until they get here. He might've broken his back."

THE WORLD FADES TO black with those words. 'He might've broken his back' is all I hear in my head over and over again. The paramedics arrive sometime later. They have to scream at me to get out of the way. I don't move. I don't even know if I can move. Someone pushes me out of the way and they take Wyatt away. They strap him onto a gurney and roll him to the ambulance.

I can't go along. No one can. They tell me and Mr. Whitewater that we can follow along behind the ambulance if we want.

I'm in a daze. I don't know what to do. I follow Mr. Whitewater to his car.

"Are you sure you want to come? I thought you wanted to leave this morning? You still can, if you want to."

I stare at him. All thoughts of leaving have all but dissipated. I don't even know what he's talking about. All I know is that I can't leave now. I don't know what's wrong with him and I can't leave until I find out. What if he needs my help?

TWELVE HOURS LATER.

I'VE SPENT the last twelve hours in the hospital looking at magazines and mindlessly reading books that I did not understand on my phone. I read the words, but they don't make any sense. I don't know who wrote them or for what reason. The only thing that makes sense to me is the pictures. I leaf through the celebrity magazines and pay close attention to which movie stars have lost and gained weight. Which ones were pregnant. Which ones got engaged and which ones got divorced. It's all things that I used to find interesting, but now none of it makes any sense.

This hospital reminds me of the one back home, where I waited for hours for my mom to get out of her various surgeries. Time stands still here. It's as if the waiting room is some secret time travel chamber in which I can go into and not age for hours and days and months. I age, of course. I noticed it whenever I went into the bathroom and looked at the horror that was my face, but I never felt time passing. Not even one second.

Breathe, I say to myself. Breathe.

I take a deep breath. And then another. And another. I feel a little better, but as soon as I look around, all of my thoughts and concerns and regrets creep back in.

A doctor who is in charge of Wyatt and his condition comes out from behind the double doors with a smile on his face.

"Wyatt's awake now," he tells Mr. Whitewater. "He's one lucky young man. Even though both of his legs are broken."

Broken legs. I sigh. He is lucky.

"Wait here," Mr. Whitewater tells me. I have no right to go see Wyatt. I'm not really anybody to him. Barely an employee. Still, I hope that I can go in to see him.

"And he doesn't have any brain damage?" Mr. Whitewater asks the doctor.

"No, not that I can tell. But it's too soon to know for sure."

I wait for what seems like a century for Mr. Whitewater to come back. Now time is positively moving backward. I wonder if it's now 1993. Finally, he comes out.

"He'd like to see you," Mr. Whitewater says.

"How is he?"

"Fine. Definitely all there."

I SMILE. A wave of relief sweeps over me.

10

WYATT

Brielle walks into my hospital room carefully and cautiously. It's as if she's walking on eggshells.

"It's okay," I say. "Don't be afraid." I sit up in my bed, trying not to look so sickly and powerless even though I have a pounding headache.

"How are you?" she asks sheepishly.

Her hair falls into her face slightly as she walks and she pushes it aside without much regard. Her lips look soft and exquisite even under the harsh fluorescent lights of the hospital room. Her skin is tan and her cheeks are full of color. Brielle is wearing a long sleeve hoodie and she wraps her arms around her shoulders as if she is trying to hold on to the entire world.

"I'm good. Fine," I say confidently. It's almost true. I want it to be true. I'll act like it is until it became true.

"Broke both legs," I say nudging at the cast. "Imagine the luck."

"It could've been much worse, Wyatt," she comes closer. I love the sound of my name in her mouth.

"Nah," I wave my hand. But she slaps it away.

"No, I'm serious. It could've been much much worse. I saw you out there. You passed out. You were unconscious. I thought you would go into a coma and never wake up."

"Hah, like you'd care. You'd just be happy that you got off the hook," I joke.

She stares at me and raises her hand to slap me again. This time across the face. But something stops her.

"Fuck you, Wyatt. Fuck you for even thinking something that terrible."

That was a pretty shitty thing to say. I shake my head. "I'm sorry. I didn't mean that. I was just trying to make you laugh."

"How would that make me laugh, exactly?"

"I don't know. I'd shrug, but my shoulders hurt too much."

This one does make her laugh. She opens her lips just a bit and lets out a small, willowy laugh. The world is alright again.

"How did this happen?" Brielle asks after a few silent moments.

"That's what you get for riding a four-year-old stallion bareback," I laugh.

Her face turns white. "What do you mean? Are you joking again?"

I shake my head no. And then suddenly, something comes over me. And I tell her something I never would otherwise.

"I was really upset that you were leaving. That I did that to you. Disrespected you like that. But I want you to know that it was really an accident. I must've not heard you or something. I would never keep going beyond what you said was okay. I'm not that guy."

I stop and look at her. She waits for me to continue.

"So I was really angry with myself over the whole thing. Over what I did. Over the fact that you were now scared of me. And leaving. That's the last thing I wanted. So this morning, I went for a walk and ended up in the stables. I saw Sebastian. He's a powerful thoroughbred. But he's not broken yet. He's wild and crazy, and I felt wild and crazy at that moment. It was like we were breathing the same air and feeling the same energy. I opened the gate and he let me get on top of him. I really thought we were connecting, and we wanted the same thing. But I was just feeling crazy. He ignited something within me, some long forgotten feeling of hope and love and wildness. And so I urged him outside of the stable. And that's when it got bad. He started to buck, and he wouldn't slow down long enough for me to get off. And then I just flew off."

"You remember it all?"

"I remember every single moment."

"And what about afterward?"

"No," I shake my head. "Once I hit the ground, I don't remember anything."

She looks at me. Tears well up inside of her eyes. One large tear breaks free and rolls down her cheek. I reach out and wipe it off her face.

"I was so scared, Wyatt. You were just laying there. Motionless. Unconscious. I wanted to shake you so much, but I was afraid something was broken. And then…"

Her voice drops off and she looks out of the window. A tiny sparrow dances on a branch. We both watch the sparrow for a moment before she turns back to me.

"And then?" I ask.

"And then I thought that maybe it was even worse than that. You didn't wake up Wyatt. Not for a long time."

I nod.

"You scare me, Brielle," I finally say.

"What do you mean?"

"I don't know exactly. But I feel something for you and it scares me."

"Don't be silly," she waves her hand and smiles. "How can I scare you?"

I try to shrug again. Again I feel pain.

"Come here," I say and wave my index finger to get her to come closer to me.

"What?" she leans down.

"You scare me," I whisper and press my lips up to hers. I lift my body a bit toward hers and my neck throbs in pain.

I sigh in pain when I pull away.

"Are you okay?" she says with a smile licking her lips.

"No," I shake my head. "But it was worth it."

THAT EVENING, the nurse gives me some morphine, and I fall asleep quickly. When I wake up in the morning, my back is throbbing, and I find Brielle half asleep in the chair.

"Hey, you're awake," she smiles at me.

"What are you doing here?" I ask. "I can't believe you slept the whole night here."

"Oh, I just dozed off. It's no big deal."

"No, it is," I say. "Thank you."

"I'm going to get us some coffee," she jumps up to her feet.

I'm jealous of the spring in her step and I wish more than anything that I could jump as well. I've only been in bed for one day and the thought of not being active for another two months scares me to death.

"Brielle…"

She turns at the door. Her hair leaps one last time before landing softly around her shoulders.

"Yes?"

"I was just wondering…" I don't know how to phrase the question exactly. She waits for me as I try.

"I was just wondering if you were planning on going back home today?"

"No," she shakes her head. A wave of relief sweeps over me, but I'm not sure if I have been clear enough.

"And tomorrow?" I ask.

Suddenly, it hits her what I'm asking. She walks back to my bed.

"I'm not going home for awhile Wyatt. But under one condition."

"What's that?"

"If you promise me that we will be friends. Just friends."

I thought about that for a moment. Just friends was better than nothing. "Okay," I nodded.

11

WYATT

How do you know if you truly love someone?

There was a time in my life when I never believed in love. I grew up in a world of privilege. My two brothers, Gatsby, and Atticus, and my sister, Ophelia, were raised by our nannies and had everything we ever wanted. Our parents had houses in Los Angeles, New York, Montana. An apartment in Paris. And another one is being built in Dubai.

When we were little, the family had more cars than I can even count – our father, Dr. Wild – is an avid collector. We each got a new car of our choosing as soon as we turned 16 and each one of us promptly crashed it soon after. I think it was O, we've always called Ophelia, O, who kept her first car, a brand new Mercedes, the most expensive class of that year, the longest. Six months, I believe.

My mother never cooked, but every night that we had dinner at home, we always had a delicious gourmet meal prepared by our personal chef. Our birthdays were lavish and expensive. Each one probably cost as much as a regular couple's wedding. They were extravagant with different themes and costumes and close to 400 guests each time. That doesn't sound like a fun birthday party for a five-year-old, but the entire school was invited so most of them were.

Our exclusive private school didn't have a school bus to get us to school, and the responsibility fell to our nannies to deliver us there and pick us up after each of our after school activities. O did theater. Gatsby and I played lacrosse. Atticus was in the band.

Our parents were always there to cheer for us – always physically present – and yet emotionally and metaphysically away. It's hard to explain now, difficult to put into words, but it was as if they were never really there.

Ever since I can remember, our parents had their own lives. My father, the renowned doctor and later the founder of a prosperous pharmaceutical company, worked late into the night and all weekends. He was always traveling and running meetings.

My mother had her philanthropic activities. She was the head of a number of boards that raised money for a variety of noble causes. She didn't get paid, but she worked nearly as hard as he did. And organized all of our days and the house staff on top of all that.

It's maybe cruel to say this, but my parents gave me the impression that love only meant one thing. My parents said that they loved us, but their love was complicated. It came with expectations and, inevitable, disappointments. It was never the kind of love often featured in movies. They were never mushy and hopeful and exuberant. They were both too busy with either work or their social obligations to really show love. Or at least, the way I expected it to be.

AND SO, coming back to my original thought. How do you know if you truly love someone? How am I expected to know if I love someone if their love was the kind of love I had only ever known?

Before I broke both of my legs riding a wild stallion, I never had time to think about these things. But now that I've been bed bound for more than six weeks, it seems all I do is think. I had to remain active somehow and my mind was the only place I had left.

Brielle enters the room carrying two cups of tea on a tray. She has been here for six weeks. Six of the happiest weeks of my life. I have never been immobile for this long before and yet her presence has made it, somehow, bearable. If it weren't for her, I'd be tearing my hair out. I'd be drunk all day just to pass the time. And yet, with her here, we find things to do that do not involve going outside much or using our legs.

I THINK I'm falling in love with Brielle. Her long hair, her tender eyes, her soft skin. I don't know anything about love, I'm the first the admit it. Yet, I also know that I've never felt this way about anyone before. Sometimes, when I see her, my heart jumps into my throat and I forget to breathe.

Other times, when she's away from me for a couple of hours, I feel anxious and uncertain. I don't know what to do with myself and spend the hours just looking out of the window or staring aimlessly at the television screen. I can't read a word that makes sense. All I can do is wait for her to return.

Brielle has been bringing me breakfast, lunch, and dinner and has made Mr. Whitewater all but useless. The responsibility of those things would've fallen to him. But she asked him if she could do it. I think she likes being useful. In fact, I've never met someone who enjoys being useful so much. It's almost as if she really loves taking care of me.

I feel myself falling in love with Brielle, even though I'm not sure if I know what that means. But does anyone? Isn't love just some sort of feeling that bubbles up from within us, from some place deep within our core that we didn't even know existed.

There is one problem, however. And it's a big one. We – Brielle and I – have decided to keep things professional. I believe that the only reason she's even here is that our relationship is now strictly professional. Or so she has called it that once. But in reality, it's not professional at all. Only a fool would think that our interaction is professional. We are more like friends. Close, close friends. And it's clear, at least I think it is, that I want more.

"What a beautiful morning, right?" she says plopping down on the couch next to me. "What do you want to do today?"

I want to kiss you and undress and lay in bed looking at and exploring your naked body until dinner. I want to say this to her, but instead I lie.

"Not sure, whatever," I shrug and remember her hurtful words.

"No more kissing, no more romance, or whatever it was that was happening between us," she said in my hospital room. I felt woozy from all the pain killers, but I remember each one of her words as if she said it a minute ago. "I just want to work here for the year, like I'd agreed, and be friends."

"Okay," I had agreed.

"You promise?" she asked.

"This is one of my conditions of staying. The only one."

I remember looking into her deep brown eyes and nodding. Then agreeing verbally to the only thing that would keep her in my life.

"You feeling alright?" she asks. Neither of us has said a word in a few moments. She touches my hand with hers sending shivers up and down my legs, as always. My cock grows hard and I press down on it trying to calm it. Ever since we'd decided to be friends, she started touching me more and more. More than she ever had before. But the touching is not sexual, at least not on her part. Just a pat of the hand, a small hug, a nudge. But each touch still makes me get hard.

I want her. I want her up against the wall. On the bed. Outside in the desert. In the shower.

"Hey, Wyatt?" she asks leaning close to me with a look of concern on her face. "How are you, today? Is everything okay?"

"I'm good," I fake a smile. "Why?"

"Something seems off," she shrugs. "Oh, I almost forgot, I got your pills, here."

I stare at her. Brielle mentions the pills in the same nonchalant way she has for the last six weeks. But this is the first day that I turn them down.

"Nah, I'm feeling okay. I don't think I need them today."

Her face lights up. "That's great!" she wraps her arms around me. "I'm so happy. You're making so much progress. Maybe you'll be able to take the casts off soon, too."

Now, there's a thought. To stand up and hold my body weight with my own two feet. I've taken that for granted for so many years. And then when I suddenly couldn't stand up on my feet and had to use crutches…the helplessness that came with that was unimaginable.

I smile with my whole body at the thought of taking the casts off.

"Yeah, I can't wait," I say. "I hate being a blimp. I feel like I'm totally useless. And like I'm getting fat."

Brielle laughs. A small quiet laugh that only gives me a small peek at her perfect white teeth. Then she looks me up and down.

"No, not at all."

"You have no idea how hard this has been for me. I mean, I know it hasn't been easy for you at all, waiting on me all the time. Which again, you don't really have to do. We have staff here for that," I say.

She starts to say something, but I cut her off. I know what she's going to say. She is the staff, she's happy to do it, or something in that vein.

"That's not what I want to say. What I mean is that it's been really hard for me to be so inactive for so long. I love being outdoors. I love riding horses. Playing basketball. Football. Baseball. Whatever. Using my body is a huge part of my life. And these past six weeks, it's like I've become someone else. I couldn't do that. And if it weren't for you…I would've been completely lost. It would've been much harder. So what I'm really trying to say, very artfully, is thank you. Thank you so much for being here. And being you."

Brielle takes a moment to internalize what I've said. Then she leans close to me. It takes all of my strength not to place my lips on hers. But I've long made myself a promise that it would be her, this time, who has to make the first move.

"It has been my pleasure," she whispers in my ear and pulls away.

BRIELLE JUMPS off the couch and the mood in the room changes. I watch her walk over to the large floor to ceiling window looking out onto the desert in front of us. A large raven perches on top of a crooked Joshua tree in the distance and then flies away.

"I finally found some tape and I'm going to take care of that bird problem," she says. By bird problem, she means that too many birds are flying into our spotless window and killing themselves. Mr. Whitewater, who washes that window almost every other day, isn't going to be happy. And we both know it.

"You know, he has been hiding this thing from me for all of these weeks," she says with a smile and picks up the roll of duct tape from the tray. "I've been asking him for it forever."

"What can I say, he loves keeping that window clean."

"I know he does, and the view from it is beautiful. But we can't just sit by and do nothing as birds continue to kill themselves on it practically every day."

"I guess not," I chuckle.

"Where do you think I should put it?" Brielle asks.

Over my hands and then to the headboard so that I can't touch you as you go down on me. And then I will wrap it around your hands and do the same to you.

Of course, I don't say any of that out loud. Instead, I point to a few spots on the window, which have resulted in the largest amount of casualties.

"You know, I talked to my mother again this morning," Brielle says as she tapes the window.

"Oh yeah, how is she?" I ask. I only mildly care. Don't get me wrong, I'm glad she's doing better but mainly because that means that Brielle doesn't have to go back home and take care of her.

"She's doing even better than before," she smiles.

The $250,000 check that I sent her for her mother's treatment was worth that smile alone. Brielle starts telling me all the details about how her mother's feeling. Her breathing is improving, not much pain in her hips, blah, blah, blah. All the information comes into one ear and goes out the other. I'm not paying attention. Not even a little bit.

Instead, my mind drifts elsewhere. I look at Brielle's round butt and the way it fills out her jeans.

Her jeans have little decorative hearts on the back pockets and they draw my eye on the roundest part of her body. I don't know why clothing designers put them there. Do they know that they make women's butts look irresistible? Is that the whole point? Do the women know just how hard it is to look away from those two little hearts? Does Brielle?

When she turns to face me and tell me something else about her mom's condition, my gaze runs up her body. Brielle's small waist accentuates her hips, making them appear wider than they really are. And then suddenly, I land on her breasts. She doesn't wear a bra often, but her breasts are firm and erect. When the temperature in the room falls below 75 degrees Fahrenheit, her nipples get erect and resemble the tips of a ripe strawberry. I've gotten into the habit of turning down the furnace and praying each morning that today would be the day that she again chooses to go without a bra.

"Hey, are you listening?" Brielle asks.

"Yeah, so your mom is happy with the new doctor?" I parrot the last thing that she said back to me. I developed this talent of reiterating the last line that someone said back in sixth grade and it served me well way after I was done with formal education.

My words put her at ease and she continues on with her story while I curse myself for ever agreeing to be this hot girl's friend.

Fuck being friends!
We shouldn't be just friends.
Friends with benefits maybe.
Fuck buddies.
Lovers.
Girlfriend?
Fiancé even.
Maybe more.

I SHUDDER at the places that mind is going. Girlfriend, maybe. I've had a few girls who I liked enough to call my girlfriend. But fiancé? Really, Wyatt? What are you thinking? That's exactly it, though. I'm not thinking. I'm just feeling.

12

BRIELLE

I don't know why the fuck I ever insisted on being friends with Wyatt. The friends status was supposed to protect me. It was supposed to make me feel safe and to make me feel as if nothing is going to happen between us. I thought that it would create distance between us and release some of the tension that forms whenever we occupy the same room. But it's only making things worse.

I want him.

I want him to want me.

He does. I can feel it. But he won't make a move. He made me a promise and he's keen on keeping it.

Even now, standing on this stupid chair, taping tape onto the glass to stop the damn birds from crashing into it every day, I feel Wyatt's eyes burning a hole in my back pocket.

He's staring at my ass and, the scary thing is that I want him to. But more than that. I want him to grab it and pull me up to his lap and kiss me.

Of course, he won't. He has made a promise.

So now it's all up to me. And I'm afraid. And I'm a coward.

AFTER I TAPED ALL the spots where birds have crashed into the past week, I get down and sit next to him on the couch, which has become his home. Wyatt hasn't moved much in weeks. He pretends that he's fine, but I can feel his anxiety growing.

"I need to get the hell out of here. Out of this room. Away from this couch. I want to see Sebastian again."

I get goosebumps at the thought. Sebastian is the crazy, untamed, four-year-old stallion that broke both of his legs the last time he tried to ride him. I don't want Wyatt anywhere near him. He was lucky to get out of that situation with only both legs broken. The doctors said it could've been much worse. He could've broken his back and ended up like Christopher Reeves.

"Can I ask you something?" I ask.

Wyatt nods and waits for the question.

"Why did you ever get on him, in the first place? What were you trying to prove?"

I don't know much about horses, but I do know that no one in their right mind rides stallions. All the testosterone makes them crazy and wild. Unbroken.

"Nothing," he shrugs in the casual way that makes me swoon. "I just felt like riding him, that's all."

I don't believe him. "I don't think so," I say staring straight into Wyatt's deep eyes.

"You don't? Why?"

"I think you were angry with yourself. And you wanted to, I don't know, take some of that anger out on yourself."

Wyatt's eyes meet mine. I can tell by the way he sits back in the couch and adjusts his stature that I've hit on something.

"Oh please," he shrugs and rolls his eyes. He's lying. Either to just me or to the both of us.

"No, I do," I smile. "Really."

Then his face grows serious. The casualness that just danced across it all but disappears.

"Listen, Brielle," Wyatt says. All I hear is the irritation in his voice. "Please don't psychoanalyze me, okay? I've been through that enough with a ton of real doctors. The last thing I need is some more psycho babble from some novice."

His words sting. More than that even. They pierce my heart. I feel tears bubbling up and I'm about to let them all out.

"Fuck you," I say and leave before I show even more vulnerability.

"Brielle, I'm sorry. I'm sorry," I hear Wyatt yell after me, but I don't turn around. At this moment, I hate him. I hate him the way I never hated anyone.

WE DON'T SPEAK the rest of the day. By the next day, my anger with Wyatt dissipates a bit. He apologizes again and, this time, I accept his apology. By the afternoon, we joke and laugh like before. I'm glad that things between us have improved, but I am still keenly aware of the boundaries that separate us. Now, I'm also more cautious. Certain things can't be talked about or joked about.

That afternoon, over a very late lunch or an early dinner, I ask Wyatt about his family. He tells me about his domineering father and the pharmaceutical company that he started when all the kids were little.

"My father's got four kids, but that company was his real baby," he says. "And we all knew that for many years."

"What about your mom?" I ask.

"Mom was there and not there. She had her own commitments, but most of the time she was absent. It's like she had her own interests that none of us kids ever fit into."

"Not even Ophelia?" I ask. I know that mothers can often be closer to their daughters than to their sons.

"Not even O. We've all had nannies, though, so that was supposed to make up for everything, I guess. It felt like they loved me, all of us, I mean, in their own way, but it was somehow never enough. You know?"

I nod. I try to understand, but Wyatt and I come from two completely different worlds.

"What about you?" he asks. "What was it like for you growing up?"

I take a moment to consider the question.

"It wasn't really easy," I say. "My father left when I was little when my little sister was only two."

"I didn't know you had siblings."

"I don't. Well, not anymore. I never know how to answer that question about brothers or sisters."

"What do you mean?" he asks. He moves closer to me with a steadfast look of concern on his face.

"Well, I used to have a sister until I was fifteen, but then she died. She was sick almost her whole little life and, after she passed, my mother was never the same after that."

"What did she die of?" he asks even though I have the feeling that he already knows.

"Cancer. What else?" I shrug.

"Like your mother?" he gasps.

I nod. "My mom was diagnosed soon after. Right when I graduated from high school. That's why I never went to college. She was the sole breadwinner and, after her diagnosis, she couldn't really work. Not with all the chemo and radiation. So I got a job at the diner. And then another one at the bar. And I've been sort of stuck there ever since."

I look at him. I like the way he looks at me. There's pity and sorrow on his face, but it isn't as depressing as the looks other people typically have.

"But it's okay now," I smile. "Thanks largely to you."

"I just wish that I'd met you earlier," he says.

A big part of me wishes that too. I've spent so many years being poor and living paycheck to paycheck, on even less than a paycheck, that having money seemed like an answer to all of my problems. People like to say that money is not the answer to all of your problems, but for many years it would've been the answer to all of mine.

WE SHARE MORE this day than any other day. I feel us growing closer and closer. Even if we don't fully comprehend or understand or conceptualize each other's childhood experiences, we are at least aware of them.

After we finish our salads, Mr. Whitewater brings us soup. I hand Wyatt his bowl and take mine. It's not very comfortable to eat soup on the couch, but I don't want to move.

"What did you want to be when you grew up?" Wyatt asks.

"I don't know," I say. "You mean for work? I thought I'd be lucky if I became a nurse or something like that. It would give me a steady job or profession. The pay is much better than a waitress's."

"No," he shakes his head. "That's not what I mean. Not just for work. Didn't you have dreams of what you wanted to do or to be when you were older? No matter how unrealistic."

I smile. I'm about to tell him that only wealthy or privileged kids spend their days thinking about unrealistic dreams and go about pursuing those. But then I really think about it and realize that I, too, had a dream once. And, perhaps, still do.

"Okay, I'll tell you, but only if you promise to keep it a secret."

"Keep it a secret? Don't you know that dreams can't become a reality unless you verbalize it? Unless you infuse them with the power of speech?"

"Actually, no, I didn't know that. But if you want to hear this then you have to promise."

He takes a moment. Then agrees.

"I've never told anyone this before, but I want to be a writer," I say.

"That's great! That's an amazing thing to want to be," Wyatt smiles with his whole face.

I feel overwhelmed by his exuberance.

"But why don't you want anyone to know? It's so inspiring and beautiful!"

Inspiring and beautiful? I'm not so sure.

"Because it's embarrassing," I mumble.

"What? How?"

I stare at him. "I just don't think you understand because you were probably raised to think that you can be anyone you want. Do anything you want. Right? But I wasn't. I don't even have a bachelor's degree, Wyatt. Only a high school diploma. I'm practically illiterate in the writing world."

"That's crap! Don't say that. Degrees don't matter. All that matters is whether or not you want to do it. And then you gotta take steps to do it."

"That's your privileged upbringing talking," I joke.

"No, it's not," he leans closer to me. His face gets really serious. "To be a writer you need heart. And you have that. I think you can be a writer. No, I *know* you can."

His words wash over me like a wave. Overwhelmed by his support and encouragement, I have trouble taking a full breath. A knot forms in the back of my throat. If I don't inhale slowly, I'm afraid that I won't be able to take a full breath again.

No one has ever believed in me so much before.

We both return to our food. Wyatt takes two last scoops of the soup. I lean across him to put the bowl on his side of the side table.

I've done this hundreds of times over the last six weeks. But today is different. There's a warmth emanating from Wyatt, the kind that I haven't felt since our last kiss. I watch him take a breath and inhale the world around us, the way people smell a bouquet of flowers.

When he opens his eyes, he catches me staring at him and sits back. He's giving me room to collect myself. He's respecting my boundaries and the rules that we have both agreed to play by. But this time, I don't, can't, respect those boundaries anymore. This time, I don't pull away. I look at his sweet, beautiful lips and press mine to them.

Immediately, his lips respond to mine. He pulls me closer to him and wraps his arms around my shoulders. In a split second, the whole world fades away. His hands move through my hair and my fingers run along his jawline. It's strong and powerful and touching it makes me want him even more.

"This is wrong," I whisper without pulling away.

"Yes, and yet it's so right," he mumbles.

And then suddenly, he stops and looks at me.

"Do you want to stop?" he asks. "Is that what you meant?"

Yes and no. I don't know.

He waits for me to answer. But I've lost the ability to speak. Instead, I reach up to him again and run my tongue on the inside of his mouth.

"Oh Brielle," he moans. He lifts up my head with his hands and then runs his hands down to my hips. With one swift motion, he lifts me up and places me on top of him.

I laugh and continue kissing him. I feel how hard he is and it makes me feel all tingly all over my body. He pulls away from my lips and starts to kiss down my neck. I tilt my head back and sigh from pleasure. His lips make his way down my collarbone and then toward my breasts. He takes one of my breasts in his hand and kisses the top.

I close my eyes. I want this moment to last forever.

"Oh my, I'm so sorry!" a female voice shatters our bliss. I pull away from Wyatt but remain firmly on top of him.

"What the fuck are you doing here, O?" Wyatt yells out. His deep voice startles me and I fall to the side. I scramble to adjust my clothes. When everything seems in place, I look back up.

There's a tall, gorgeous woman in five- inch heels standing before me. Her hair is jet black and cut in an aggressive slant. Her makeup is flawless and her eyeslashes are long and powerful. She has pale skin and her blood red lipstick makes her look like something of a clash between a 50's pinup and a vampire.

"I live here, too, remember?" she laughs and tosses her hair. "Besides, I've come to see how you were feeling. And from what I can see, you're doing quite well."

Neither Wyatt nor I say a word. I probably look as dumbfounded as he does.

"Well, since my brother seems to have forgotten his manners, I'll introduce myself. I'm Ophelia, Wyatt's older sister."

Ophelia extends her hand to me. When I shake it, what strikes me most about it is how cold it is. Her fingers are long and her long gray nails are filed down to a point at the end. In fact, come to think of it, everything about Ophelia is pointy. She has pointy heels, a pointy nose, pointy nails, and even pointy elbows.

"I'm Brielle. I'm Wyatt's personal assistant," I mumble.

"Yes, I see. You're definitely assisting him on a very personal level," she says lifting one of her eyebrows.

"O, please. Play nice," Wyatt says. "Brielle's a friend."

Ophelia puts her sunglasses back over her eyes, turns on her heel and waves her hand. "Well, I gotta get my bag."

Wyatt and I watch her walk out. Before she reaches the end of the hallway, she turns around briefly and says, "Brielle, can you help me with something here?"

I look at Wyatt, unsure as to what to do.

"No, O, take care of it yourself," he yells back.

"No, it's okay," I get up. "I'll help her, it's no problem."

ADVANCED READER TEAM

Sign up for Charlotte Byrd's mailing list and get notifications of New Releases, access to exclusive giveaways, and a chance to be on her Advanced Reader Team:

http://eepurl.com/btLdbT

You will only receive e-mails about new releases and you can opt out anytime

BOOKS BY CHARLOTTE BYRD

Billionaire Matchmaker Series
(standalone novels)
1. Malibu Connection - April 2016
2. Book 2 - May 2016
3. Book 3 - June 2016
4. Book 4 - July 2016
5. Book 5 - August 2016
6. Book 6 - September 2016

WILD BROTHERS SERIES (both standalone novels)
1. Falling for the CEO - out now
2. The Debt - out now

ONE SEMESTER SERIES (both standalone novels)
1. One Semester - out now
2. Accidental Wedding - out now

OTHER BOOKS
Wrong for Me - out now

**ALL BOOKS ARE available on Amazon, Apple, Barnes & Noble, Kobo, Scribd, and all major retailers.

Printed in Great Britain
by Amazon